*Lieutenant Leroy Powder books
by Michael Z. Lewin*

NIGHT COVER
HARD LINE
LATE PAYMENTS

# NIGHT COVER

# NIGHT COVER

*Michael·Z·Lewin*

A Foul Play Press Book

The Countryman Press, Inc.
Woodstock, Vermont

Copyright © 1976 by Michael Z. Lewin

This edition published in 1995 by Foul Play Press,
a division of The Countryman Press, Inc.,
Woodstock, Vermont

All rights reserved. No part of this book may be
reproduced in any form or by any mechanical or
electronic means, including information storage and
retrieval systems, without the publisher's express
written permission, except by reviewers
who may quote brief passages.

ISBN 0-88150-345-2

10 9 8 7 6 5 4 3 2 1

Cover design © 1995 by Honi Werner

Printed in Canada

**To Uncle Don and Aunt Louie**

**AUTHOR'S NOTE**

Because there are a number of superficial exactnesses in this novel, I feel bound—for the readers' sake as well as the sake of those who live and work in places apparently described—to emphasize that it is a work of fiction. There are many people, particularly G. M. Miller and R. W. Jehs, whose time and effort were generously expended to provide me with background details, but I alone am responsible for the differences between the real world and its fictionalized appearance in this book.

# NIGHT COVER

# 1

"Look, I'm forty-eight years old and I only got seven toes. I don't have the time or the wear left to spend all night teaching a kid how to write a duty roster."

Though six two and looking down a good five inches, the young officer felt his shaking knees put his whole body's balance in question. "Gosh, Lieutenant Powder, I looked at the last two rosters and saw you been on Cover Shift eight straight weeks. I thought you was about due to come on days."

Powder rubbed his face with both hands, as if he had been asleep within the hour. The young officer read it as a gesture of disgust aimed his way because of his stupidity. Powder had been asleep an hour ago; and he did think the young officer stupid.

"Sonny, you go upstairs to the Assembly Room, take your new roster off the board and rewrite it. And when you start, remember I'm the easiest guy you do because you just write my name at the top of Cover Shift and then you start worrying about guys' days and nights."

Powder turned around and left the kid struggling to find something to say that wasn't stupid. But he was too slow and Powder walked away.

On the two flights of stairs up to the detective Day Room, Powder rubbed his face twice more. Didn't help much, but it didn't hurt. He always rubbed his face twice on the stairs.

The kid must have been told about me, he thought. They always tell the new roster men.

There were only two detective sergeants using a room full of desks. 6:46 P.M. Powder walked past the desks to a row of

NIGHT COVER

lieutenants' cubbyholes. He looked in each open doorway. Only the last compartment was occupied and the lieutenant there looked up as Powder passed.

"Roy," he said by way of greeting.

"Morning," said Powder, and he walked past to the desk at the end which, in a strange way, he thought of as home. His home-hold on the past—the desk maintained for him in the Day Room as if sometime he would work days regularly again. A choice desk, with the wall behind the swivel chair so he could lean back and scratch his dandruff off on the crags of the plaster. It wasn't the cubbyhole he would rate if he were really on days, but it was a choice desk.

Powder checked for messages, special assignments, projects, phone memos. There weren't any. Sometimes there were.

He turned around and walked slowly back the way he had come in.

"You're working late, Miller," he said to the lieutenant he'd greeted on the way in.

"Yeah," said Miller. He rustled a handful of papers with his left hand.

"Tell me," said Powder, "what's the story on the body we brought in for you last night?"

"Homicide," said Miller without looking up.

"I knew she was killed."

"That was obvious."

"What were the details?"

With a sigh, Miller leaned back and pursed his lips. "What do you want to know, Powder? Chest size? She was kind of flattened out because rigor set in after she was put on her back."

"Information, copper," said Powder. Half pulling rank, though their ranks were equal. He'd been a lieutenant nineteen years and Miller only a year and a half. Half he was pulling race because Miller was black, though in the Indianapolis Police Department all races are equal. "Cause of death. Time of death," said Powder. "Individualizing details," measuring all the syllables, showing he was equally comfortable with long words or short.

Miller sighed and thought he should know better by now than to work late. "Strangulation, but it didn't take place where she was found. Long time since she last ate. It's hard to pin a time," said Miller.

Powder frowned. If he'd been talking to a doctor, he would have asked aggressive questions, but if Miller said it was hard to pin a time, it was hard to pin a time. Reputations abound in a closed society like a police department.

"I know what you're thinking," said Miller. "No, she wasn't raped. We have no apparent motive, and no ID yet. But . . . someone went to some trouble to step on her fingerprints."

Eyebrows up. "With what?" asked Powder, remembering she'd looked messy.

"Blunt, heavy, hard object something like a sledgehammer. Put a few on her face for good luck, but all after she was dead."

"Which means the killer thought fingerprints would help us."

"So it would seem," said Miller, not without interest. He didn't dislike Powder, but there was a presumptuousness about him which didn't fit smoothly into a working team.

"I wonder," said Powder. "Is there any relation between toe whorls and finger whorls? You'd think there would be. They might not be exact, but you'd think out of a thousand sets of fingerprints you could eliminate most of them from the toe prints."

Miller smiled wryly. "Down the corridor, turn right for ID. E411."

"Yeah," said Powder. He pushed off the door frame. And walked downstairs to the Night Cover Room of the detective division.

The first call requiring a detective presence didn't come until 7:40. Plenty of time before it for Powder to impress on three detective sergeants just how much confusion the new roster man was going to cause. His fourth sergeant was late.

**NIGHT COVER**

The call was an armed robbery in Edward-4, a near-northside neighborhood. No shots fired, but the owner—it was a liquor store—had suffered a suspected heart attack after calling the police, so Powder sent a man to take over from the uniformed patrolman first on the scene.

He sent Alexander Smith, his aged probationer. Alexander Smith, as opposed to Sid Smith, the kid with the beard. Worlds of difference.

"Let him make something out of this one," Powder said to no one in particular after Alexander Smith was out the door.

Stretch. Yawn.

An hour later things were in hand. The fourth cover detective, Salimbean, had arrived at last and was duly put on report. A couple more calls, but no one hijacking the mayor. Powder caught up with the paperwork in his In-Tray. He'd left a few reports over day because the woman's body had come near the end of the shift the previous night, at 2:15 A.M.

The Cover Lieutenant goes out to take care of bodies himself. And that slows down his read-through of the night's reports prepared by the sergeants, because it gives him a report of his own to write. Not a long one; just enough to give the day man a solid platform to start his work from. Get a medico in, the lab; take some pictures. Follow up any hot leads.

No hot leads last night. Unidentified female body on a vacant lot. Strictly cold last night. And took too long, too.

There's no way you can get through a 2:15 body and all the night's reports before the end of a 3:00 A.M. shift.


At 9:15 Powder had just decided to go downstairs to the coffee machine in the Vending Canteen. But he looked up to see a high-cheeked man in a green shirt and brown jacket come to a halt in front of his desk.

"Lieutenant Powder?" the man asked nervously.

"Who the hell sent you up here?" grumbled Powder. He looked past the man over the half-walls which separated his niche from the desks of his sergeants. Schleutter and Sid Smith were in, working hard with heads low. Jokers.

"I asked downstairs . . . I don't know who it was . . . and here, at the door, a man said you were in charge."

Powder leaned back and nodded. At that moment Alexander Smith, the probationer, walked into the Night Room leading a handcuffed man.

Now, what had he been sent out to? Armed robbery? Armed robbery. What the hell was he doing bringing him in here?

"Smith! What the hell are you doing bringing a prisoner in here for?" Powder stood up and said to his visitor, "Just a minute."

"I've brought him in for interrogation," said Smith obliviously. "Just wanted to explain why I've been so long. You see, I went out to the liquor store, and the owner there had died, and—"

"Get this man out of here. Don't you know enough to deal with a prisoner before you come in here to tell me how smart you've been?"

Alexander Smith looked chagrined.

"Doesn't anybody know anything?"

Dale Schleutter came over and took the prisoner's arm. "I'll take care of him until you finish with the boss." Before Powder or Alexander Smith could think whether they should complain, Schleutter had led the prisoner out of the Night Room.

"This was your armed robbery, then?" asked Powder.

"Well, no, not exactly," said Smith, who was still excited. "Not the same one. Another one."

"Another one?"

"See, we was inside talking to the guy's wife that died in the first stick-up when we heard a shot around the corner and this guy I brought in was sticking up an all-night grocery around the corner from the liquor store."

"Anyone hurt?"

"Naw, he just wanted to scare the old man that runs it. Boy, Lieutenant, I never seen anybody get his hands up so fast as this guy I brought in when five of us come around that corner. I had to laugh, I really did."

Powder just shook his head. If Alexander Smith had anything to offer the Indianapolis Detective Division, it was luck.

"I'll take him, shall I?" Smith was asking about the interrogation. "I wouldn't be surprised if he was the same guy held up the liquor store. Wouldn't be at all surprised. The description is close."

Powder rubbed his face. Night Cover is one of the assignments probationary detective sergeants get broken in with. They can't do so much harm. "You take him, Smith. He's all yours."

"Gee, thanks, Lieutenant."

Alexander Smith. Thirty-nine and too old to make the change from uniform department to detectives. Too old—anybody knew that. Except the fools at Personnel.

The man with high cheekbones was still standing in Powder's cubicle.

"Sit down, sit down," said Powder as he came back.

The man sat down quickly. "Name is Wilkins," he said.

"How do you do," said Powder, over-enthusiastic by way of emphasizing his pleasure at any relief from Alexander Smith. "I'm Detective Lieutenant Leroy Powder. What can I do for you this fine April evening?"

"Well . . ." The man hesitated, despite all the time he'd had to prepare his little speech. "You see, I'm a student at IU Extension." Cough. "A 'mature student' and I'm studying Traffic Management."

"A course of some kind, this is?"

"That's right. City Planning 204867b, Traffic Management in a Congested Society. Tuesday and Thursday." The man coughed again, a nervous little cough. "I've never been in a, um, police station before."

Powder turned slightly in his chair to show his holstered gun more prominently. "Relax. It's just like being at home," he said, and looked at his watch. To offer the guy coffee or not. Would it keep him here longer? Yeah, it probably would. "What can I do for you, Mr. Wilkins?"

"Well, I have a report to do. A term paper, and I had this idea."


Twenty-two minutes later Powder felt martyred. So he sacrificed quality for speed and instead of going downstairs to the Vending Canteen he just walked down the corridor to the Forensic Laboratory. It was still early enough. Forensic works late night but not all night.

"Lock up your daughters," someone said as Powder pushed the lab door open.

"I haven't got the time to mess around. I want some coffee."

"We know, we know. You only got seven toes."

Powder walked over to the large flask which was kept at a perpetual simmer. When some of the putative coffee had passed into a beaker, Powder held the flask up to the light. "Why don't I ever see coffee grounds in this thing?"

Someone across the room mumbled, "Don't ask."

Someone else said, "Make a note, Charlie—we gotta work on some synthetic coffee grounds."

"There's not much left," said Powder as he put it back. "You guys had a lot of time on your hands?"

"You don't think *we* drink that stuff, do you?" From across the room again.

"Naw, just the freaks down the hall have been celebrating."

"Celebrating? Who?" asked Powder.

"Didn't you hear? Drug Squad got some fancy citation today. Some national thing. You may not have realized it, Lieutenant, but for a city in our classification Indianapolis has an outstanding record against drugs. Recently anyway. Figures are down over the last couple of years."

"I hadn't heard," said Powder. "And they celebrate with your coffee?"

"We offered them some of our other special mixtures . . . but they're a pretty straight bunch."

"Freaks," somebody said.

"Well, maybe they get their pleasures elsewhere."

"Freaks."

"Cool it, will you? The lieutenant here will think we don't appreciate our best customers."

"Well," said Powder, "it's rough duty. I wouldn't want it."

"Who would? That's what makes you think; but we figured they ought to be providing *us* with the party supplies, rather than us them."

"Why?" asked Powder.

"We do all their work for them. We spend all day and most of the night telling them what's in the sugar cubes they bring in. Let me tell you, if we didn't have to deal with all this drugs stuff, we'd have a pretty well-staffed crime lab here. But analyzing pocket scrapings for aspirin fragments, it distorts our whole perspective. If we only—"

"Booooo," from the back.

"Don't get him started, Lieutenant."

"Give us a break."

"Yeah," said Powder. "Only we don't make the rules, do we? We're just the slobs who fill the jobs."

"I just wish I got a chance to do my job."

"Boooooo."

"Well, gentlemen," said Powder, "much as I enjoy your uplifting conversation . . ." He poured a little liquid down the sink and rinsed out the beaker.

"Aw, he didn't finish it, fellas. What's the matter, Lieutenant, didn't you like it?"

"Let him go. He's got to get back to work to win himself an award."

"Hey, we never asked him if he wanted a sugar cube for his coffee."

"Hey, Lieutenant, do you . . ."

Powder walked slowly toward the Night Room. But before he reached the door, Alexander Smith came out of an interview room and accosted him. "I've interrogated the prisoner."

"Oh?"

"And I don't really think he did both jobs."

"Can't get him to confess to the liquor store while he's at it, eh?" said Powder sourly.

"Well, I'd like to see you do any better with him," said Smith earnestly. The refining of a raw detective is a wondrous thing.

"You didn't really think he'd done them both, did you?" asked Powder.

"Well . . ." said Smith.

He did. Christ! He gets an armed robbery walking straight into his arms, and he's not satisfied. He has to have two armed robberies.

"Did the man who robbed the liquor store have to fire a shot to scare the liquor-store proprietor?"

"Well, no."

"And how much did he get away from the liquor store with?"

"About three hundred."

"And how long after the liquor-store job did the grocery store happen?"

"Twenty, twenty-five minutes."

Powder shrugged. "Take what you're given, Smith. You got the cleanest, easiest armed-robbery arrest that you'll ever get. Just because a dumb kid tries his first stick-up at a two-bit grocery store around the corner from where someone better at it has just done a liquor store. Rotten bad luck which is your good luck. What do you want for nothing?"

# NIGHT COVER

"I didn't realize you were back," said Powder as he re-entered the Night Room.

"Just a few minutes ago," said Sid Smith. The other Smith, Sidney R., was a different case. An opposite. Shrewd, ambitious; bearded to disassociate himself from the old guard. At twenty-five, young to be a detective and impatient with it. He was already most of the way through the report on the case he'd been sent to cover.

"I had a guy in here a few minutes ago you would have liked," said Powder. "A student. A scholar. He thinks the booze people get on airplanes is a menace to society."

"Oh?" said Sid Smith. He felt obliged to pay attention. But he felt Powder resented him because he, Smith, was clearly on the way up and oozed competence. While Powder was stuck as a Night lieutenant. How someone gets stuck like that, Smith didn't know. "How does a guy just walk up to the third floor to come to you? I thought they screened them on the first floor."

Powder shrugged. "I got a friend down there who sends them up."

"Some friend," said Sid Smith.

"Particularly businessmen. He figures the plane people pour alcohol down their passengers' throats to keep them from being scared of flying. They don't think about what the booze might do after they get off the plane. He says you just gotta think about all the guys who go straight from the plane to a rented car. Particularly the ones who are in unfamiliar cities." Powder chuckled.

"I hope you told the guy what he could do with it," said Smith.

"No," said Powder abruptly. "I think he has a point."

Crazy to waste time on cranks, thought Sidney Smith. He stroked his chin whiskers.

No sense of justice, Powder thought. "No, I told him how to get in touch with the traffic boys. I think if he goes through a few years' auto accidents he might find a pattern. Kind of interesting, I thought."

"Car-rental people will tell you quick enough, if you're really interested," said Smith, and turned back to his report, having paid attention the requisite time.

Half an hour later Powder was talking to Schleutter. "All right, Dale, here's a hypothetical question for you. Help you become a better cop. You arrest a guy in the act of holding up a grocery store and twenty-five minutes earlier a liquor store is held up a block away. You want to know whether the same guy did both jobs. What's the first thing you look for?"

"A six-pack and some peanuts?" offered Schleutter and scratched at his stomach through his shirt. Dale Schleutter had been a detective sergeant for a long time, had worked with Powder often enough to know how to handle his hypothetical questions. The men were, relatively speaking, friends. To the extent that Schleutter had even once told Powder he shouldn't "dwell on things so much."

"Stick it up your twinkie," said Powder.

Six burglaries, an armed robbery, two assaults and a bomb scare later, Powder was within a half-hour of the end of his shift.

Harold Salimbean, who'd had a busy night after he'd managed to come to work, hailed Powder across the room. "Phone, Lieutenant. He'll only speak to you."

Looked up, squinted. Salimbean was a responsible type. But late too often recently. Powder picked up his phone. "Powder."

"Roy, that you?"

"Who's talking?"

"This is Johnny Uncle, Roy. Look, I was walking along the street and I saw something I thought you'd want to know, maybe help you out."

"What, Johnny?"

"Well, I don't want no trouble. I'm doing you a favor. You understand that, don't you?"

"What did you see, Johnny?"

"A stiff. I just seen a stiff."

"Oh yes?"

"A lady stiff at that."

"Where, Johnny?"

"You know the demolition they're doing out Tremont?"

"Haughville?"

"That's it. I was wandering around there, you know . . . like I do. And next to one of the walls I found this lady stiff. I thought you oughta know, Roy."

"Why tell *me*, Johnny? Why not just an anonymous call? Why tell anyone?"

"I want to do you a favor, Roy. You know your Johnny Uncle."

Powder paused. He knew his Johnny Uncle. "Put it back, Johnny."

"What back?" A nervous whine.

"Whatever you took off the body."

"I didn't take nothing, Roy, honest. She was as clean as a whistle."

"So?"

The phone was quiet for a moment. "It's just that when I found it, her, I got scared."

"Yeah . . . ?"

"Well . . ."

"You're trying to tell me something, Johnny."

"It's when I was on my way to where I was going."

"Before or—?"

"Oh, before I found it, before. See, I was walking up Tremont and one of your cars saw me and pulled up close and followed me."

"One of mine?"

"Aw, I don't know whether he was one of *yours*, but my time of life I know a car with two cops in it when I see it. I mean, they *followed* me, Roy. They drove along right beside me for a long time."

"Was it a patrol car, Johnny?"

"Naw, it was a plainclothes car. But, see, Roy, I got nervous and I kinda slipped behind the demolition—which I didn't intend to be going to. Then later when I found it, her, I got scared."

"Yeah?"

"Well, I figured once they found the body, well . . . these guys will remember me and I might be in trouble when I didn't do nothing to get in trouble for, you see? Now, I wouldn't stiff nobody, Roy. You know that. So I says to myself, Johnny, it's your public duty to report that stiff you saw to your old friend Roy Powder which will know you was just an accidental bystander."

"Why'd you kill her, Johnny?"

"Aw, Roy."

Powder laughed. "How long since you found her?"

"Maybe fifteen minutes, half an hour."

"Or maybe a couple of hours?"

Quietly. "Maybe."

"How long had she been dead?"

"Now, how do I know that?"

"Well, you know if it smelled."

"It didn't smell none."

"Was she still warm?"

"Now, Roy, how would—"

"Was she warm?" Powder demanded.

Quietly. "Pretty warm, Roy," said Johnny Uncle.


"Come on, Harold," said Powder.

"Give me a break, will you, Lieutenant? Smith will be back in a couple of minutes. He hasn't got a wife and mine's going to divorce me if I'm late home. It's bad enough being on nights." Salimbean hesitated. Then said resignedly, "I know I don't rate a break, being late again and all."

Powder stopped in the doorway to put on his raincoat. Harold Salimbean sighed. If he hadn't been tired he would never have

# NIGHT COVER

spoken to Powder that way. Powder had a reputation for being a real driver.

Powder said sternly, "You call Communications and tell them to send me George-1 and a couple of other Georges to Tremont and Tenth. And you get the homicide technicians over there, too. But make sure you don't tell the Georges it's a homicide; I don't want all the young bucks from Charlie, David and Edward busting into George on the chance they can pick up a runaway murderer."

"Right, Lieutenant," said Salimbean resignedly.

"Then you come back up here and send me Smith."

"Which one?"

"There's not much to choose."

It wasn't till Powder had left that Salimbean realized he could go home on time. It was an unexpectedly benevolent response to his request. He didn't understand.

## 2

At ten to three Powder rolled up at the corner of Tremont and 10th, where there were two police cars, one behind the other. Two uniformed officers walked over as Powder rolled down his window. Cool drizzle; April night.

"What's up, Lieutenant? Why the mystery?"

"Can't quite see your face, you're . . ."

"Sergeant Mildmay. George District. This is the section patrolman. I've got another man on his way."

"Mildmay," said Powder, trying to place the man. He couldn't. "What time is it?"

Mildmay squinted at his left wrist to get the minute right. "Two fifty-two A.M."

Powder rubbed his face with both hands. "I gotta get out, I suppose."

Patiently the two uniformed officers waited and watched. Powder turned his radio up and got out. "Over here," he said, and led them to the base of a streetlight. "Like to have something to lean against," said Powder and slouched against the pole.

The section man, who read two papers a day and a couple of weekly news magazines, stood back and thought to himself, Perfect fucking target. He studied the windows in buildings nearby.

"You know," said Powder, "when I was about thirteen I had a girl friend who hated me to lean against a pole like this." He exaggerated his slouch. "She said it looked common." He chuckled.

There was no answer to it, so the three men stood in silence.

Then the section man said, "Here he comes." Seconds later a fourth police car pulled up, with a screech of tires, behind the other three. Powder, still in no hurry, put his hands over his ears. "Enough noise to wake the dead," he said conversationally.

"What's up?" asked a tall young officer with a coppery mustache as he joined the crowd.

The section man shrugged and smirked. He took life seriously.

"We just standing around and waiting for something?" asked the second patrolman, who had made noisy time all the way from his own patrol section.

"This," said Mildmay, "is Lieutenant Powder."

Since Powder was obviously a detective—in plainclothes—and a lieutenant, the number-two knew something was happening. There are poles to lean on closer to Headquarters than the streetlight at Tremont and 10th.

The section man straightened suddenly. "Man crossing the street," he said. He hadn't seen any movements in the windows.

**NIGHT COVER**

But to see an actual human being walking toward them rather than away, that had startled him. An involuntary thing.

Everybody looked.

"Just a bum," said number-two.

"Bad leg," said Mildmay.

Powder shifted up off his pole. "Anybody got a cigarette?"

Mildmay won the race. Powder took two sticks out of the sergeant's pack.

"He's stopped on the corner across the street," said the section man. "Hey, you know I saw an old guy with a limp around here while I was patrolling."

Number-two, anticipating, whipped out a pistol-shaped lighter and bared a flame for Powder's light-up.

"Wonder if the old guy has a light," said Powder. In such a way as to make clear he didn't want company, Powder crossed the street to the old man.

According to Johnny Uncle, the body was a few blocks away, straight down Tremont.

"Ride in my car," said Powder.

"No, I'm gonna walk," said Johnny firmly. He buttoned a pocket flap over the two cigarettes.

"What do you mean, you're going to walk?"

"I can still walk, you know."

Powder frowned. Crossed the street back to the leaning lamp. "All right, get your cars. Follow me."

One after another the three patrol cars U-turned on 10th Street to line up behind Powder as he drove at two miles an hour alongside Johnny Uncle. Number-two made the loudest squeal on the U-turns, but it was the section man who came closest to hitting the back of the car in front of him.

Powder called Communications. He wanted to tell them where he was going to be so they could give more exact directions to Smith and the lab team.

"Where are you, Lieutenant?" said the radio.

"South of Tenth Street on Tremont."

"Would you please call in on the North and West Frequency and repeat your instructions? Thank you."

Damn. He switched from 158.85 mhz to 155.01 mhz and repeated his message.

He'd left the radio on East and South after going to see the body the previous night. The fact he hadn't been out this whole shift showed it had been a quiet night till now.

And now Johnny refused to ride in a warm car. Something new every day. And two bodies in two days. That was something old. Ho hum, another body.

Powder unhitched the heavy-duty flashlight from its clip.

Johnny stopped after nearly three blocks and pointed to a gap between two partly demolished houses. Powder got out of his car and told the following officers to wait where they were. He brought the flashlight up and turned it on Johnny's face.

"Hey, Roy, cut it out. Come on, stop it."

Powder held the old man firmly by an arm and used the intense beam to examine Johnny's clothes. Brown spots on his jacket and more on both sleeves.

"You old reprobate," Powder swore.

"You call me old, you call yourself old," Johnny squawked. "You know I ain't three years older than you."

"No wonder you were afraid someone would remember you."

"Let go!"

"If you disturbed anything around that body . . ." said Powder furiously.

"I didn't disturb nothing, Roy, honest. Honest!"

Johnny led the quartet between the two houses. Through the rubble of an erstwhile kitchen to the body.

That she had been a big woman was clear. Not tall but heavy. Lot of dead weight. She lay uncomfortably at the junction between wall and floor of the derelict half-room. As if to emphasize the unlikeliness of her living presence, she lay with a pile of bricks under her back. There were several other bricks around. Her face was a pulpy mess.

As the other officers lined up behind him, Powder panned around the body with his light beam.

"So that's what it's all about," said the number-two, exhaling what the three uniformed men felt.

"Well, what does it look like to you?" said Powder.

"She's dead, I suppose," offered the section man.

The lab team arrived about ten minutes later. Illuminated the area of the corpse, took a lot of pictures, discovered a blood-covered brick and little else of interest.

"Hey, Lieutenant Powder!" called a voice from the road.

Powder left the kitchen.

"Look what I found!"

Near the row of parked cars two men stood.

"Make him let me go, Roy," a voice whined.

"He was creeping away as I rolled up."

Powder flashed his beam in the face of the man who held Johnny Uncle by the arm. It was young Smith, Sid.

"You," said Powder with some distaste.

"Hal Salimbean said you wanted me. And like I say, this guy was sneaking away. And look." Smith covered Johnny's arms with his own flash beam. "He's got blood all over his sleeves."

"Yeah," said Powder. "I know."

"I wasn't going nowhere, Roy," whined Johnny.

"Yeah, yeah."

"He's covered with blood," repeated Smith, confused at Powder's indifference.

"He's covered with blood," mimicked Powder. "What do you want me to do, give him a bath?"

"But . . ."

"I didn't do nothing, Roy, honest."

"He didn't do nothing, Smith. Honest." Powder mimicked Johnny. "All he did was find a corpse and give it the once over, looking for something he could take off it. And he looked at the hands for rings, only he found there weren't any fingers left to have rings on."

"Someone bashed 'em," said Johnny quietly.

"And that's why he's covered with blood. And the blood's why we're here at all instead of letting this body cool and harden and age until some kid found it. Thank the kind man for giving us a call, Smith. We should be grateful."

Smith released his hold.

"Aw, Roy, I—"

"Shut up," snapped Powder. "Smith, take our friend into your car and get his statement."

Powder walked away and left the two men looking at each other.

At 5:15 Powder was starting on a double portion of barbecued ribs and a green salad. The place was on Northwestern Avenue, near the canal, and it was called All Knight Ribs.

"You're in late tonight," said Knight, an amiable man with the girth of Henry VIII and a gold tooth.

"Found a body. You know anything about it?"

Knight laughed hugely. "When have I ever known anything about anything?"

"Wouldn't want you not to tell me because you thought I wasn't interested," said Powder, stripping a bone.

"Got a letter from Alaska," said Knight. Alaska was his darkest son. "He say everything's fine."

"Liar," said Powder.

"Yeah, he is," said Knight. "Man, I hope he be OK."

"Never give up hoping. Where's Ella tonight?"

"I'll tell her you asked."

# NIGHT COVER

"Just don't tell my wife," said Powder.

"Naw. Tuesday is a quiet night. She don't feel so good."

"You're all heart."

"Not quite all," said Knight, then held his stomach and roared with laughter.

"Better watch out," said Powder. "You gonna die young."

"Shit, man," said Knight, "my grandfather, he was twice as big as me and he lived to a hundred and fifty. I'm only half so big. I gotta settle for seventy-five."

"If you die when you're seventy-five, what am I going to do for ribs?"

"I teach you. Then you take over for me."

"There are days that's positively tempting," said Powder, sounding more serious than he intended. He finished his meal in silence. Paid the bill.

"Very kind," said Knight as he rang the money up.

"Look," said Powder. "Here's a hypothetical question that will make you a better cop."

Knight laughed.

"You pick up a guy in the act of robbing a rib take-out place and it happens that a liquor store two blocks away was robbed twenty minutes ago. Right?"

"Yeah . . ." said Knight speculatively.

"And you want to know whether maybe he did the liquor store, too. What's the first thing you look for?"

"What he take from the liquor store," said Knight slowly, as if he was expecting there to be a lot more to it.

"Exactly," said Powder. "If he picks up three hundred bucks and then fifteen, twenty minutes later he hasn't got it, he never picked up the three hundred bucks."

"You have a hard night?" Knight asked.

Powder rubbed his face with both hands. "Yeah, I guess so."

Pushing six, with more than an hour to kill, Powder drove to the hill in Holliday Park and watched the sun come up.

## 3

The phone rang and rang and rang. Go away. Go away. Go away.

But it didn't. "Hello," finally.

"Glad I caught you at home, Lieutenant Powder," said a wide-awake voice.

Powder was not yet awake enough to tell the voice what it could do with its gladness.

"You there, Lieutenant?"

"What you want?"

"It's about that corpse you covered last night."

Last night? Last year. Oh yeah, last night. "What about it?"

"Oh, this is Brindell. Well, the guy who found it, John Daeger, you know him? He says he knows you."

"I know him."

"Well, we ask him about his involvement and he keeps crying. We ask him anything and all he does is cry. He's been at it for hours, I don't know what the hell to do. So I thought I'd try you. Sorry if I bothered you."

"Just a sec." Powder pulled his jacket off the chair next to the bed. Took his date book out and opened to a page headed *Memoranda.* "What's your full name, Brindell?"

"Huh?"

"Your name, damn it."

"Howard. Howard Brindell, Detective Sergeant."

"Home phone?"

"864-1101."

Powder wrote it all down and memorandamned (sic) the man: "Call at 3 A.M."

"Tell you what you do, Brindell. You take old Johnny—now, the way to make him feel secure is to give him a good meal, a high-class hamburger, Salisbury steak because his teeth are bad. And you let him rest on his own for a while and then after a couple of hours he won't cry anymore."

"How the hell am I supposed to get money for a Salisbury steak for a guy like that?"

"Do you want to get what he has to tell you or not?"

"Well . . ."

"What you so concerned about Johnny for?"

"The report I got made it look pretty bad for him. One of your men. Here, Sergeant Smith. Look, Lieutenant, since you know him, I thought you might come in a little early and help us out."

"Gee, I'd like to, Brindell. I really would. But you take Johnny out and then give him a rest. It's the only way. Even if I did come in I couldn't help you until he's more relaxed. Pity you didn't call me earlier."

"Yeah," said Brindell, who didn't know whether he'd been helped or not.

When the phone was back in its cradle Powder leafed through his date book to the page headed *Wednesday, April 25*. At the bottom he wrote "See Memoranda." At the bottom of the 26th and 27th he wrote "Ditto." Three lashes for a first offense.

Powder threw the book against the bedroom door hard. Then he turned over and went back to sleep.


They learn fast enough how to be tough, Powder thought as he drove in. And they learn fast enough how to break the tough ones who'll break. But it never occurs to them that they might get soft ones. They just don't know how to talk to people who are soft.

It's a hard, hard world, he thought later, in the elevator up to the fourth floor.

"You're early, Roy," someone said. He didn't notice who.

Not all that early. Then checked his watch. Five to six.

"Somewhere around this place," he said chattily to Sergeant Mabel, Homicide and Robbery reception officer, "there is a sergeant with a checkered future called Brindle. Where do I find him?"

It took awhile, but after she reduced the problem to "Brindell," it all worked out.

"You do what I told you?" said Powder to Brindell when at last they met.

"Yeah, but I don't know how it helps. The old guy cried all the way through the meal."

"But did he eat it?"

"Oh, he ate it. How do you happen to know this guy, Lieutenant? If I may ask."

"We were in grade school together."

Johnny Uncle was brought downstairs to an interview room where Powder was perusing Smith's report. He'd *told* the damn kid how Johnny came to be bloody. Damn the Sid Smiths of this world. They know a lot, but they can't ever learn anything.

"Hello, Mr. Daeger."

"Oh my God, Roy, am I glad to see you," said Johnny, and began to cry.

"They giving you any rest?"

No answer. Boo hoo. Boo hoo. Powder waited it out. He guessed well enough about Johnny's rest, lack of it. Been sent home at 4:30 in the morning and told to stay available. Can't have slept while waiting, waiting. Then 8:00 Brindell reports to work and draws the case. 9:30 he's had time to read the reports; get the preliminary lab report. 10:00 Brindell's taken a deep breath and said, OK, let's go bring this John Daeger in for a chat.

Boo hoo. Boo hooooo.

"I feel so hopeless, Roy. So damn hopeless."

"C'mon, John," said Powder gently. "You gonna make me look bad if you don't talk to me. This guy's a friend of mine, I told them. A friend. He'll chat to me."

"But I didn't do anything," whined Johnny Uncle.

"Fine. So you'll be out on the streets in an hour or so."
"And I'm so tired. I sleep during the day, you know."
"I know."
"It's warmer in the day."
"You want a warm place, is that it?"
"Wouldn't mind."

Powder nodded. "So tell me just what happened, just what you saw, so we can get on with our job."

"All right," said Johnny, and then didn't say anything.

"What happened first?" said Powder finally.

"Well, I was walking along Tremont last night."

"Shuffling," said Powder.

"Yeah, kinda shuffling," Daeger said with a glint which would grow into a smile. "And thinking. You know, about what a hopeless failure I made of my life." This time, strictly matter-of-fact. "When I look up and see a car coming toward me."

"Yeah?"

"Just a car. So I don't think nothing until it turns around and pulls up beside me and these two guys look at me hard. They gotta be cops. I told you last night. Well, I don't know what they're thinking about me, but I can see they're talking. So, you know, kind of natural I slip aside."

"Behind houses?"

"No. These are already pulled down, and besides," the smile fruiting, "I did them the night before, see? But I step aside. And after a minute the car goes away."

"And you stay off the road?"

"Yeah."

"What time was this?"

"Nine, ten."

"And?"

"And I find the stiff." Pause. "I get away as soon as I can, but my luck, I'm not hardly back on the road but what do I see but a patrol car."

"A patrol car?"

"Yeah . . . And *he* notices me, I can see. I thought it over and I called you."

Two hours later. A lot of thought.

"I go days without seeing a cop," Johnny said. "Days!"

"Well?" said Brindell when Powder came back to the Day Room after arranging for Johnny to spend the night on the fifth floor in a warm cell.

"Go home, get a good night's sleep," said Powder. "Read my report in the morning." Powder left the room and went to the Canteen.

Brindell was gone when Powder came back to the Day Room. He had a look into Miller's cubicle as he went by, but it was empty.

Powder sat down at his desk. Looked for messages, but there was none. While he was there he picked up the phone, dialed a few digits.

"This is Lieutenant Powder," he said crisply. "Who'd you give lab reports on that body I dug up last night?"

Wait.

"Well, who the hell besides Brindell!"

Wait.

"Look, I want to see a copy."

Interrupting.

"Well, I'm entitled to be interested. Maybe she reminded me of my grandmother. You damn well send me a copy tonight." He slammed down the receiver. Rubbed his face.

9:00. A busy night but no more bodies. Seem to come in pairs. He thought back the three months to the week before his January vacation. There was a pair of murders then, too.

"Sergeant Powder?"

"Huh?"

"I was directed to you, if you're Sergeant Powder," said a thin boy in a blue suit. His hair was straight, straw-colored and lay flat on his head. It looked funny.

"Lieutenant Powder," Powder said. Defensive. "What do you want?"

"I have a problem. If you have a few moments. If it's not convenient, however, I can come back another time."

They looked at each other for a few seconds.

"Hell," said Powder, whose anger with Brindell had cooled with the routine of work. "Come in, sit down. You want some coffee?"

The boy limped to one of Powder's chairs. His left leg was less functional than his right.

"Well . . ." The boy hesitated.

"Look, I'm going to a machine for some for myself. You want a cup, I'll get you a cup. I'll be back in a minute."

"I don't like coffee," said the boy. "But if there's tea, I'll have some of that."

As he went past the seated boy Powder saw why the hair looked funny. Pulled back tight into a pony tail.

Alexander Smith, the old probationer, was in the office and working single-mindedly on a report. "Keep an eye on the kid over there while I'm gone," said Powder.

Smith stopped what he was doing and watched the boy intently.

Powder frowned as he left. For crying out loud!

But he was smiling on the way back. Realizing the kid probably had combed his hair special. Making the effort to clean himself up for the unaccustomed voluntary visit to the police station.

Powder re-entered his partitioned space with the two cups. Black coffee and black tea.

"Here you go. Now tell me. What are you? Mature student?"

"Well," said the kid. "I don't know about mature." He drank heavily from the hot tea and smiled. "Thank you."

"So?" said Powder. "Problem?"

"Yes," said the boy. Twenty, give or take a year. He put the paper teacup on the edge of Powder's desk, folded his hands in his lap and began. "I'm a student at a private high school called the University School."

Powder nodded in a vague way; he knew the name in a vague way.

"There are about a hundred and eighty of us in the four years, though some are in one year in one subject and in another in others."

"Could you spare me the background? If your problem is a police matter, there'll be time enough for all that."

The boy stopped and rubbed his chin. The chin was reddened and a little rashy. Could he have shaved a ragged teenage beard just to come in to talk tonight?

"I'll try and say it as briefly as I can. But I need you to know how important it is." Intent stare.

Powder raised an eyebrow.

"In this school," said the boy, "they have two-way speakers in every room. From the office they can talk to any room or listen in to any room whenever they like. Like Big Brother."

"Oh yes?"

"Well, without commenting on the moral position about such two-way speakers, not only for the students but for the teachers, last week I was working late in one of these rooms—"

"A classroom?"

"A classroom. And in the office a teacher was having a meeting with the owner."

"Yes?"

The kid smiled, unable to control it. "And someone had left the intercom thing on."

"Very titillating for you, I'm sure." It didn't quite wipe off the juvenile grin.

"Well, he, the owner, was telling the teacher about grades at the end of the semester."

"Look, son, if you got a grade you don't like, that's no business of mine." Powder's patience decreased with the coffee in his cup.

"My name is Rex," said the kid. "Rex, not 'son.'"

And touchy with it. Powder pulled a piece of paper out of his drawer. "Rex what?"

"Rex Funkhouser."

"Where do you live?"

"Fourteen Alberta Street, Eagledale."

Eagledale; worth two eyebrows. "They let you live around there?" asked Powder, more than half serious.

"My parents and their neighbors are not the subject of this visit," said Rex Funkhouser seriously. "We coexist."

"Oh," said Powder.

Rex Funkhouser rubbed his chin.

"Go on," said Powder.

"Well." Tight-lipped now. "I overheard about grades."

"Delivery, Lieutenant!" Schleutter passed a small collection of paper over the half-wall. "Medical report from last night." Schleutter looked down at the back of Rex's head, up at Powder's face, which appeared to frown even in repose. Schleutter winked and left.

"Go on," Powder said.

Rex squirmed slightly in his chair. "I heard the school owner change the grades that the teacher wanted to give some of his students. I heard him *fail* one boy because his parents won't send him to the school next year if he passes. And I heard him pass another kid because his parents won't send him back if he fails again."

"I'm sure there was more to it."

"On my life," Rex said, breathing heavily. "It was as coldblooded as that. There just wasn't any question."

"Well," said Powder, and took a breath. "And which one were you? The one who failed?"

Rex grunted; he was emotionally worked up. "No. I'm one of

their 'good' students. I work hard. They're not used to it, which is why they didn't expect anybody to be studying in the school that late."

"I see," said Powder.

"You don't understand what that cruddy school means to those kids. For most of them it's their last chance. And that . . . fat . . . bastard just plays with their lives for the profit motive!"

Feeling scorched by Rex's fired-up passion, looking at the medical report he wanted to read, Powder tried to cool the kid down. "I'm afraid, son—Rex—that I still don't see what all this has to do with me. With the police."

"I thought if a school which purports to be, you know, a school gives out grades which are supposed to be, you know, grades, but which aren't true grades . . . I mean, isn't that like fraud? You people are concerned about money and buying goods and services. If you send your kid to a school and pay for it and then the school owner gives out grades in order to get more money out of you, isn't that extortion or fraud or something?"

Breath. Over Rex's shoulder Powder saw Schleutter lifting eyes to the heavens. "You've got to appreciate my position. However unfortunate the situation you describe may be, morally, it's not a crime. It doesn't seem to be something I can do anything about."

"OK," Rex said abruptly. "I tried. He says to try, so I tried." He rose, with difficulty, to leave.

"Who said to try?" asked Powder.

"You wouldn't understand."

"And what's that supposed to mean?"

"It means you wouldn't understand. It means you wouldn't like it. It means you'd foam at the mouth. I should have known what kind of answer I'd get here. I *did* know. But he says to try, so I tried."

"Someone advised you to consult the police about the problem you've described."

"As a first step. In a kind of way. Yes." Rex standing, with Powder sitting. Rex no longer wanting something, feeling more belligerent.

"Who?" Powder asked.

"You wouldn't like it," said Rex.

"How do you come to know what the hell *I* like, kid? Don't you come in here and tell *me*. I'm perfectly capable of doing my thinking for myself. Now, who told you to come in here with a problem like that?"

Rex Funkhouser sat down again. "Mao Tse-tung."

Powder leaned on the palm of his left hand, not quite believing.

"I told you you wouldn't like it."

Powder raised his voice. "When I don't like something, it's not ambiguous, damn it. I shout and swear and stamp my fucking feet." He stamped a foot, and kept shouting. "God damn it, I don't like people telling me what I think!" Pause. Then quietly, "But I don't mind your coming to see me because Mao Tse-tung told you to. Why should I mind that? In fact, I like it, I like it."

Rex had to smile. And whatever else he'd done, Powder had given this kid what he didn't expect.

"And how is Mr. Tung these days? Lumbago not acting up again, I hope?"

"It would be Mr. Mao," said Rex, eager to impart knowledge. "His last name is Mao even though it's said first."

"I see," said Powder. "And just when did he tell you to come to me?"

"When you are faced with a problem," said Rex Funkhouser formally, "you must try to use all the resources available. It's called pragmatism."

"Oh yes?"

"That's the essence of one of Mao's thoughts. You see, the police can be thought of as one of the resources that might be available for solving my problem. However reactionary much of your other function may be. You see?"

"I see," said Powder, his interest fading again.

"But you only deal with crimes. Ruining people's lives isn't a crime for you. I understand now. I tried. So now I must try something else."

"Anything particular in mind?"

Funkhouser spread his hands, palms down. Powder thought he was saying, Mind your own business. But he wasn't. "May I tell you the famous story of the Foolish Old Man Who Removed Mountains?"

Over Rex's shoulder Powder saw Schleutter collapse in his chair in silent laughter. It was enough to make Powder listen to the kid again and say loudly, contrarily, "Sergeant Schleutter, no work to do?"

Schleutter didn't like being called in front of the kid; he stopped laughing.

Powder nodded to Rex.

"It's about an old man in ancient times whose house faced south, but whose view was obstructed by two great mountains."

"Oh yes?"

"Together with his sons he began to dig the mountains away. A so-called wise man saw them and he laughed at them for attempting the impossible. But the old man was not daunted."

Perversely, Schleutter began to act out the parable in mime.

"He replied to the wise man: 'When I die, my sons will carry on; when they die, there will be my grandsons and then their sons and grandsons and so on to infinity. High as they are, the mountains can never grow any higher. Every bit we dig away will make them that much lower. So why can't we dig them away?'" Rex stopped.

"That's the end?"

"Yes."

"Did they dig them away?"

Rex sighed. "That's not the point."

Shrug. "I just like to know how things come out," said Powder. "Seems like a lot of trouble for a better view. Even so, I don't quite understand how this applies to the problem of your friend getting failed when he might not deserve it."

"He's not my friend. I don't even know the person involved. But Mao's story applies in two senses."

"Oh yes?"

"If we keep chipping away at injustice we can conquer it, and—"

"But," interrupted Powder, "the mountains can't grow any bigger. Injustice can."

"But the principle applies," said Rex pedagogically. "And it applies to the specific case in the sense that one must not be afraid to tackle a problem just because it seems to be impossible."

"Yes, I understand that," Powder said.

"And now that you won't help, I just have to try something else." Rex rose again. Again with difficulty. "But thank you for listening to me."

The acknowledgment took Powder a little by surprise. He said, "If you ever have a crime . . ."

Rex pivoted on his better foot. Limped out of the room. Powder watched him go. It took quite awhile.

Schleutter watched, too, then got up and came over to Powder's desk. "Did I ever tell you the famous story of the Senile Lieutenant Who Listened to Fools?"

"Don't make fun of Mao," said Powder crankily. "If you'd listened to him, you'd have been a lieutenant by now yourself."

Schleutter smiled. "Why ain't you that patient with me?"

"You're not a member of the public; I expect you to be moderately sensible."

"Roy, you got anything special against Sid Smith? You don't like his beard or something?"

"What is this, the Heart Line? What's the matter, he think I have a down on him?"

"I was just thinking about patience."

Powder took up the medical report. "He needs humanizing."

The medical story on the new body sounded much like what Miller had told him about the previous body. Strangled elsewhere, dumped. And the fingers mutilated again, but this time not so well. Done with a brick, but one whole finger had been left intact and bits of others.

The face was ruined this time, though. The battering brick was left on the scene. Rather than a hammer taken away. Fingerprints on a brick? No, but, ugh, gruesome, the print pieces of fingers. Bit of luck to have a whole finger left. Powder looked for identification details. Nothing. Another department.

Still, how many women forty to forty-five years old, five feet four inches, 210 pounds, would there be around who were likely to get themselves murdered? Identification wasn't likely to be difficult.

No sexual assault. Just a plain, vicious, violent murder which had taken place the same night.

Still pretty warm, Johnny had said. Warm.

You occasionally get people putting corpses in freezers, which could slow decay processes enough to confuse time of death. Wonder if anybody ever heats bodies up a little to make a death look more recent? Full of good ideas, Powder thought.

A sluice of break-ins, robberies, and armed robberies. They all come the same night; television shows must be bad. At 2:15 the phone rang again and Powder was alone in the office.

"A break-in, Lieutenant," said the officer from Uniform.

"What happened?"

"Someone broke into a hardware store and stole fifteen clocks."

"Fifteen clocks?"

"That's it."

"Cover it yourselves. Good opportunity for one of your youngsters to crack a big case and make a name."

"Thanks a lot, Powder," said the voice. "I have to tell you about all of them even if you don't want them."

**NIGHT COVER**

"Yeah. Nothing but fifteen clocks?"

"All wind-up. Didn't even take electric ones."

"And nothing else stolen?"

"Not that the guy noticed. He was on the scene and reported it himself. He'll check stock thoroughly in the morning."

"How does he happen to come to the store at this time of night?"

"Fight with his wife, he says."

Speaking of fights with the wife . . . , thought Powder as he hung up.

## 4

Powder woke up not long after one. He had a shower, got dressed and gathered a selection of freshly laundered heavy work clothes. He loaded them into a paper shopping bag.

Then he went downtown. Curiosity. Also to get some gas from the police pump.

He was looking for Brindell. And found him eating a sandwich on the second floor, surrounded by vending machines.

"I've been looking for you," said Powder.

Brindell made a meal of swallowing the bite in his mouth.

"Have you made the two mashed-finger bodies yet?" Powder swung into a seat across the table from Brindell, oblivious to the conversation with two other young sergeants he had interrupted.

It took a few moments for Brindell to find his voice. "Not both, not yet."

"But you found one?"

"Yeah, the second one. She's called Hilda Chaney. Was."

"Should I have known her?"

"Thought you might have," said Brindell. "She was in the

shake-out in drug arrests twice in the last five years and she had quite a history before that."

"Who's the other one?"

"No idea. Yet. We're liaising with the Drug Squad, though."

Powder nodded. Similar murders suggest victims with something in common. "Let me know how it comes out."

"What's it to you, if I may ask, Lieutenant?" asked Brindell, who was no fonder than most cops of being questioned himself.

"Look, sonny," said Powder. "You may think of night people just being there to hold cases for you guys, but if we didn't do it right, your arrest record would drop through your drawers."

"I'm not talking about that," said Brindell. "Nobody said you didn't do a job. But once you're finished the first night, I mean, what do you care who we've identified? I mean, to make a special thing of it?"

"You've never worked with me, have you, Brindell?"

"No."

"I think I'm going to try and have you spend a month on my shift. Help you be a better cop. Hey, I'll teach you something now. How many hours a day do you work?"

"Eight hours a day, five days a week. A shift like anybody else."

"Not twenty-four hours? Not seven days a week?"

"What's the point?"

"The point is what happens to your goddamn cases while you're home trying to talk your wife into it."

"There's an overlap system and a case sheet."

"But suppose I pick up someone for shooting rabbits in the city limits and I find he's got a bloody sledgehammer in his trunk. You figure it's better for me to go through a stack of paper looking for 'hammer, sledge, bloody'? Or should I know because you told me that Janice Bloggs had her hands done with a hammer? It doesn't cost you anything to keep me up to date if I'm cop enough to want to know. If I come down here out of time to ask you, or if I was to call you up, does that hurt you? Christ, you should be happy. Because if I do come up with

# NIGHT COVER

anything that might help you, you get it, it makes your job easier. You—"

"All right! All right! I get the idea, Powder."

"Lieutenant Powder to you."

"Yeah. All right. I'm sorry I called you on it. You got every right to ask questions."

"All right. Keep me informed. You got egg salad in your lap, you know that?" Powder walked away.

Brindell looked down. He couldn't see any egg salad.


Anyhow, Powder thought as he walked along the second-floor corridor, I like to know how things come out. And as long as he was on second, he'd decided to stop at Rosters.

Nobody was at the desk. He banged on it, half expecting the roster kid to crawl out from under. Or maybe appear in a puff of smoke to do the master's bidding.

He started to write a note.

"Looking for me, Lieutenant?" said the young officer, coming through the door behind Powder.

"Yeah," said Powder. "Chairman Mao wouldn't approve of you being out of the office when you're wanted."

"What?"

Powder crumpled up his note. "Doesn't occur to you to leave some indication of where you're going?"

"I just went to the can, Lieutenant. Sorry if you were inconvenienced."

"You got the next roster set up?"

"Yessir, you want to look at it?"

"Not if it's right. You're in the statistical department, aren't you, son?"

"The statistical side of Planning. Yessir."

"Working in pretty well now?"

"It's getting better."

"Keep trying, it will come."

"Yessir."

"One thing I wondered if you would do for me."

"Yes?"

"There's an officer I would like to have with me on the roster you just finished. Sergeant Brindell. Howard."

The kid wrote it down. "I'll do my best, sir. Unless he's on reserve."

"Thanks," said Powder. "Good luck." *You'll damn well need it, you stupid . . .*

"Thank you, sir."

*Forgot to give Brindell a little phone call last night,* Powder realized as he went to the stairs. *Make up for it when I have him for four straight weeks.*

*Checking drug files, eh? Well, Hilda Chaney would be nobody's loss. Who the hell is the first one?* He tried to remember whether the first body'd had obvious needle marks. He remembered; she hadn't.

*Had a feeling she was a prostitute,* he thought.

In the police parking lot he nodded to Marlon, the attendant, and went to his car. He drove steadily out old 37, the Allisonville Road. A little past 56th Street he turned onto a gravel road across from a mailbox which presented the number 5650 in phosphorescent red. The road went due west from the northeast line of 37. Powder could see the sun, bright, leading him from high up and a little to his left.

A hundred fifty feet in, he pulled over on a shoulder only slightly more grassy than the track. A regular parking space off an irregular road.

A large plot, cut off the end of the adjoining field, was marked out. The ground cultivation had a different texture, and some young peach trees were planted along the southern boundary. They would make a delicious wall one day.

Near the parking spot was a shed. On the door Powder had painted: CLANDESTINE SHED. Clandestine because the seven-eighths of an acre was Powder's little secret. He'd bought it three years before from a farmer called Cyril and the idea then was to have a place to grow things, more room. But room had grown on him. It was one of the few things he was aware of being soft about. One day maybe a house. Call it Off Duty, he thought. If I live that long.

Inside the shed Powder changed to his gardening clothes. Carefully, not to knock potions and pots from the shelves which lined the walls.

He took a spade from the array of carefully maintained tools, and went back into the sunshine to do some digging.

About five he quit. He toweled down. There was a little breeze. Trees flanking a drainage ditch across the access road swayed. He carried his city clothes from the shed to his car. He drove back to the Allisonville Road. From there to the police parking lot. He was thinking of snap beans when he nearly hit a patrol car coming out.

The problem with coroners is they don't get paid piecework, he thought as he climbed the stairs after a shower and changing from his garden clothes. They try to figure what to look for— maybe just a little bit—before they start. Like if I had died in that crash I just didn't have. Would the coroner ever have checked whether my muscles were aching and stiff?

As he turned onto the fourth floor, he didn't remember what this perception about coroners had to do with anything.

## 5

At 9:00 Powder told Alexander Smith that they would be going out on a case together that night. Part of Smith's evaluation during his detective probation.

Powder looked for Smith to show visible shock, or nervousness, or something. But he was oblivious, which was bad. The man was hopeless.

The call came at 9:42, a break-in at Rock Electrical Supplies, a small store in the Sylvandale Shopping Center. The break was spotted by a private patrol guard who came on at 9:30. He'd noticed the hole in the door, panned inside carefully with his high beam to make sure there was nobody left in the shop. Then he'd called Crime Alert.

Adam-3, the section patrolman, was there first, closely followed by his sergeant, Adam-1. But when he heard that detectives were coming, Adam-1 left.

Powder and Alexander Smith arrived a few minutes after ten. At least Smith hadn't used the siren. It showed Powder he could be worse.

Alexander Smith, in fact, did all right on the basics. Largely because the task was so like ones he'd done hundreds of times in fifteen years as a uniformed cop. Point of entrance, center of attention inside. When the store's manager arrived, they were able to fix the losses, which were just cash and were only $160 from a small stainless-steel box kept in the stock room. The float was still locked in the cash register. Nothing was damaged.

The manager wondered what had happened to his alarm. Smith found quickly enough that it had been jumped.

Powder stayed in the background as Smith ordered a lab man. Let the patrol cop go. Tried to soothe the manager, who was more shocked than upset. He never kept big money around; he'd never had a shop robbed before.

"More exciting than watching television," Smith told him.

The manager had to agree.

Smith had used the line for years.

When some superficial work showed a scrupulous lack of additional evidence, Smith let the lab man go. A few pictures and he was off.

Smith assured the manager that they would do everything possible and that he could go ahead and have the door with the hole replaced.

"The door will cost more than they took," said the manager. He was getting irritable; the shock was passing.

Powder and Smith rode back in silence. In the elevator Powder said only, "Try and get the feel of the thing when you write your report."

Alexander Smith went back to the Night Room alone. Powder went for coffee. Therein lies the difference, Powder thought as he sat alone in the Canteen. The difference between Detective and Uniform. The feel of the thing.

The feel of this apparently simple break-in bothered him. Ever use a rifle to kill a fly?

As Powder walked in, Sergeant Salimbean was on his way out.

"Where to?" Powder asked him.

"A shooting on the War Memorial Plaza. A couple of shots fired, anyway. I don't know if anyone's hurt."

"Smith is downstairs."

"Which one?"

"The young one, Sid. Take him with you."

Salimbean nodded. "Oh, another of your favorite people was in here while you were out."

"Who?"

"A kid, skinny kid with a pony tail. Came in about ten, but he left."

"Oh."

"We told him to come back tomorrow, catch you about seven. Not my idea, Lieutenant." Hands raised to disassociate himself from the prank. "But I don't remember whose it was."

Powder was tired without all this. "So I don't owe a favor to you," he said, just earnestly enough for Salimbean to wonder.

"You want to see this kid? An informant or something?"

Powder tried to work up an enthusiasm which would irritate Salimbean. He said, "He holds some very important information." He realized it didn't mean anything as he said it, but didn't have the energy to care.

Salimbean wasn't irritated, but he was confused, which was almost as good. "Oh yeah?"

"And before you go. I want to see *you* tomorrow, too. Say six forty-five?"

"I may not be able to get in quite that early tomorrow, Lieutenant."

Powder just said, "All right, we'll catch some time," and Salimbean left.

Powder dropped into his chair and rested before he looked in his In-Tray. Where he found Alexander Smith's report on the break-in at the electrical-supply place.

He knew what he would find. He knew what he wouldn't find.

He leafed through, there were no surprises.

Smith had missed the feel. That something was wrong about it all. Careful, highly professional work; timed so that they were well away when the patrol guard made his first round. Not only were the alarms spotted, but they were recognized as ones to bridge rather than cut. All for $160. It didn't add up.

Smith considered it fortunate that was all there was to take.

And no damage. Frustrated villains often do wanton damage; and they're rarely careful with odds and ends as they do their work. But this was very clean.

Smith did suggest questioning employees. Powder wanted the employees questioned, too.

Smith suggested that, because nothing had been forced inside, an employee might have provided information.

But an employee also knows how much money there is around. It just can't be worth it for $160.

How do you train a Smith to think right? How do you give someone a feel? Someone who'd lived thirty-nine years without it.

Powder was tired. The excesses of the afternoon. All that digging.

The shift ended quietly. Powder was almost asleep.

---

He ate at Knight's again. When he went in only Ella was behind the counter. She was an attractive but fashion-conscious woman who never quite looked in her element behind the counter of a rib joint.

"Where's the man?" asked Powder.

"Nice way to greet me!"

Powder just smiled and took his usual seat, back against the wall at the table closest to the counter. "You know," he said, mustering absolutely the last iota of graciousness left in his none too gracious body, "that I mean no offense."

"You want me to get him? He's in the back," said Ella. "Having a little rest."

"No, I just wondered," said Powder. He took off his coat.

"You want double tonight?" asked Ella.

"No."

"Tired and not hungry, that's it?"

"That's it. Warm weather this afternoon."

"Oh, better get used to it. I understand they have warm weather here several days each and every year."

Powder smiled. "You haven't killed anybody recently, have you, Ella?"

"Oh, nice thing to ask me! You eat that, see if you want to ask me about killing."

Powder started on his food. Two young men laughed in the doorway and cool-walked across the room. One of them acknowledged Powder by making an exaggerated face, mask surprise, as he passed the table.

"Yes?" Ella said.

"Give us all your money," said the young man who arrived at the counter first.

"What?" said Ella.

"Yeah!" said the other man. "This is a stick-up."

Powder reached quickly into his jacket pocket. Without looking up from his plate he pulled out his ID wallet and slapped it open on the table. The slap of leather on laminate was loud.

Everyone turned to look. Powder's police shield sparkled in the fluorescent lights.

"Oooo," said the first man. "Yeah. Hi, Ella. You remember me. James Jeffer. I was in school with you, couple years behind. You remember me?"

"No," said Ella, who struggled to keep from laughing.

"No! Damn, that's the world for you. Impersonal. Look, maybe you remember my friend Loco here. Look." Jeffer turned his friend from Powder's shield to face Ella. "Look, remember him? He makes funny faces. Make a funny face, Loco."

Loco made a funny face.

"Remember him now?"

"No."

"Damn!" said Jeffer with frustration.

He turned to face Powder now. "It was just a joke, man. Cop, sir. Loco here, he gets some funny ideas for some funny jokes. He say, Look, there's a nice-looking piece in that place. I wonder if she remembers us. That's all it was, man."

Powder looked up, rib in one hand. Staring at Jeffer, he picked up his ID wallet and put it away. "Pull up a chair," he said affably. "Maybe you guys would like to confess to a couple murders I got going?"

"He did it," pointing to Loco.

"She did it," pointing to Ella.

"Just a little joke," said Powder, and went back to his sustenance.

Loco whispered something into Jeffer's ear. Jeffer whispered the same into Ella's ear. A middle-aged couple came in the door, Jeffer and Loco slipped out.

Ten minutes later the couple left with food for six.

Ella said to Powder, "Those two kids, they said you sober them up faster than a quart of black coffee."

"You know them?"

"Hell, no," said Ella proudly. "Those are what we call niggers, excuse the word. Dumb kids, Southern-born parents. Come in here and everyplace, act like clowns. You won't find island people acting like that."

"I thought you didn't know them?"

"I don't. But they're all the same."

"I thought they were pretty funny," said Powder.

"Each to his own taste, I suppose," said Ella. She went through the back door into the back room.

Powder finished his meal. Stood up and was trying to find the exact change when Ella came back. "Papa's asleep," she said and took his money.

"That's where I ought to be," said Powder.

"So?" she said, meaning why aren't you.

"Maybe I will. It's just my wife thinks I'm out with another woman and she'd be upset if I came home early."

Ella smiled formally without understanding, and counted out his change.

Ella tipped the balance. A man ought to have the right to go home and sleep. So Powder decided he would. Sleep in Ricky's room. No need to disturb anybody.

It wasn't until he killed the headlights and pulled into the driveway that the grim possibility of confrontation seemed important. Before eight. Possible hassle.

He sat in the car, trying to decide whether to put it in the garage or leave it out.

Screw it. He was tired. Leave the car out, don't take the chance of waking her up. Leave a note on Ricky's door: "Sorry, very tired. Hard day."

He wasn't allowed in the house before 8:00 A.M. She before 6:00 P.M. Except weekends, of course, when he got the house to himself, except for the first weekend in every month, when she got it. And the four weeks a year of his vacation she also got it. Somehow the four hours each day that she got the house more than his ten balanced the yearly total of hour occupancy.

He didn't quite remember the drawing up of the arrangement. But he entered quietly. Scribbled the note on a paper bag and left it on the floor outside Ricky's room door.

Then slept. His marvelous do-it-anywhere skill: sleep.

When he woke up in the afternoon and found his watch, it read 3:15. She hadn't been annoyed enough to pour water on his head or throw the cat on him when she saw he was home early. Must be in a good mood.

But when he got to the kitchen, he realized mood had nothing to do with it. There he found a note: "Away for a week. All yours."

It annoyed him. But he was annoyed anyway. The problem was that his sleep, easy as it was and refreshing, didn't seem to solve problems like it did for other people. He woke up just as angry or frustrated or curious as he'd been when he hit the pillow. It never did him any good to have a night's sleep on a problem.

Maybe because I almost never sleep at night, he thought, and made some hot chocolate.

## 6

When he came through the stairwell door and turned to the Night Room, Rex Funkhouser was waiting for him in the corridor.

Powder passed him and said, "I'll call you in a minute."

Rex nodded. Powder walked through the room to his night desk. Hadn't had a chance to stop upstairs at his erstwhile day desk. No messages here.

Only Sid Smith was in. Just didn't look like a cop with that full beard, however closely cropped. Odds on, Salimbean would be late again. What was it he wanted to talk to Salimbean about? Damn.

He thought about the kid waiting outside the door. "Rex."

Slowly, apparently with pain, Rex Funkhouser came through. Sat down. Powder had a chance to study his movement. It was limited.

When Rex sat down, Powder said, "What you want?"

"There are two things. The first, I've come to admit a mistake."

"Oh?"

"About the Foolish Old Man Who Removed Mountains, you remember it?"

"Pretty much, yes."

"I said that it applied to injustice and you didn't think it did because injustice, unlike mountains, can grow larger even though you attack it."

"I did?"

"Well, I just wanted to tell you that you were absolutely right. It doesn't apply the way I said. I was wrong not to understand when you explained to me. It was egocentric of me. I had preconceptions about what you would be like and what you would be able to understand, and I let these preconceptions get in the way of my judgment."

Powder was not the receiver of many apologies, and the sheer novelty disposed him toward the kid.

"Mao says," Rex Funkhouser said, "that we must face our mistakes without embarrassment. Mistakes which are hidden only perpetuate themselves, but mistakes which are admitted freely and understood become the foundation stones for superior understanding in the future."

Powder was not unaffected by this truth. If it came to truths, Powder had certain preconceptions about boys with pony tails —not to mention detective sergeants with beards. This strange young man had managed to slip inside them. "I just hope you're so quick to acknowledge important mistakes."

"It was important to me. I was conceited and arrogant, and

such feelings get in the way of clear-headed decisions and judgments."

OK. OK. "You said there was another thing."

"You said to come to you if I had a crime?"

"Yeah."

"I realize now," Rex said crisply, "that injustice isn't enough. So I want to make a complaint. A specific complaint. As a citizen. I have a friend who goes to this school. She's told me that if she fails this year and has to go back, she's going to kill herself. She's told me that on six different occasions. Here." From the inside pocket of his jacket. "These are dates and locations and times. Each one Cherry told me in complete seriousness she was going to kill herself if she failed." Rex pushed the paper forward.

Powder took the list, but he put it on his desk without looking at it.

"What am I supposed to do?" Powder asked.

"Can you let her life, whether she lives or dies, depend on the school owner's wallet? It's tantamount to murdering her."

Powder leaned back. You get them all. "You make it hard for me to be polite to you," he said, back to the comfortable preconception.

However, instead of being belligerent, Rex Funkhouser looked puzzled and asked quietly, "Why?"

"Whatever sympathy I might have for you and your friend as a private citizen," or however little, "as a policeman my job is to deal with crime."

"Never prevention of crime?"

"Look, you're not a stupid kid. I can't sit in judgment on people I don't know because other people I don't know come in and tell me bad things about them."

"Even if the bad things are true?"

"Really now, what can you expect me to do?"

"I didn't really expect anything from you. But I tried," said Rex, without the resignation he should have had. But he didn't rise or suggest he was leaving.

They were both quiet for a few seconds.

"If you overheard what I heard, what would you do?"

Powder looked at his watch. No Salimbean. Ten past seven.

"Well, I see why you thought about coming here. You feel powerless and you think we have all the power."

"You do, if you'd use it for the benefit of the people." Bitter now.

Kids. "How did you get started on this Mao stuff?" Powder asked.

"It's not 'stuff.' Like . . . like . . ." Grasping for . . . "It's not like catching measles or something. It's the first attempt at a rational government committed to solve the problems of its people since . . . Well, the first almost ever."

"It's just I don't run across many Maoists in my work."

"There aren't many in Indianapolis."

"And the ones I read about in the papers . . ." said Powder, never intending to finish the statement.

"I consider it unrealistic to expect a peasant revolution in the United States," said Rex definitively.

"So do I," said Powder, unable to suppress completely the amusement provided by this earnest but very young man. A change from reading reports.

"But!" said Rex, responding to the wisp of smile with extra decibels. "The principles Mao has discovered, his thoughts, provide the only rational basis, the only moral basis, the *best* basis for living your life for yourself and your brother, wherever you are."

Getting into deep water.

"I can see that the amount of time you're willing to spend talking about the problems of this particular brother human being is nearly up," said Rex Funkhouser. "May I ask if you can make a constructive suggestion about what I should do next? Or do you not make constructive suggestions?"

Deep breath. "Yes, I have suggestions for you. I advise, unofficially, that you talk to your principal—"

"Owner," Rex interrupted him with distaste.

"You want my advice or not?"

"Yes. But I couldn't actually denounce him myself," said Rex.

"Why not?"

"Because I can't afford to get kicked out of the school. I've got to graduate so I can go to college and learn Chinese."

Powder shrugged. "You could try a lawyer. You might even try someone like a private detective."

"I don't have any money."

Powder shrugged.

"OK," said Rex. "I guess I'll have to *get* some money, then."

"Just like that?"

"If you have to, you have to."

"Stop in again. Let me know how things come out."

"Why? What do you care?"

"I like to know how things work out, that's all. Besides, it's not every day a real live Maoist comes in voluntarily. Makes a change. Maybe I'll learn something."

"If you're really interested, I can recommend some books."

"I don't get a lot of chance to read."

"I see. Just making conversation."

"I do have other problems, son."

"Yeah, so you tell me. One other thing. Can you suggest a private detective? I don't know anything about them."

Powder smiled. Private detective sounded more appealing to the kid than lawyers. He tried to remember if he'd ever met a private detective. "I'll ask around."

"Yeah," said Rex, who was rising to go. He said it as though he meant thanks. Powder accepted it as such. Watched him leave.

Sid Smith was at Powder's desk before Rex had made it out the office door. Powder looked at Smith. Smith watched until Rex was gone.

"Was that wise?" Smith asked with a harsh frown. "If you'll pardon my asking."

"Was it wise for you to eavesdrop on my conversation, you mean?" said Powder. He'd let things slide a bit. 7:20, and everybody was in now.

"I mean, to tell a kid like that to go and put pressure on his school principal. Kid like that is nothing but trouble, Lieutenant Powder, he really is. I don't understand how in hell's name you can talk like that to him."

"I like him," Powder lied. *And I don't like you.* "I'll talk to him if I want to. If it gets me in trouble, then there's one more vacancy among lieutenants. I thought you'd like that."

"I worry about the department. We've been getting a lot of bad exposure. You go around giving advice like that—"

"Here's some more free advice. When you work for me, you do what I tell you to. You don't like what I say to a member of the public, then you see what you can do about it. It upsets you? Next time he comes in I'll take him into an interview room so my talking doesn't make your stomach churn, OK?"

Smith was subsiding, retreating under the onslaught of Powder's loud words.

"Go to your desk and write some anonymous letters to the Chief." Smith sat down. But Powder pursued him. "Go on, get out a piece of paper. Dear Chief, Lieutenant Powder listened to a kid with a pony tail who talks about Mao Tung. Lieutenant Powder didn't kick him in the ass. I write you this so you should do something about it, but I don't sign it because it might affect my promotion chance. After all, Chief, I'm after your job."

The whole room, which now included Salimbean, was still in the face of Powder's fury.

When he paused, Powder noticed it. Round it off. Quieter, but not yet able to speak quietly, Powder said, "For a smart ass, Smith, you're pretty goddamned dumb. Doesn't even occur to you that this kid might even turn into an informant, does it? How many Maoist informants do you have? Or does everybody you talk to have to have a tie on and be able to give you thirty percent off a used car?"

Powder posed, lower lip puffed out, leaning over Smith at his desk.

Then suddenly, "I'm going to the Canteen. Salimbean, I want you to come with me. Rest of you know where I am. Schleutter, you catch my phone. And keep Smith out of my desk, will you? I mean, if he wants to search it for the Thoughts of Mao, tell him not to screw up all my papers, it's in the bottom lefthand drawer."

Powder left the room, followed at a distance by Harold Salimbean, who was taking deep breaths because, of all the moods to catch Powder in for a personal chat, this had to be the worst. They tell you about Powder's temper. He quick-stepped behind the lieutenant's lengthening strides.

Powder was wishing the mousetrap in his lower lefthand drawer were set.

Then he thought that he really did rather like poor old Rex Funkhouser. At least he wasn't airy-fairy like his own son, Ricky. Even if he had the thoughts of Mao, at least Rex had thoughts of something.

As they entered the Canteen, Powder whirled suddenly and was surprised to see Salimbean jump. Powder laughed. "What can I get you, Harold? Coffee, tea or me?"

"Coffee," Salimbean stammered, utterly confused.

"Fine, sit down, I'll bring it. And before we talk about your problems, try and think if you've ever heard anyone say anything about knowing a private detective."

# NIGHT COVER

## 7

Salimbean's problems were more suited to the Canteen than they would have been to the open-plan Night Room. He was fraying and didn't have the perspective on himself to admit it. He'd been in detective division for two and a half years. The vastly increased responsibilities which detective sergeants carry were straining him on the job and the job was straining him at home. Powder knew Salimbean's situation cold.

"You ever think of going into some other kind of work, Harold?" Powder asked. No point in beating around the bush.

"What?" said Salimbean, his worst fears seemingly coming true. All he needed now was to be chucked out. Or demoted. His wife called him "the big hot-shot detective." His middle child's grades had taken a sharp dip since he came into detective division. "The big hot-shot detective. Hot shit!"

"Sugar?" Powder asked.

"Thanks." Salimbean stirred in two.

"You're a pretty good detective, Harold," said Powder. "Pretty good cop."

Quizzical frown, but, "Thanks."

"But you're having troubles at home, aren't you?"

"Well..." he began, feeling that loyalty required him to deny the obvious. "I think my wife would have preferred me to take Traffic," he said. That wasn't disloyal, was it? Preferred wasn't the word. "Got to be a big hot-shit detective!" over and over, night after night.

"Can't think of a sensible wife who wouldn't," said Powder, though he could think of some wives who weren't sensible.

"I didn't want to write tickets all day."

"I can see that," Powder mused. "But your problems at home have been showing here, Harold."

"They have?"

"Late a lot. Tired. The edge is off. What is it, she just beginning to realize that things don't get better for cops' wives?"

"I don't honestly know what she thinks anymore," said Salimbean, and he knew that more than the hem of the slip was showing.

"What you going to do about it, Harold?"

Silence for a few moments. "I'll just have to try harder, I guess."

Powder shook his head. "You can't try harder. You don't have much try left in you. You're a responsible cop, you're giving it what you've got."

Salimbean nodded. It was true.

"I'm making you an appointment with Lieutenant Gaulden. When's your next day off?"

"What the hell will Lieutenant Gaulden be able to do? What can anybody do? It's my problem, Lieutenant Powder, I'll just have to work it out."

"Look," said Powder gently, "it's just not worth ruining your home life about. I know. I've seen it. I've been through it. I've got a wife I don't talk to except the kid's home from college. It's not worth it. Makes you cranky. You don't want to end up like me, son, believe it. Gaulden has seen it, too; he's in charge of personnel. I want you to talk to him, see what we can find you in the force. If not, my advice would be to consider looking around outside. I'm not talking about becoming a night watchman. Something to use your training. When's your next days, Harold?"

"Sunday and Monday." He knows, Salimbean thought. We're on the same shift.

"All right, I'll get you an appointment on Monday. It's off the record, by the way. You're not so far over the edge that I have to put it on paper, don't think that."

"I didn't."

"I'd just hate to see you get stuck in a groove because you thought there was no way out. Only difference between a groove and a grave is the depth. That's why I'm sending you to Gaulden on your off day. Let you know the time."

"OK," said Salimbean, who was thoroughly dispirited. He was getting used to a cloud over his world at home, but he hadn't thought the sunshine had ended at work. God, what a life!

Leave him to get used to it, thought Powder. "I gotta go back upstairs now," he said, rising. "Take your time." Powder walked to the stairwell. Now, an intelligent guy like Salimbean in the statistics department, he thought, and we'd get decent organized rosters out of them.

She'll kill me this time, Salimbean was thinking. Having to come in on an off day.


As he unlocked the stairwell door at the fourth floor, Powder ran into Brindell waiting for the elevator.

"Wouldn't expect to see you around here this time of day," said Powder.

"Things are moving. You got the summary I left on your desk up here, didn't you?"

"Yeah."

"Well, then you know. We think we're getting places. Oh . . ." The elevator came, Brindell stepped into it.

Powder walked smartly to the desk in the Day Room which he had told Brindell he'd already been to. Lo and behold. A file just for him. He picked it up, then looked around for what he had come up for. Any lingering day lieutenants. But the copboard was bare.

So Powder went back downstairs to the Night Room, the file hugged tightly under an arm.

"Where is everybody?" he asked when he walked into the room. Only Schleutter was there.

"Smiths are both out. Harold Salimbean came back, but went out again—to make a call, he said."

"Anything exciting?"

"Somebody cleaned out a house on the east side. Couple just got back tonight. Other was an armed robbery."

Powder looked at his watch. Just past 7:30. He took a few steps toward his desk. Then turned back. "Dale, you don't know any private detectives, do you?"

Schleutter shrugged. "Know or know?"

"Know anybody who does?"

"They say Miller has a friend. Lieutenant Miller. You know him?"

"Yeah."

"They say he knows one who's been some help to him, you know what I mean."

"I remember now," said Powder. Nodded slowly, went to his desk to read Brindell's offerings.

Which turned out to be a few notes made to look more significant by a folder on the outside.

Records appeared to have made the first of the week's two bodies. The woman on the south side.

No prints at all left. But they had most of her face. And from size and shape and age they'd got a couple of reasonably possible names from the arrest files—assuming the fingers had been smashed to cover up records of a local arrest. One of the likely names answered the door when a man was sent around. The other, a Leonora Ellyson, hadn't been seen for a week. That was Brindell's hot prospect. Because she'd been convicted twice for solicitation and once for accessory to obtaining by deception. She had a husband, and Powder could see Brindell's line of thinking. Wasn't too farfetched to think he had a drug tie, which would tie to Hilda Chaney. And give Brindell a little gold star on his sheet. The problem was finding Les Ellyson. The first problem.

Well well well, thought Powder. Lucky old Brindell.

By eleven o'clock Powder had another body.

**NIGHT COVER**

---

It was on the east side, this one. In Boy district. The discovery had been broadcast for all the east and south cars to hear. When Powder arrived, it was a convention. Not only Boy-1, Boy-6 and Boy-7, but two Adam cars and a Frank. And B-5, the Boy accident car, pulled in right after he got there. They were lining up on 21st street near Sherman Drive. The body had been spotted floating in Pogues Run under the bridge at 21st Street. It was still in the water. The teenage couple who'd found it were standing in the middle of a group of cops; a crowd of spectators was growing either side of the bridge.

Just the sort of thing Powder hated.

Boy Sergeant Duhamell was the first Powder spoke to. "Damn it, get rid of those people. Tell them there's a maniac with a machine gun who's about to open up."

Duhamell went to talk to the people.

"Why the hell are there so many of you here?" Powder asked the patrol officers standing around the teenagers. "Give me your names."

"Uh oh," he heard one of them mutter. "It's Powder."

"Name and badge. You." He picked one at random.

"Look, Lieutenant," said the smallish crew-cut cop, "some of us shouldn't be here, but we thought maybe you could use some extra hands. Asking people whether they saw anything. Thought it would speed things up, maybe catch your . . ." he looked at the teenagers, remembering they had found the body, decided to say it, ". . . killer for you a little quicker."

Powder turned to him. "Who's covering you?"

"It's real quiet tonight," said the man with a smile. He looked around for a little support from his peers and got it.

"You bronco over here when you hear about a body just in case you might get lucky and pick up a good arrest cheap? Now, who's covering your sector, cowboy?" It was apparent Powder was not pleased. The man didn't answer.

Powder took all the names and badge numbers. He promised to check them against the log to see which were the chosen few who'd been requested.

"Now go home, if you haven't been sent for. We want you, we'll call you."

It left him with two cops and the two kids.

Jackrabbiting to where the action is happens all the time. It's all tied to the recruiting problem. The kind of recruits who are helped into the force by having a car of their own are too often the kind who get restless when novelty wears off. Who see the promotions of officers with flashy arrests more clearly than the promotions of the men who slogged it out. Powder could teach them a thing or two about being a cop.

Problem is, he thought, as he walked down the bank of the run, so many of them don't take it as seriously as we used to.

The body was floating face down. Nothing to do for it. Powder walked back up to the road.

The lab people directed the removal of the body from the water.

It had been a woman, young. Her hands and face had been largely obliterated.

## 8

Saturday. Rain. A reminder that spring is not all May flowers.

The rain kept Powder in and he spent the afternoon restlessly, rebuilding shelves in the garage that he'd built only a year and a half before.

All the things he'd done around the house. All the years. All the things he'd made, remade, refined. There was a lot of him in the house. Too much.

By the late afternoon he was thoroughly irritable. Why does it rain me out of my garden when I'm just coming up for my day off? He didn't answer himself; he just hit the nails harder.

Shortly before he left for the department, the phone rang. He picked up the receiver and said, "Hello?"

After a pause the caller hung up without a word.

"Don't you know it's *my* house in the daytime?" he asked the dead receiver.

He left his car in the Police Garage at five past six. Went out to pick up coffee and Danish, then came back in and, because he was irritated with his life and his routines, he took the elevator to the fourth floor instead of walking.

When he got there he felt cramped from the elevator and wished he'd used the stairs.

The Day Room was still pretty busy. On his desk Powder found a memo from Gaulden giving Harold Salimbean a Monday appointment. Powder wondered if Salimbean would manage to solve his problems. Who ever solves his problems? Powder had been trying to figure the best configuration of shelves in that garage for what seemed forever.

Not expecting anybody to be there, Powder popped his head into Miller's cubicle. That's the difference between day and night. In the day, lieutenants get walls that go up to the ceiling; downstairs, night lieutenants only come up to the waist.

Powder was startled when he saw Miller working at his desk. Why shouldn't he be there? It was his desk. Saturday was a busy day.

"What you want?" asked Miller when he saw movement out of the edge of his eye. He didn't look up at first.

"Two things," said Powder.

Miller looked up. "Powder," he said.

"What of it?" said Powder.

"What is it you want?"

"Two things."

"So you said."

"First," said Powder, "the body we brought in last night."

"We've got a busy little bee," Miller said. He was telling Powder that the superficial details were the same as the two previous killings of the week.

"Second, I've been told you have a friend who's a private eye."

Miller sat up. "Who said that?"

"What I hear," said Powder. "It ain't a crime, you know. I just wondered, what's he like, this guy you know?"

"Why?"

"Touchy, aren't we?"

"Look, Powder," said Miller, "I know a guy from schooldays who happens to be a private detective. Tell me what you want a private detective for, I'll tell you whether he'd be right for it, OK?"

"What's the matter, he don't take divorce cases or other refined work?"

"He'll take divorce cases, if that's what you're looking for." Miller eyed Powder privately. "But he works on his own and he's not fancy."

"What's the matter, he stupid?"

"No," said Miller, trying to find words for his friend which he'd never bothered to look for before. "But he's not what you'd call ambitious."

"Cheap?"

"As they go, yes. Look, what the hell is it you want done?"

"What I want done? An act of God to make the sun shine in the day and all the rain come at night so my plants can grow good."

Miller sighed.

Powder said, "Kid came in a couple nights ago wanting us to rout injustice from his private school. I talk to him because it's part of what I do. If I throw him back in the ocean with the other hippie fishies, he may do something dumb, so I figure an ounce of prevention. Maybe I can find someone to carry the can for a while, till he cools down. So I ask around, so I come to you. Your friend isn't stupid, you say; he's cheap. Has he got enough judgment to cool the kid off some? Give him something to hope for until he gets a new girl friend? Your friend up to this kind of work or do I go elsewhere?"

After a pause Miller said, "Samson. Al Samson. West Maryland; number in the book."

"No wonder the bum's poor if his friends are so cagey about recommending him." Powder walked away.

What you don't know, Miller thought, is that he's not so keen on cops, cops like you. Where was I? "At that point Sergeant Oranen requested the suspect to . . ."

It was still early. Powder walked through the gray-green corridors. To E411. Identification. Where, to his surprise, he found the young officer who'd messed up the rosters. "What are *you* doing here?"

"We rotate assignments on Statistical Training, sir."

"What the hell does that mean?" No answer. "Roster drawn up?" Powder asked abruptly. It's not what he'd come to ID to find out, but while he had the kid on hand . . .

"It's posted, sir."

"Get Brindell on my shift?"

"I did, sir, at first, but then Captain Graniela called down to take him off it. So I did."

One eyebrow up. "Oh, he did, did he?"

"Yes, sir."

"Who's in charge down here these days?"

"Right now, sir? It's Sergeant Tidmarsh, sir."

"Where is he?"

"I think he just went out."

"Where?"

"Not sure. He was going upstairs to Fraud."

"Call them to see if he's there."

"Yes, sir."

Nervously the young officer called Fraud. Tidmarsh wasn't there. "They say he's gone, sir."

"Well, ask them where he went."

Done. "They say he went downstairs to Operations.

Spelling it out. "Well, call Operations."

Seven minutes later Tidmarsh was located in Vice. Powder arranged to meet him in the Canteen, but left the roster kid without having asked what Tidmarsh looked like. Didn't want to go back. Decided he didn't like the kid. Where do they get them so weedy? If I were in Personnel . . .

Powder was surprised by the crowd in the Canteen. And annoyed. Why don't they go home to eat? He almost called out, Go home! but restrained himself. Then was irritated at his own restraint.

"Which one of you is Tidmarsh! Where the hell is Tidmarsh!"

No one volunteered, though many turned to see who was shouting.

Powder got a cup of vended coffee.

Three minutes later a middle-aged man whose face looked like a contour map of the Alps walked through the Canteen door, looked around and came straight to Powder's table.

Better known than knowing, Powder thought.

"I'm Tidmarsh," said the man and extended a hand.

After a round of coffees Powder had established that though he'd only been in Identification for two months, Tidmarsh thought he was settling in pretty well.

"What did you do before that?"

Tidmarsh laughed. "You're going to laugh," he said, forgetting what he'd heard about Powder. "I was in Traffic for thirteen years."

"Christ!"

"Don't knock it. I developed the Monodirectional Traffic Flow Grid we use downtown in the city now."

"Christ!" said Powder again. With more feeling.

Tidmarsh shrugged with a smile. "So now some One-Ways in ID and Stats."

"I always thought someone from Detective ought to be down there."

"They tested some of your boys, I know. Either they don't really have the right kind of mind or maybe they think Statistics is a comedown. I don't know. I enjoy it. I did pretty well in Traffic, but a change—" he spread his hands and caused landslides with an alpine grin—"keeps you young."

Powder had been on nights for nineteen years.

"So," Tidmarsh said. "What was it I can do for you?"

"I don't know whether you're going to be any help," said Powder sourly.

Expansively, "Tell me your problems. I'll take a stab at anything, you know. Helps get me familiar with things."

Powder paid attention to this. "I got a probation detective who's stuck in his old habits. Been Uniform too long. He's too fixed on facts; he's got to learn to let his imagination run a little bit. See the possibilities a case might have."

"I don't quite follow."

"He gets a crime and he doesn't think about it. He sees what's there, but he doesn't ask why the individual pieces occur together."

Tidmarsh nodded. "Got to learn to think like a crook, you mean. Without becoming one."

Powder rubbed his chin. "That's about what I mean."

"This an older guy?" asked Tidmarsh.

"You know him?"

Tidmarsh laughed. "You said he'd been in Uniform *too long.*"

Powder nodded. "I was wrong about you," he said.

"But you didn't know me."

"Look, I want to have this guy work on some problems with you guys. That OK?"

"Sure," said Tidmarsh, and finished his coffee. "Friend of yours?"

"Why's everybody got to be a friend? Personnel ought to know better than to wait till a guy's thirty-nine to try and make a detective of him. But now they've done it, I want him to have his shot."

Tidmarsh nodded slowly, but said, "Thirty-nine ain't that old."

"All right," Powder said stiffly. "I'll send him down with some jobs to do."

Powder left abruptly. Looks like the lieutenant got up on the wrong side of his wife, Tidmarsh thought. Looked at his watch. Corrected the minute to the Canteen clock.

Alexander Smith was alone in the Night Room when Powder walked in at five to seven. "Smith."

"Yes, sir?"

"Come on in here a minute."

They went to Powder's retreat.

Rubbed his face and had a look at Smith. "How are things, Smith?"

"All right, sir. Fine."

"Settling in?"

"Doing my best."

Take a breath. Big, strong guy. Could use someone like him to help get the garden dug. Damn, what are we thinking about? "I've been thinking about that case we went out on together. The electric-supply place up at Sylvandale. You remember?"

"Sure. What's the matter, did I do something wrong in the report?"

"No, no," Powder said. "I just been thinking about it. Pretty sophisticated job for a hundred and sixty bucks, don't you think?"

"They're all doing things fancy these days. Sir."

"Yeah, but . . ." Powder mused. Mind away, like anchors.

"I think it's television," said Smith. "You just don't see the crappy break-ins like you used to."

Powder didn't encourage him. "Look, Smith, I want you to do

something for me. I turned over that case to the day boys, but it worries me. I want you to go down to ID. Look through the records and see if you can turn up anybody with the same MO. Got your book?"

Smith got his book out, but looked upset.

"You have your notes on it, then," Powder said. "It just doesn't feel right to me."

"Think the store manager wasn't telling us everything that got taken?"

Powder perked up. The first bit of speculation he'd ever heard from Alexander Smith. "You talked to him, what'd you think?"

Smith shrugged.

"Well," said Powder, "I just think it's too small a job for this quality of work. Like a dry run or something. I was thinking maybe somebody teaching somebody else how to do it." Ask for response with eyebrows up. None. "Anyway, go down to ID. Guy called Tidmarsh. Help him set up a search for people with the MO, the technique. Only established pros, now. It wasn't beginners' work."

"Right," said Smith. "Sir?"

"Yeah?"

"You're not taking me off real work, are you, sir?"

"I told you to do something. So do it. One more ignorant question like that and I'll throw you back." Powder intended to go on, but realized what he'd said was closer to his real feelings about the man than he'd intended.

"Yes, sir." Smith got up, left the cubicle.

"And Smith . . ."

"Yeah?"

"That guy Tidmarsh. He gives you lip, tell me about it. He's new. I think we'd be better off with someone from Detective down there."

"Yessir." Smith left the Night Room. Everybody else was in now. Even Salimbean.

"Watch out, Lieutenant." Snide voice from the side. "You'll

make Smith cry if you don't put him on real work."

Powder didn't have to look to know it was Sid Smith making the crack.

"Besides," Sid Smith continued, "everybody knows Tidmarsh is some kind of genius or something. Been working in Traffic and they gave him some test. He went off the chart. Smitty will have a hard time if he complains about that guy."

"Go clean the latrines if you think you know so much how things ought to be done."


A little before nine o'clock Powder went out of the Night Room for a cup of coffee. Schleutter found him in the Canteen.

"Soon as you leave, things happen," said Schleutter. "Get a big armed-robbery call and in the same minute China Charlie walks in."

"China Charlie?"

"That kid who wants his grades fixing."

"Oh yeah. Rex."

"He came in, asked for you. Four guys with shotguns took the Riley House."

"The Riley House!"

"Yeah. Good old-fashioned line-yourselves-up-and-put-your-wallets-in-the-hat."

Rex Funkhouser sat on a chair just inside the Night Room and rose, with difficulty, when he saw Powder.

Powder brushed by him. "Just a minute, kid." From his office where he gathered his overcoat Powder called to Schleutter. "Look, Dale, get out there and find someone who saw how they got away and get the whole fucking city after them. Sid Smith'll cover things here. Go on, Dale."

Schleutter left quickly. As Powder walked to the door and stopped in front of Rex.

"Look, I've asked around and got you the name of a private detective who maybe won't set you back so much as some. I don't know anything about him, but you can try him. I got his name here somewhere." Powder tried to find the page in his notebook he'd written Miller's friend's name down on.

"I've managed to come across a little money," Rex said. "I passed the hat at school."

"Good, good," Powder said impatiently. "Where the . . . Here it is. Guy's name is Samson. Lives on West Maryland or maybe that's his office, I don't know. But it's the best I can do for you, kid. Good luck. Hope you make a million."

"Just a minute, Lieutenant."

"Yeah?" said Powder, one hand on the door.

"I just wanted to show that I appreciate the time you've taken with me." He handed Powder a small paper bag.

"What's this, a bribe?"

"Thank you for talking to me." Firmly, Rex took hold of the open door and limped out while Powder tried to snap the cellophane tape on the bag and put his coat on at the same time.

Finally the bag yielded a small red book: *The Thoughts of Chairman Mao Tse-tung.*

Oh yes, thought Powder. There's something you can buy influence in the Police Department with! He put the book and the bag in his coat pocket. And went off to find some hold-up men.

Two patrolmen in Charlie district made the big arrest. Getaway car inside rented furniture truck. The patrolmen were talking together when they saw a car fitting the Riley House getaway-car description. But before they could follow it, the truck opened and the car drove in. They waited for the truck's driver to close the occupants in. They collared the driver and slapped a handcuff into the hole on the back where a padlock would ordinarily be. So the people inside couldn't get themselves out. One cop kept close guard on the driver. The other called in the rest of Indianapolis's police. *Voilà,* big capture.

Only two things made the night slightly less than a complete triumph for the two patrolmen. First, one of them dropped the key to his handcuffs and had to spend two or three minutes groveling for it in the oily dirt of the parking lot spotlit by half a dozen flashlights.

Second, Powder, when he arrived, questioned both men aggressively about just what they thought they were doing parked together in a dark corner of a parking lot when they were supposed to be patrolling Charlie-7 and Charlie-9 sections. Powder said he wouldn't accept that they were just talking. "What's to talk about in the middle of the night? And we know you weren't asleep because you heard the description of the car we wanted and saw it come through." Powder walked away and wouldn't let them try to convince him.

It was quarter to two when Powder got back to Headquarters. Back to stay, he hoped as he walked up the stairs. Rough night already, one way and another. Rough way to end the week. Cops in Indianapolis work five days a week on assigned shifts which change every fourth week unless they have a permanent assignment. On his two off days Powder's authority was covered either by a lieutenant from Homicide and Robbery or one from Vice, or by the senior sergeant on duty. It was a matter of how the rosters worked out. Though procedure wasn't left to chance. After his first four years on the job Powder produced a seven-page document outlining correct procedures for night responsibilities in the detective division. The Notes were accepted by the department as policy and, in theory, every officer supervising night cover studied them. I've made a few One-Ways in my time, Powder thought, recalling his meeting with Tidmarsh. Speaking of whom.

Sergeant Alexander Smith was alone in the Night Room when Powder came in. "You've been out a long time, Lieutenant."

Powder shrugged. "Anything happen here?"

"Nothing desperate. Couple of stick-ups. Break-in at a school. Pretty quiet, really."

"How'd you get on with Tidmarsh?"

"Well, all right, I guess."

"Got me the guy who broke that electric-supplies store?"

"Not exactly, no."

"Did you and Tidmarsh turn anything up or not?"

"I told him about it. He worked on some cards and checked some books and pushed it into this big computer. I have to admit I didn't realize what information they have in machines now. I always thought you had to put a guy looking through books and things."

"And that's what you thought I sent you down to do?"

Smith shrugged.

"And?" It was like pulling teeth.

"Well," said Smith, "in the end Tidmarsh came out with eight names."

"Eight?"

"Well, only three of them really made much sense, I mean if you figure he always does jobs like this one was done."

"Cleanly. Intelligently."

"Yeah and without busting things up. A lot of them bust things up for the hell of it when they break into a place."

"So the three most likely candidates?"

"Well, one of them, he looked pretty good for a while. Thirty-one years old. Convicted for a string of eight break-ins, all one-man jobs and seven electronic-equipment places. And thing is, he cuts round holes like the one at the place we were at."

Powder sat up sharply. "For crying out loud, that's almost enough to convict him."

"I thought it looked pretty good for a while."

"But it doesn't look good to you now?"

"No. The guy's in jail."

Powder felt the lateness of the hour, the endness of his work week. "Oh."

"I went and looked up his record file, see."

Powder nodded. "What about the other two of your hot prospects?"

Smith shook his head. "I . . . I didn't do them. By the time I had done all this with Tidmarsh and talked to him and so on and had read this guy's file it was near midnight and I came back here in case you needed me. Saturday being a busy night, see?"

"You just got yourself elected to continue this another night. That's what I see."

"Yes, sir."

"Smith, do you still feel it makes sense that there's a sophisticated robbery for only a hundred and sixty bucks?"

"He could have just been unlucky. That was one thing against this Wendell Walker, the guy who's in jail. He never got less than a grand and usually three or four between cash and small equipment."

"He knew his stuff, did he? Knew what kind of equipment was worth taking?"

"They say he knows electronics. I don't know where he learned it, but he knows it."

"I don't know," said Powder. "Maybe I'm wrong."

He left Smith and went to his desk.

Just had this feeling that maybe the break-in was by way of teaching someone else how to do it. A small place, just as an example. On-the-job training, like. I must have been watching too much TV, Powder thought. Though he hadn't been watching any. He turned to the pile of reports on his desk.

Every time he finished a report, someone brought him another. What's this? Jesus. Three cartons of wind-up clocks. Some lucky day detective was going to be scratching his head. What the hell could someone want with—how many now? Two dozen per carton?—getting on to a hundred and a half wind-up clocks? To strengthen their wrists winding them up? Jesus.

"D'ja hear?"

Preoccupation broken. "Hear what?"

It was Schleutter. "In Richmond they just found a guy tonight who has papers on him saying he's Les Ellyson."

"Ellyson?"

"The dead women with smashed fingers."

"Did he do it?"

"Well," said Schleutter, "they're not so sure now." He let it hang, didn't often get to dangle Powder.

"Why the hell not?"

"Because he's been dead a week, that's why."

Powder rubbed his chin. "If it *is* Ellyson."

"Yeah," said Schleutter, who hadn't really considered the possibility that the body might not be Ellyson even though it had his papers. "I'm glad I'm not upstairs for this one," he said then.

"Why not? No ambition!"

"I got enough problems."

"I'll arrange to get you on nights permanently if you like."

"Without making any more for myself," said Schleutter.

Powder went back to surveying reports. One of the innovations from his Notes. Each case report to be checked by the supervising officer.

The next report stopped him cold. Forced entry at premises corner Berkeley Road and Rookwood Avenue. 4400 North. 600 West. Premises a private high school called the University School.

Patrol Adam-3, Officer Hursh, was cruising and noticed the front door of the premises apparently open. He stopped to investigate. The door was open and a pane of glass had been broken to effect entry. Internal office door was forced. Officer Hursh made sure there was no one on the premises, that nobody was injured, then called in. Detective Sergeant Alexander Smith was assigned.

Was assigned! thought Powder. Then looked at the time of the call as Smith, in the report, had noted it. 23:52. That's it. While we were all out chasing night-club robbers. Smith takes it on himself to go out to the first call that comes in. Though, with his luck, the guy who did the electric store was the same one who did this.

Powder exhaled heavily.

The owner of the premises had been summoned. Arrived at 00:40. Confirmed break-in, estimated losses. Petty-cash box with $408 in it was empty.

$408 like hell, thought Powder. $8 more like, plus quick calculation of how much the insurance company would bear.

Also willful damage inside to an intercom console in the office. Owner to prepare more detailed listing, ready tomorrow. Today.

Powder picked up the phone . . .

And then put it back in its cradle. Almost put the long arm on Rex Funkhouser, 3:00 A.M. style. The kid was in here at about nine. Gave me a book.

Powder looked for the book. Coat pocket. He got up and checked. There it was, with a paper bag. *The Thoughts of Chairman Mao Tse-tung.* A little light bedtime reading, he thought. Short enough. Maybe the guy doesn't have all that many thoughts. Powder turned the cover. An inscription: "To Lt. Powder in the hopes he may find it possible to be a friend and comfort to the people."

Jesus. Jesus!

Powder opened the book to a page.

"The only way to settle questions of an ideological nature or controversial issues among the people is by the democratic method, the method of discussion of criticism of persuasion and education, and not by the method of coercion or repression."

And then, "We must undoubtedly criticize wrong ideas of every description. Mistakes must be criticized and poisonous weeds fought wherever they may crop up."

He closed the book. Oh yeah. Good stuff. Well, you've grown yourself a poisonous weed with your little adventure tonight, Mr. Funkhouser, Powder thought. Angrily. And after thinking for a few minutes he put the University School break-in report aside and went through the rest of the pile.


Powder went straight home when he finished his reports. He didn't stop to eat because, with his wife not there, he had free rein of the house. But it was a mistake because there wasn't anything to eat. Nothing in the freezer, except . . . But he didn't feel like having a pie shell for dinner.

He ended up with two cans—cans!—of ravioli. Left over, it seemed, from before they invented freezers. When did they invent canned food? Napoleonic times. When did they invent ravioli?

For a change, Powder didn't get to sleep very easily. Just having the University School break-in report in his pocket instead of turned in with the others made him uncomfortable. Or maybe it was the ravioli.

Decided to read a little.

What else does a detective lieutenant of police in Indianapolis, Indiana, USA, read to get himself to sleep but the Thoughts of Mao?

"We should rid our ranks of all impotent thinking. All views that overestimate the strength of the enemy and underestimate the strength of the people are wrong."

And "Ask your subordinates about matters you don't understand or don't know. And do not lightly express your approval or disapproval."

And "Cure the sickness to save the patient. The mistakes of the past must be exposed without sparing anyone's sensibilities."

They have a preoccupation with mistakes, Powder thought. Unable to adjust to people who never make mistakes. Like me.

But he found one for himself, too: "Many things become baggage, may become encumbrances. Having made mistakes you may feel that come what may, you are saddled with them and so become dispirited. If you have not made mistakes you may feel that you are free from error and so become conceited. Modesty helps one go forward, whereas conceit makes one lag behind."


Powder woke up sweating. The noonday sun was streaming, burning through the window onto his face. Forgot to draw the curtains. Face. Through the window, a kid staring in. Is that Ricky?

No face. Bent branches dovetailing with the pane frames. Which tree was that, outside the southern window in the bedroom? Oh yeah. Silver birch. Little thing, never really took a hold on life in this climate. Fighting gamely. Definitely not Ricky.

Powder sat up. Fully awake now. Oh yeah. I remember who I am. What I am. Where I am. How I am. Why I am. King Siam.

"Screw it," he said to no one in particular, and rose, dumped his sweat-wet pajamas in the dirty clothes and took a shower.

April Sunday, Indianapolis, a summery one for spring. Where is everybody going? Everybody else. Picnics and early baseball and late basketball and drives to grannies. And to Police Headquarters on days off, sure.

Where else is there to go on a Sunday in Indianapolis?

Powder walked up to the sixth floor. To the uniformed secretary outside Homicide-and-Robbery brass offices he said he wanted to see Captain Gartland.

"I'll see if he's in," said the secretary.

"He's in," said Powder. Old cops have routine. Us old cops.

The secretary disappeared after walking around her desk. Powder passed the time thinking about what it was that made an ankle "well turned." A chronic problem, worked on it off days only.

Gartland was in.

"What can I do for you, Roy?" asked Gartland, who didn't stand on ceremony. They were not exactly friends. Powder had been a sergeant under the then Lieutenant Gartland. Not exactly friends, but each appreciated that the other did his job better than most.

Powder pulled up a chair informally. "I want to save you guys some work."

"Oh yeah." Gartland lit a baby cigar. "And how you going to do that?"

Powder produced the report on the University School break-in and passed it across. Gartland skimmed it and looked up. "So?"

"I think I know who did it."

"If that were all, you'd fill in the name on the dotted line and go home and beat your wife. You stopped beating your wife yet?"

"Yeah, well, I'm kind of involved."

"Oh yeah?" It was the first light relief he'd had all day.

"Kid came in and I PRed him because he's John Public. He wanted us to clean up the corruption in his school and I tried to let him down easy. He persisted. I suggested maybe he wanted a private detective instead of public nothing. I think he cracked the school to pay for the PI."

Gartland cracked a smile and shook his head. "You deserve it, Powder, you really do. Some stray dog and he bites you. You take the cake, chum."

"No comment."

"I could tell the punks downstairs some stories about you that would bring tears to their eyes, I really could."

Powder cleared his throat, an emotional period. New paragraph. "Now you've rubbed my nose in it, can I go and get to work?"

"Yeah, yeah. Get out."

"So initial it."

"How long you want it?"

"Couple of days, I'm not going to kill myself."

Gartland initialed the report, assigning it for investigation to Powder for the next two days.

From Gartland's office Powder went down the stairs to the Day Room to let the paperwork people know he was working and what he was on.

From there he went to his car and grabbed a sandwich on the way to North Indianapolis.

## 9

Powder felt some pleasure from being on casework again. And a caseload of one was more congenial than it was when . . . A thousand years ago. Nineteen.

A couple of days, then throw it upstairs, finished or not. After he'd atoned for causing the case to become bigger than it need have done. Two days on my own time, Powder thought. No one can complain about that.

Except possibly the garden. As living and loving a person to him as any.

The University School looked like a house except for the garish No Parking Zone striped along twenty feet of street in front of it. Large, redbrick. Sparsely covered with ivy; part of the sales image, no doubt, along with the location: a few blocks from Butler University on the one side and from the Governor's Mansion on the other.

A brass plate visible from the sidewalk announced the name of the school and in letters equally large named a Benjamin Jefty as the 1948 "Founder." It also read "Education: Keystone in the Arch of Life." The building was surrounded by fir trees except for a cervical clearway from the sidewalk to the front door.

Powder rang the bell. Two panes of glass were missing from the outside door. No one answered the ring.

Powder walked back to his car and looked at the report on the break-in. It located the owner, Jefty, at 43rd and Graceland. One block south, three blocks east. Powder sighed, and decided, while he was here, to have a look around the outside of the school.

The building walls were actually moist to the touch. The trees ran all the way around the building and effectively prevented direct sunlight from getting through to the lower windows.

The place was bigger than it looked. The basement had been fully exploited, a cafeteria in the front half and two classrooms in the back. Every other room he could see into seemed to be a tiny classroom.

There would have to be a principal's office. But he couldn't find it.

No clue from looking up. There were two floors above, but books appeared to fill each windowsill. Every inch of space. It didn't make a good impression on a man who'd come, late and lately, to take pleasure in the outdoors of life.

He worried about the location of the office and walked around the building again. One possibility, one window with closed Venetian blinds. But it looked, through cracks, like a book storeroom.

"Hey, you!"

Powder turned to the front of the building, where a corpulent man with a stick was holding some tree branches out of his face.

"Yes?" said Powder.

"This is private property. What do you think you're doing here? Come out of there immediately. I've called the police. And don't threaten me, I'm not alone." The man vanished as he stepped around the corner back to the front of the building from which he'd come.

Threatened with a stick in broad daylight. The school was becoming a high-crime area.

Powder walked to where the man had been. He considered getting his ID out; he considered drawing or showing his gun. But he just walked to the front of the building.

Where the man no longer stood.

"Come on, off the property!" The man was on the sidewalk now. The stick was raised. Powder took a step forward on the path; the man took two steps back.

"Who are you?" said the man. "What do you want?"

"Police," said Powder forcefully. "Now who the hell are you and why are you threatening me with that stick?"

Powder followed Benjamin Jefty's car the four blocks to its home. The car ride gave Jefty time to find a less hostile self, and when Powder parked in front of a brick house, Jefty opened Powder's car door for him and was sweating. The stick was now a twig on the tree of the past.

"I'm terribly, terribly sorry, Lieutenant," he said unctuously. "A terrible little misunderstanding."

Powder got out.

"This robbery has upset me so. Then when Mrs. Oxwald called and said she'd seen a suspicious man prowling around the school, I thought, Heavens! and I called the police and I came straight over. It was just too much."

On the drive Powder had restrained the forces which Jefty's call would have unleashed.

A frowning woman dressed in a white T-shirt and black shorts appeared in the hall as they came into the house. Every visible square inch of her flesh was supported by hardened muscle.

"It was just police, dear. I'm going up to get my statement about the stolen property and damage. See to the lieutenant, will you? Perhaps some coffee if he takes it." Jefty hurried slowly up the stairs.

"Where were you last night when we needed you?" asked the woman.

She seemed to wait for Powder to answer. Till snowballs in hell. Finally she motioned him through an archway to the living room. Powder went in; unasked, he sat down.

Mrs. Jefty followed and stood. "We hadn't been out in six weeks, but last night we were out."

"Do you think the perpetrator or perpetrators knew you were out?"

She shrugged. "We hardly ever go out. When you're in the business we're in, you can hardly go anywhere in town without seeing someone you know. I mean, from the school: kids or their parents or teachers who used to work for us."

"You have a high turnover of teachers?"

"Teachers are a dime a dozen."

They paused to listen for the rescue of footsteps coming down the stairs. But no aural lifeline. Upstairs a toilet flushed.

"Do you work at the school?" Powder asked.

"Yes."

"Teach?"

"Yes," she said. "French." She did a deep knee bend. "Everywhere you go, kids. You can't call life your own."

Jefty came down the stairs. "Here we are," he said as he entered the room. He handed Powder a typewritten sheet; Powder read it. Knee bend.

"If you must do that, dear, please go back to the kitchen!"

Mrs. Jefty complied silently.

"Isn't four hundred and eight dollars a lot of money to have around a school?"

"I explain, if you read on, it was petty cash plus the cafeteria's float."

"You kept them together?"

"Over the weekend, yes."

Powder looked back at the sheet of paper. "There was damage to your intercom console. And the only other thing that was taken was an Adler electric typewriter?"

"That's right. All the doors were still locked."

"The officer last night reported that the front door was open."

"I meant apart from the front door. They got in the front."

"Is there no other equipment in the office? Besides a typewriter. Film projector? That sort of thing."

"There is an electric mimeograph machine. The rest is locked away."

"And they didn't take the mimeograph? You left it out because it was too large to carry easily?"

"The electric typewriter is too large to carry easily, Lieutenant. Very heavy."

"You have samples of work typed on it, I suppose?" said Powder.

The question surprised. "Why, yes, I suppose we do. Why?"

"It might help identify the machine if we do find it."

"I have the serial number, but it's at the school."

"We'll take that, too. You were out last night?"

"Why, yes."

"Where did you go?"

"To the theater."

"What time did you get back?"

"We were home before midnight. We go to bed early and we rise early. I don't understand why you're asking me these things, Lieutenant."

Good. "You were insured against theft?"

"Well, essentially, yes." Jefty frowned.

"What is 'essentially'?"

"For the damage and the typewriter, but not all the cash."

Powder let Jefty's wrinkles relax. Then asked, "Do you have any idea who might have robbed you?"

"None," Jefty said quickly. "Just a thief I suppose."


Powder drove Jefty back to the University School. The only words spoken were Powder's, telling Communications he was returning to Berkeley and Rookwood.

It was coming back. Powder never had liked victims who took their victimization with good humor. Let me have indignation about me.

By the time the two men were walking up the steps to the school's front door Jefty realized that a crime you call the police into is a serious crime.

"They came in here?" said Powder at the door.

"Yes. It was open. Two panes of glass were broken—there, and there. You see?"

"And there's a latch on the inside so you can open the door without a key?"

"Yes."

"So you've been protecting the school with two panes of glass?"

"I suppose so. Look, Lieutenant, you seem to be blaming me for what happened here last night. *I* didn't break into the school to steal things."

But if you're disturbed you'll think more actively about who did, thought Powder. "We must clear away all ideas of winning easy victories, without hard and bitter struggle." Chairman Mao. What the hell am I thinking about!

Powder rubbed his face. "Do you have any idea who might have broken in here last night?"

"None at all."

"Have you tried to think of anyone?"

"Well, I just assumed it was . . . well, someone off the street. Some professional or something."

"Why here?"

"I don't know. I didn't think about it. I suppose it could have been someone I . . ." He followed Powder inside. A gray, musty, sullen place. Maybe it was lighter with the happy voices of enthusiastic children burbling in the background.

"Your office?"

"That door. A pane of glass there, too. When I was over here this morning I swept up. I chipped the sharp edges out."

"Open the door, please."

With a key Jefty opened the door to the room which bore the title: "Principal's Office." The electric light was necessary, as it had no windows. Powder found it a cluttered, compact room, with two desks, three filing cabinets, stacks of paper, books and one electric mimeograph machine.

"The door there is my storage cupboard. The portable machines and books. Nothing was touched."

"May I see it?"

"I . . . Nothing was taken."

"May I see it, please!"

Jefty sorted tintinabulatorily through his keys and found the correct one. He revealed a room as small as the office, but long and narrow. At the end there was a window darkened by its Venetian blind. The lefthand wall was covered with shelving, intricate and almost full. Books, a movie projector. Boxes of supplies.

On the right behind the door was a tall cupboard filled with stationery supplies and next to it along the wall was a narrow leather couch.

Jefty stood by the couch, a little embarrassed. "I like to lie down occasionally," he said. "When I get the chance. And sometimes students rest here when they aren't well and perhaps their parents are going to come and pick them up. The ones who don't drive. There should be a first-aid kit around here somewhere."

He looked around for the first-aid kit and with some difficulty finally pulled a dusty box up from the floor shelf near the window.

Powder walked back into the office. "And where was the money kept?"

Jefty pulled the bottom door of a filing cabinet open. From it he took a small cashbox.

"Not locked?"

"No, I thought . . ."

"How did you find it? Was it open on the desk, or what?"

"Why, no, it was the first thing I checked. I didn't even notice the typewriter was gone till this morning. When the police called, I came over and I opened the drawer to check the cashbox. I found it . . ." He turned the box over to show that nothing fell out.

Powder sighed and decided to sit down. Ninety-five years old and tired with it. He couldn't find a chair on his side of the desk. He pushed a pile of paper out of the way and sat on the corner of the desk.

"Did anyone dust the box for fingerprints last night?"

"Well . . . not that I remember."

Trust Alexander Smith to miss the obvious. "I'll take it with me, then." Pause. "Mr. Jefty. Do you have any idea of someone who might have done this?" For the third time.

Powder left Jefty at the school. Stewing. "You don't mind walking back?" Powder had asked in a statement-like way. Powder called in when he got into his car. He told them he was on his way to Eagledale.

Thinking all the while that you don't really appreciate the training and perceptiveness of a cop, even an imperceptive cop, until you compare it to a civilian's.

Even Alexander Smith would have seen the obvious at the University School.

Powder hoped.

Oh yes, he must.

Look at it. No wastage. Go directly to the cashbox. How do they know where it was?

That fact alone. Must be some contact in the school, wouldn't you think, Mr. Jefty? A student, a former student, a teacher, a former teacher? Or a student . . . ?

Who would know where the cashbox would be? Set aside the typewriter and the smashed console for a moment.

"Who?" Jefty had said. "Gee. Well, it couldn't have been students."

Which had surprised Powder. "Why not?"

A chuckle, patronizing. On his own ground. Teacher revealing all to tyro. "You have to understand the function of this school in the overall educational situation in the community."

Which was prelude to a speech the gist of which was that the University School accepted—was offered—only pupils who had had extreme difficulty elsewhere. Behavioral problems which had forced their ejection from public schools; psychological problems. "We do have a few students who just seem to function better in a small-school environment. We have a few with physical disabilities who are better able to cope with the situation here. We're a kind of catch-all for children who need another chance or special treatment. Considering what we get, our record is pretty admirable."

The gist was that Jefty couldn't conceive his students being intellectually capable of a stunt like this. "Besides, none of them know where the cashbox is kept, so that theory is out."

Let's say set aside for the moment.

"What about teachers or former teachers? They'd know where the cashbox is kept, wouldn't they?"

"Well . . . some of them might."

"Cafeteria staff?"

"Mrs. Pirgos? Never Mrs. Pirgos."

Ho humm.

"So this robbery never took place. The only people left are you and your wife. What did you say you were doing last night?"

"There's no need to be insulting, Lieutenant."

"Teachers, Mr. Jefty. In your long career here are there no teachers who have left with bad feelings?"

"I think," convincing himself, "that we've had pretty good faculty relations on the whole." Unconvincing.

But he'd let it rest. That was Day's job. Powder was concerned with the Rex Funkhouser side of things. If Funkhouser had used Powder as an excuse to . . .


The house at the address given by Rex Funkhouser was a fifties prefab and the yard was maintained as if the world still thought prefabs were the latest in cat whiskers. Powder walked quickly up to the door. It was getting hot inside his suit. Good gardening weather. There was a dark aquamarine Chrysler in the driveway. A couple of years old.

Powder rang the bell, stepped back and waited with his hands in his pockets.

The door opened six inches. A face looked up at him. He saw the top of a little blue hat and some netting pinned carefully about the head. "Yes?"

Powder pulled out his identification wallet and opened it to the face. "I'm Detective Lieutenant Powder from the Indianapolis Police Department, ma'am. I want to speak to Rex Funkhouser. I believe he lives here."

The woman's face showed shock. She opened the door wide without hesitation. "Lieutenant? Police?"

"Yes, ma'am."

She unlocked the half-screen, half-storm door and held it open. "Please come in, Lieutenant." Powder entered. The woman called, "Burl! Burl!" She pointed to a chair in an immaculate living room, but Powder stood and watched as the woman took a few steps in the direction she had shouted. She was about five feet tall, in a conservative blue dress of some shiny material printed with small pink flowers. Petticoats, so it stood out. "Burl, come here!" Turned back to Powder. "Sit down!" she said. Powder remained standing.

The woman stared blindly at Powder, and just as she was about to fetch Burl by force, the hall filled. A stocky man of medium height was slipping into a dark blue jacket as he backed toward them, closing a door. He said, "We're not late, are we, Nicki? Who was that at the door? I was on the . . ." He turned around and saw Powder. Burl wore a dark maroon tie. "Who are you?" he asked Powder. "Some trouble?" he asked Nicki.

"This is a policeman, Burl. A Lieutenant . . ."

"Powder."

"Powder. He wants Rex."

"What about?" asked Burl.

"Is Rex Funkhouser your son?" asked Powder.

"He is. What do you want him for? What's he done?"

"I want to talk to him," said Powder patiently, "because I think he may be able to help us with an investigation we're conducting."

"Please sit down!" said Nicki Funkhouser urgently. Both men felt the urgency and complied.

Burl looked at his watch as he sat. "Will this take long?" he asked Powder, but without giving him a chance to answer, he

said to Nicki, "Call Baba and tell her we may be late. Go on."
Nicki went.

The men watched her leave. Burl said, "She's going to be a mess for a week," to nobody in particular. "Look, Lieutenant Powder, I'm not the kind of guy to give trouble to a cop, excuse me, a police officer who's doing his job. But Rex is my only kid and I got a right to know. And he is under twenty-one. Or doesn't that matter anymore? I ain't no lawyer."

"Is Rex here, Mr. Funkhouser?"

"No. He went downtown. Said he had to see a man about some business. What kind of business *he's* got I don't know. We gave up a long time since trying to get him to come to church with us. But if he made some special excuse, there must have been something. What kind of business . . . on a Sunday . . . ?" He made it clear he feared to think.

"When do you expect him back?"

"Hard to tell. This must seem bad to you, having a kid and not keeping tabs on him. He ain't twenty-one, after all. Only nineteen, but we can't do anything with him."

"It's a common problem," said Powder formally.

"Yeah, yeah," said Burl Funkhouser, making it clear that was no more consolation now than it had been the first hundred times he'd heard it. "I suppose we could throw him out, but it would break his mother's heart. I wouldn't like it neither, that I gotta say. Ever since the accident he's been a different kid. Was a good, tough boy before that," remembered pride, "but he's gone . . ." He scratched the back of his hand as if trying to peel off a word to complete the idea. None came; the idea was already complete.

Powder said, "What accident?"

"Oh, you wouldn't know the kid, would you? When he was sixteen he had a crack-up on a bike, motorcycle. Broke his back and his neck. Not severed, though, so he gets around now. With a terrible limp. He was in bed for about sixteen months. Still goes to therapy."

"I see," said Powder, who had wondered why a kid of Rex's

age was in a high school, private or otherwise.

"Nicki thinks he hit his head, too. I think it was just having to lie around while all the—"

Nicki Funkhouser burst back into the room. "It's that girl, isn't it? That Cherry Whateverhernameis."

"—other kids were playing football," said Burl.

"It's her, isn't it? Baba wants to know what's going on. So do I. She's terribly upset."

"Did you have to tell her the whole thing?" said Burl sharply. "Couldn't you just do what I said and tell her we'd be a little bit late? Why couldn't you just do that?"

Nicki looked like she had a ready answer, but withheld it in front of Powder.

"It's my mother," explained Burl. "She's got a heart condition."

"Do you know where Rex was last night?"

"No," said Burl.

"Yes," said Nicki.

They looked at each other, then at Powder, both said, "Out."

"But where in particular, and until when?"

They both shook their heads.

Powder got up. "There's not much I can do, then. Will you please tell Rex to call this number—" he handed Burl a card with his name and the division number—"and ask for me. Tell him," forcefully, "to do it as soon as he gets home, or as soon as you hear from him. If I'm not in the office, they'll know where to call me. Whenever he gets back. You understand?"

"It's that girl, I know it is."

"What girl is that, ma'am?"

"There's a girl at this school Rex goes to. She's new there this semester and he's been seeing her a lot. She's no good, but you can't expect him to know that, can you? There's something wrong with that boy. I could tell you things, things I know, things I've found—"

"Shut up!" said Burl, his tackle nipping a ninety-yard runback in the bud.

"I'll call Baba and tell her we aren't coming," said Nicki.

Powder took a few steps toward the door.

"We *have* to go now, now that you blew your big mouth off."

"Not in front of the lieutenant."

"All right!" Burl escorted Powder to the door.

"I'm staying here, in case Rex comes back," Nicki said, following them. "You go to Baba's alone." She began to unpin her hat.

"All right! All right!"

Nicki disappeared into a room at the back of the house. Burl said, "She's never liked Baba. All these years."

Powder rubbed his face with both hands as he walked back to his car.

This was the time when a real day cop would shift gears to another case. Powder wasn't ready to put out a pick-up on Rex. Yet. But he wasn't willing to shift to other lines of inquiry before he had interviewed his prime suspect.

Let things rest till Rex turns up, he thought happily. He headed for his garden and thanked the gods for letting him have his cake and eat it, too.

## 10

By 5:30 Powder was covered with sweat and had planted six rows of beans. Both facts pleased him.

In Clandestine Shed he toweled himself off and changed back to duty clothes. He was bothered that Rex had not surfaced. He'd left the car's external speaker on throughout the late afternoon. For more than two hours police calls had boomed through the otherwise quiet field. But no call for Powder.

Not that there was a rush. But he decided it couldn't hurt to look at the likely spot of Rex's "business" in town.

Powder came into town on Pennsylvania Avenue, turned

right on Maryland, which is one-way west. Parking was easy.

The building he was looking for was on the north side of the street, but he didn't see the doorway at first.

A window, filled with an enormous announcement: ASTOUNDING APRIL SALE, seemed to occupy the whole site. But at the side of the window he found a dirty door and, screwed to the frame, a clean, well-lettered sign: "Albert Samson. Private Investigator."

Powder tried the door. It was open. Powder frowned. Took a breath, and climbed the stairs to an unlit landing. He heard a voice in the distance.

His penlight showed another posted door: "Albert Samson. Private Investigator. Walk Right In." He put the light away and tried the handle. The door didn't open, but it wasn't locked. He pushed again, near the top, where it was sticking. Then pushed at the door and hit the sticking point with the heel of a hand.

Which put him in the open doorway of a dark room. He walked right in. The voice in the back was clearer now. Singing "Swing Low."

Powder got the penlight out again and found the light switch. It revealed an office about twelve feet square, sparsely furnished. Desk, filing cabinet. Two chairs, a bench against one wall.

"Anybody here?" Powder called.

The singing continued.

There were two doors leading from the office. Powder tried one on the right of the room, but it was a closet filled top to bottom with photographic equipment, including an enlarger. The other he walked to, knocked on hard and called again, "Anybody there?"

The singing stopped. Powder stepped back to the middle of the room. The door finally opened and a thick, wet man walked into the office. He had a flowered towel wrapped one and a half times around his waist. His bare feet left large wet tracks as he walked across the floorboards and extended a hand.

"Crusoe, I presume; my name's Sunday." The hand, at least, was dry.

"Samson?" said Powder formally.

"Sunday. Samson. Something like that. If you can wait a minute, I'll change into something more comfortable. This business?"

Powder pulled out his ID. "Name's Powder. Police."

"You can wait," said Samson and went back into the other room, closed the door.

And began to sing again.

After a minute Powder banged on the door. "Move your ass in there!"

The singing continued, but only a few more moments.

Dry and more fully covered by a patched bathrobe and cotton slippers, Samson came back to his office. Sat behind the desk and pulled out a notebook.

"Now, Officer. Was it a parking ticket you wanted me to fix for you, or is that level of corruption too low for the police of this fair city to bother with?"

Powder frowned.

Samson said, "This glib talk is all an act to cover up my quivering fear of the police."

"You always leave the door to the street open? It's a pretty stupid thing to do."

"I see," said Samson, sitting back and showing green-and-orange striped undershorts. "You're on the crime-prevention squad. That's why you've come around on a Sunday evening. Pretty keen, aren't you? Well, sorry I can't stop to chat now, I have a date."

"This isn't a social call," said Powder menacingly.

"So . . . Get to the point. Powder? Powder. What kind of name's that, then? Arabic? Onomatopoeaic?"

"If you don't shut up, I'll damn well run you in."

"Don't get tough with me, cop. This room is bugged. Tapes are being made for posterity. And I ain't big enough to buck a subpoena. Get to the point. I'm in a hurry."

"Do you know a Rex Funkhouser?"

"I've met him."

"Did he hire you this morning?"

"I don't think it's beyond the scope of possibility."

"What did he want you to do?"

"Nice to have met you. Don't bother to close the door as you go out, it's sticky and requires delicacy."

"Get your clothes, Samson."

"You arresting me?"

"I'm taking you downtown."

"Look out the window in my bedroom. We're already downtown. You want me to come to Police Headquarters, you have to arrest me because I won't come voluntarily because I've got a date and my woman will kill me if I'm late, which I almost am already, and then you'll have a real crime to solve. If you are investigating some crime, say so. But you know damn well that I don't have to tell anyone except my client what my client's business is. If you've got some questions that I can answer, fine, ask them. If not, get out so I can dress."

Powder shook his head. "I thought you were a friend of Lieutenant Miller's."

"A friend. Which doesn't mean I'll break the law by blabbing my client's business to any stray cop who walks in off the street. Yes, Rex Funkhouser came to my office today; yes, he retained me." Samson spread his hands as if there could be no more answers in the universe.

Powder said, "Did he give you a cash retainer?"

"Why?" Firm.

"Because he talked to me four days ago and said he didn't have any money. Then yesterday he comes to me and says he has acquired some money and in the meantime we find out that the school he goes to was broken into and money taken. If he's hired you for the same sort of thing he talked to me about, then you can see—Miller said you weren't dumb—why it is reasonable to explore the possibility that Funkhouser cracked the school. Now, did he give you a cash retainer?"

"Yes."

"How much?"

"Fifty bucks."

"You have it here?"

"Yes."

"I want it."

"So do I."

"It's evidence. I'll give you a receipt for it and you can have it back when we're finished with it."

"And I give the receipt to my landlord, I suppose?"

"You do for your landlord whatever you were going to do before this long-haired kid walked in off the street one Sunday morning. I'm amazed he could bring himself to come up here. This is a pretty crappy set-up you got here."

"It looks better in the sunshine," said Samson, now clearly less manic. He lifted a cake box out of the bottom drawer of his desk and pried off the top. He took out a stack of small bills and pushed them across the desk toward Powder. Held the box upside down. "And then the cupboard was bare."

"You're breaking my heart," said Powder as he counted the money, then wrote a receipt for $50.

"I want to know what you guys are going to do about this missing girl."

"What missing girl?"

Samson thumbed through his notebook. "Cherry Cable."

"Never heard of her." Powder got up after wrapping the bills carefully in his handkerchief. "Look, Samson. I'm just doing the preliminary investigation here. We'll have more people around to see you. You keep available, hear?"

"You want me on call, you arrest me. Then see how good my lawyer is."

"Going tough again? Huh. We'll see."

"Look, you come here and talk effluvia to me, I deal it back. You talk sense and we can work all right. I spend my spare time reading lawbooks, so don't think you can belt me around."

Powder looked at him and yawned.

Samson looked back and yawned.

Powder said, "I don't know many private detectives. Is your life as glamorous as it looks on TV?"

"You're the cop Funkhouser talked to, are you?" More speculative.

"In one week I meet a Maoist and a private dick. I think I prefer the Maoist." Powder got up.

"Watch yourself. I'll tell the American Legion you've been reading dirty books."

"You annoy me, Samson."

"Because I don't like you walking in here without asking if it's convenient? And then boring me with empty threats if I don't tell you my granny's shoe size? As a Gestapo agent you're really punk, Powder."

Powder was getting tired and got out his notebook. Memo: "Look up Samson, Albert."

"While you're taking notes on the chat, whyn't you write down you'll get a lot more help from me with a few pleases and thank yous?"

Feeling stupid, but too tired to wise up, Powder grabbed the door. "Like I say," he said, "keep available."

Powder walked out the door, slammed it, but it hit the frame behind him and flew back open.

Samson stood behind his desk and smirked. "Delicacy," he said. "It takes delicacy to close my door. Tact. You've got to say please to it."

Powder walked back into the office from the landing, around the desk. Samson turned to meet him. Powder slugged him hard in the gut and felt good.

While Samson lay gasping on his desk, Powder left, closing the door, delicately, behind him.

---

From West Maryland it was a short drive to the police parking lot. Powder took the elevator to the third floor and marched to the Forensic Lab.

"Lock up your daughters!"

"Why're you all sitting around?" Powder asked. "No work to do?"

"Even the world's drones get to rest now and then."

"It's our ethanol break."

"Hey, we're nearly out of coffee! Where are the sodium-arsenate crystals?"

"Look," said Powder, "I've brought you some work. Top priority."

"Next month soon enough?"

"Work?!"

"What is it, Lieutenant? Not unidentified capsules, I hope. We've had our fill of those this week."

"Drug Squad has run out of dope peddlers, so they're busting people with hay fever now."

"Got to protect society."

"I think I've missed something," Powder said.

"What have you got, Lieutenant?"

"Fingerprints on this metal cashbox." Powder produced Jefty's box. "And there's this money. . . ."

"Don't try to buy us, you pretty boy, you."

"There's this money," Powder repeated. "I think it came out of the box, but I'd like you guys to prove it."

"Prove it?"

"You know, dust fragments that match. Something like that." Powder shrugged. "They do it on TV."

"So take your money to TV."

"All right, Lieutenant. We'll have a look."

"Thanks," said Powder. "And hey, do you have a Band-Aid?"

"What's the matter?"

"I cut my knuckle. Must have hit a button."

**NIGHT COVER**

**11** At 10:45 next morning Powder sat at his day desk. After a night's sleep, taken at night for a change, he was writing up his report for the previous day. Jefty's cashbox had provided one set of prints, all recent. They were certainly Jefty's, all put on after the crime—thief must have wiped the box carefully. As well, the $50 confiscated from Samson had turned up nothing. The odds against matching fragments on used bills uniquely with dust particles in Jefty's cashbox were prohibitive. It had been a nice idea. As he'd driven to the department, Powder had developed some enthusiasm for the notion of going to the University School to bring Rex Funkhouser ostentatiously in for questioning.

But when he'd arrived at his desk he'd found a message saying Rex had called in the previous night and would stay at home today.

With a little luck Powder reckoned he would be able to salvage half a day at the garden again. His strange ally, the garden. For whom he was a fair-weather friend.

Powder finished his account of the background to the case, but he was uncertain whether he must turn in the copy of Mao's Thoughts. Thought not, since it's obvious where it is. It was the smallest book, physically, that he'd ever owned. An appeal in its own right.

"There we are," he said to nobody in particular as he affixed his initials.

"Lieutenant Powder! Surprised to see you here today." It was Harold Salimbean.

"I was just leaving."

"So am I. I've been to see Gaulden in Personnel."
"Oh yeah. How he treat you?"
"Pretty well."
"You look a little happier; what you going to do?"
"I don't really know. But he was straight with me and he's got me thinking. Just what part of my job my wife dislikes most. The irregular hours and that. It was good to talk to someone. He didn't make me feel bad. I . . . I may look for a job elsewhere." It was rolling out.

"Good," said Powder without thinking about whether the remark might be a little tactless.

"You going out, Lieutenant?" Eager to show his appreciation of Powder's understanding.

"No, I want to see Miller."

"Well then, I'll see you tomorrow night."

"On time, I hope."


Miller, however, was not in his cubicle. Powder would abuse him about his friends another time.

Decided to go down to the Canteen. Where he found Howard Brindell sitting with a uniformed officer. Brindell looked terrible.

"Wait there, Brindell," Powder said when he saw him. "I got something to say to you."

When Powder came back to the table with his coffee, Brindell looked grimmer than before. The other man, whom Powder didn't know, said, "Give him a break, Lieutenant. He's had a hard day."

"Try prunes," said Powder and sat down backward on a chair, feeling tough. "I want to know what makes you think you're so important you can have your roster assignments fixed for you. Everybody takes a turn on night shift; where do you get off having Graniela take your name off the night roster? I asked you a question, Brindell."

Brindell didn't answer.

"What's the matter with him?"

"He's just been bumped off his prime case."

"Tough. Which one was it?"

"Some murders last week, ten days. Three women with their fingers mashed up."

"Oh!" said Powder. "What'd you do wrong, Brindell?"

Brindell got up from the table.

"Don't you leave, Sergeant. I've got some questions to ask you."

"Fuck off," said Brindell and walked out of the room.

Powder snorted, but was not unpleased. "So what happened?"

"Don't be too hard on him, Lieutenant."

"What happened, damn it?"

"Well, he got these three bodies and they're all dumped and they've all got mashed fingers and they're all women. Brindell figures they've all been killed by the same hand."

"Yeah?"

"So he gets an ID on the first two, then gets a make on the guy who probably bumped off the first one."

"Yeah, I kind of remember all this. Name was . . ."

"Ellyson. Les Ellyson, who probably bumped off the first woman, who was Leonora Ellyson."

"Right."

"But then they find the body of Les Ellyson in Richmond. He was around when Leonora got dead, but definitely was dead before the third body appeared and maybe before the second."

"Huh!" said Powder, who found it interesting. "So he's got two or maybe three murderers to catch instead of one."

"Yeah," said the man. "So it turns out."

"So, what'd he think?"

"Well, he kind of gave the medical man in Richmond a hard time."

"Oh," said Powder. "And for his efforts . . . They took him off the whole thing?"

"Yeah. And he's taking it hard."

"Huh," said Powder. "It's what he deserves."

Brindell's friend scowled. "He's got a right to ask Richmond if they've made a mistake. So maybe he did push it, but if they knew this guy maybe killed three people, maybe they'd be a little more careful fixing time of death."

Powder scowled and he was a lot better at it. "Bull."

"What?"

"You're full of shit and so is Brindell. He wants to tell the medicals when it would be convenient for the death to have occurred before they look at it to see when it really did."

"These guys don't know nearly so much as they think they do," protested the friend.

"Not as much as Brindell, huh? At least they know better than to try to cram a square peg into a round fucking hole."

The friend got up and left Powder alone at the table.

Powder smiled to himself. And then frowned. It was one thing to invoke a bit of hindsight to think that the first body hadn't really *felt* like the other two. But it left the need to explain why the later killings were superficially so like the first.

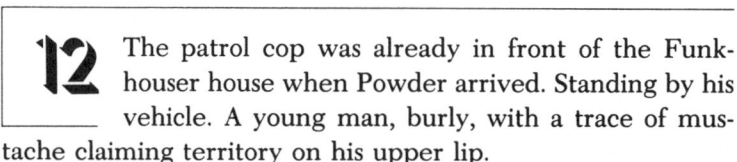

## 12

The patrol cop was already in front of the Funkhouser house when Powder arrived. Standing by his vehicle. A young man, burly, with a trace of mustache claiming territory on his upper lip.

"What's your name?"

"Latchman, sir."

"All right, Latchman. We're going to interview the young man in the house."

"Yes, sir. Shall I take notes?"

"Yes."

The two policemen walked slowly up to the front door.

Which opened before them quickly. "I said *I'll* talk to them, Mother! Just go away. Go piss in the garden or something." Then Rex turned to the officers who were stepping onto the porch.

"Am I glad to see you, Lieutenant!" he said. "The most terrible thing has happened! Cherry is gone!"

"Into the living room," said Powder. "We'll talk there." Powder walked straight into the living room. Latchman followed behind Rex, slowly. Nicki was nowhere to be seen.

"This is not a social call. Officer Latchman will take notes. You aren't obliged to answer my questions, however advisable it might be, and you can have a lawyer present."

"You're not arresting me!" said Rex, as if being arrested had never occurred to him.

"You're in trouble, kid. You've strained my good nature."

Latchman coughed. He'd heard about Powder. Legend in his own time.

"I don't know what you're talking about," said Rex. "But I do know that Cherry is missing and you could have done something about it."

"Where were you Saturday night, Rex?"

"What are you going to do about Cherry?"

Powder paused. "Where were you Saturday night, Rex?"

"What about—"

"Saturday night! Where? Where were you Saturday night?"

Having settled who was asking the questions . . .

Rex's alibi was largely by way of being no alibi. The only time he could establish his location was the period on Saturday he'd been at Police Headquarters to give a copy of his favorite book to Powder. Until, roughly, 9:00 to 9:30. Apart from that, Powder had the statements from Rex's parents that he had been "out."

"Why are you so interested in Saturday, Lieutenant?"

"I know you were involved in the robbery."

Rex smiled broadly. "Robbery?" he said. "What robbery?"

Powder would have put his life on being face to face with the University School burglar. "The University School was broken into. I know you did it. So let's have the details."

"That's ridiculous," said Rex, still smiling.

"Where's your mother?" asked Powder.

Smile gone. "What you want her for?"

"I want her permission to search the house. I don't have a warrant, but I can get one easily enough."

"Well, she's out. She's two doors down crying on Charlene's shoulder about what a hard life she's got. But you have my permission. Search the house. Anywhere but my father's account books. They're broken; he hasn't fixed them yet."


Eleven Mao posters and no electric typewriter later, Powder and Latchman returned to the living room. Where they found Rex full of confidence. "Now that we've finished playing cops and robbers, I want to know what you're going to do about Cherry."

Powder said, "Where were you yesterday?"

"I went to town to try this private detective you told me about."

Latchman looked up from his notebook; looked down again. "Yeah?"

"He seems to be pretty intelligent, considering."

"Where did you get the fifty dollars you gave him as a retainer?"

Rex grinned again. "I'm not impoverished, you know."

"Where did you get it?"

"I have bonds that Baba, my grandmother, bought for me when I was a kid."

"You told me you didn't have any money."

"Well, I was saving it for college, but when I thought about it . . . well, justice is more important than college."

Powder paused, then said, "Where and when did you cash your bonds?"

Rex was immediately nervous. Powder knew, *knew* that the break-in at the school was an impulse, something Rex had worked himself up to, and that he had not cashed any bonds yet. "I . . . well," said Rex.

"Just where and when?" said Powder. "So we can confirm your story."

"I don't want to answer that question."

"Why not?" said Powder sweetly. "Because you're lying?"

"I . . . I . . ." Then he was silent for a minute. Powder felt him come to the decision that anything was better than telling a lie which would be found out easily. Rex said, "I haven't cashed the bonds yet."

Both Rex and Latchman were surprised when Powder changed his attack and said gently, "Do you know what a forensic lab is?"

"I . . . Yeah, I think so."

"Let me tell you one of the things it can do, son. If you have some money in a cashbox"—Rex reddened—"there's dust and fibers and all sorts of microscopic stuff in that box. Now, a forensic lab can tell us whether some bills, say fifty dollars, came from a box or not."

"But I had the fifty dollars already! I was going to cash the bonds in case Mr. Samson, the detective, needed more."

"You'll never be able to spend that money, son."

"But I didn't take any money," said Rex, without convincing the fly on the wall.

"Let me tell you something else about a forensic lab. Every typewriter in the world is different. It's like fingerprints. You'll never be able to use the typewriter either. Or sell it. When you got this bright idea, son, you got yourself involved in business a lot bigger than you expected."

Hotly Rex said, "I didn't take any typewriter!"

"Because," Powder finished, "believe me, they don't teach Chinese in any prison I ever heard of. You think about it, son. Think about what you told me about that intercom in the school."

"Yeah," said Rex, acknowledging.

"Yeah what?" Powder snapped.

Both Rex and Powder knew that Rex had been admitting knowledge of the damage done to the University School intercom console.

"Yeah nothing," said Rex hastily. Then, "I mean, yeah, I remember talking to you about it."

Powder stood up.

Latchman also rose and said routinely, "Shall I handcuff him, sir?"

Rex paled.

Powder said, "I'm not going to take you in, Funkhouser. That's because I'm a nice guy. I'm known for being a nice guy, isn't that right, Latchman?"

"I . . . Yes, sir."

"See? He thinks we ought to take you in and lock you up. But I want to give you a chance to think about what you've done. I want you to turn yourself in. Believe me, it will go easier on you if you do. Come on, Latchman."

Powder and Latchman walked quickly to the door. Rex limped after them.

"But what about Cherry?" he asked plaintively from the door.

Powder turned to face the house door. "That the one who was going to kill herself if she didn't pass some course?"

"That's right."

"Did she pass the course?"

"She's missing. She hasn't been home since Friday after school."

"Tell you what, Rex. You come in and tell me about your own misadventures, and then we'll talk about your girl friend's problems."

"But . . ."

Powder turned and walked quickly to his car.

Latchman was already there, looking puzzled. "Why didn't you take him in, sir? I'm sure you could break him."

**NIGHT COVER**

"Sweet kid like that? Do you want him to have the trauma of an interrogation at Headquarters on his mind for the rest of his life?"

"Hell," said Latchman, but he knew Powder knew his own mind.

I should spend the rest of my last off day for a week breaking a cracked China plate?

Powder drove back to Headquarters and concluded his report, the fruits of his two-day investigation. He turned it over for reassignment to a day officer and left. Rex could wait a day; but the garden couldn't.

## 13

There were no messages on his day desk when Powder checked it Tuesday night. So he was in the night saddle before seven. The four detectives whose shifts coincided with his own were all in on time: the Smiths, Schleutter and even Harold Salimbean.

"Well, class," Powder said as the big hand passed twelve, "I see we're all here. I just want to thank you for the apple that was left on my desk. Now if you'll all get out your Bibles . . ."

They walked together to Detective Assembly, where Lieutenant Octavian gave them a condensed rundown of the week's action and whatever else crossed his mind. Since the night detectives had limited responsibilities for their calls, their briefings were less frequent than those for patrolling uniformed men. Uniform got assembly in some form each new shift.

On the way back to the Night Room, Powder asked Alexander Smith chattily, "What you been up to the last two days?"

"Not much, Lieutenant. Out flying some models with the kids. Resting."

"Really? I thought you'd have spent your time here."

"Here?" Smith asked.

"Yeah. Down ID working with Tidmarsh and his computer."

Smith bristled, but didn't say anything.

"If you don't mind," Powder said, "I've been thinking of something I'd like to have you dig up down there." He'd thought it up while digging in his garden.

"I mind being shuffled down to Tidmarsh when I'm supposed to be up here doing my detective probation."

"If that's what you think, then screw it," Powder said.

The phone was ringing when they walked back into the Night Room. A borderline armed robbery; Powder sent Alexander Smith out to tend to it.

He took a deep breath and rubbed his face as Smith left the room. The annoyance was that he had something that did want checking whereas last week it *had* been an excuse to see if Alex Smith could be taught anything.

7:10 and already thinking about nine-o'clock coffee.

He wondered how the other Smith would like to go down and answer some questions with Tidmarsh.

Hell, Sid Smith would probably enjoy it. Powder decided to ask Tidmarsh himself. Despite not wanting to get too pally with the man.

But Tidmarsh was pleasant enough. Sure. Happy to look through the last eighteen months at the murder records.

The conversation left Powder disquieted. He was deeply suspicious of people who seemed even-tempered.

But then the phone rang and Powder was invited to a shooting.

According to two neighbors, a man had been shooting randomly from an upstairs window of a small apartment building. When Powder arrived, no shots had been heard for more than half an hour. No one appeared to be hurt; but the first patrol officer on the scene found four holes through the roof of a yellow Ford parked in front of the building. No one knew whose car it was. The two neighbors didn't agree about which window the firing had come from.

Shooting in a public street is taken seriously. It's against the law for a private party to discharge a firearm within the city limits. The police cleared the street and then planned their approach to the two apartments nominated by the reporting neighbors. One on the third floor had an open window. It seemed more likely than the one with the closed window on the fourth floor.

Powder designated an entry team including the district sergeant. Three men. Two at the door each time, one with a protective angle on the doorway from the corridor. Auxiliary men assigned to keep civilians from wandering into the action.

When everyone else was in place, Powder went up to join the entry team outside the suspect third-floor door. "Hear anything inside?" Powder asked the sergeant.

He pointed to a tall officer standing against the wall by the door, gun in hand. "He says he hears voices."

"Mmmmm," said Powder. "Knock on the door."

"Knock on the door?"

"That's what I said, if you're asking. Or are you an echo?"

"Isn't it safer to go right in?"

"Knock on the door, damn it."

From the shelter of the wall—nobody stood directly in front of the door—the tall cop knocked hard with the knuckles of his left hand. He had to contort to do it, but he wasn't going to take the revolver out of his right hand for anything.

After a pause in which nothing was heard, the young cop looked at Powder.

"Again. And not like a pansy this time."

The young cop dented the door with the butt of his gun.

Powder swore. "Nobody never tell you they can go off that way?"

But the answer came from inside the apartment. "Who's there?" Male and tentative.

"Police. Open up!"

"Who?" Unbelieving.

"Police!"

The door opened slowly. The entry team flowed in and turned over three cups of coffee. They left four unspilled.

"Not here," said Powder, after the obvious had been acknowledged as obvious. "Upstairs."

The members of the Committee of the Irvington Golden Years Society reseated themselves and Powder sent for a young patrolman to ensure their safety.

On the fourth floor the entry team got no response at the door. There were no sounds of any kind. After three separate and severe dentings by truncheon.

"Break it in, Lieutenant?"

"Try the handle first."

The tall cop turned the knob. The door opened. He pushed it hard so it would open all the way.

The room was dark. Everyone waited outside this time; no point in rushing in when the only light would be a powder flash.

Nothing happened except that the door hit the wall inside with such force that it swung slowly closed again.

"You," said Powder to the tall cop, "in first. Look for a light. Sergeant, you cover him from the doorway. Ready?"

The door was thrown open again; the first man in tripped over a table; agonizing wait. Light on in time to be closed from view as the door swung back again into the crouching sergeant's face. Angrily he pushed the door aside, third time lucky.

Nothing much was happening.

In the room which contained the window over the street, they found four cartridge casings. In the bedroom, on their left, they found John Lee and a single-shot twenty-two rifle.

The rifle was empty. Lee was asleep, though restlessly as if disturbed by his dreams.

"See if he's hurt," said Powder to the officer who found Lee. "And the rest of you, I want this place turned over for drugs or alcohol or anything."

Before they left they found Lee's wallet with $28 in it and a driver's license which showed he was thirty-three. They found three bottles of beer sitting in a warm refrigerator. They found a receipt for repairs carried out on a '67 Ford, yellow, to the amount of $92.

They did not find any evidence of alcohol that had been consumed, any containers full or empty of sleeping pills. Any indication of illegal drugs. Or, indeed, any unspent cartridges for the rifle.

Powder was unable to displace the theory which said that Lee had pumped four bullets into his own car because it cost him too much. That he had then gone to sleep because he was tired.

Powder started down the stairs to return the street to normal, but he was stopped one flight down by the young cop he had left with the old people.

"Lieutenant?" Powder heard urgency and confusion in the voice.

"What's up, son?"

"I . . . I think we have a problem. With . . . with . . ."

"What are you trying to say? No one hurt, is there? Need an ambulance?"

"I'm not sure, Lieutenant, but is there anyone here who can identify marijuana?"

Powder peered past the young cop through the open door into the continuing meeting of the Golden Years Committee. A white-haired woman noticed him, smiled and waved.

"No, I don't think there is," Powder said, taking the kid by the arm. "Let's go down and wrap it up now. Say, did you ever hear the one about the Foolish Old Man Who Moved Mountains?"

"No," said the young cop uncertainly, allowing himself to be led by the venerable Powder.

Driving back to Headquarters, Powder found himself wondering what would have happened if a wife had cost Lee too much. Maybe a deeper, more contented sleep?

---

It was past 9:30 when Powder got to the Night Room. Because of the time, he went, reluctantly, to the Forensic Lab for his coffee instead of all the way to the Canteen.

"Lock up your daughters," someone said as Powder walked in the door.

"Your daughters are safe enough," said a tall technician whose name was Oliver. He waved a newspaper pointedly. "You see this, Lieutenant?"

"What?"

"This letter to the editor. It casts aspersions on the discretion of the guys in your department."

"Where?" said Powder and took the paper.

"There."

"This paper is five days old!" Powder said.

From the back: "When you're on the frontiers of science, you lose contact with the ordinary values of human life."

Oliver said, "Henry's wife put it in the bottom of his dinner box, that's the only way we came across it. Nobody reads letters to the editor."

Powder read the letter, which responded to the news of the award to the Drug Squad. It drew to the attention of the world at large that the Indianapolis police were unnecessarily rough —physical and mental violence—with people suspected of having any association with drugs. "I was bruised in four places," said the letter writer, "when the police turned over a friend's apartment I happened to be at. I think something should be done to curb these brutal people."

"What's this got to do with me?" Powder asked as he returned the paper and began the coffee routine. "You guys are always bitching about the Drug Squad. Why don't you go down the hall and make your complaints direct?"

"I don't want to get my head beat in," said Oliver. "Those boys are rough down there."

It wasn't a rest night: the phone rang as soon as Powder got back to his desk. It was a west-side appliance warehouse. A watchman had been hit hard on the head and his dog shot, but a second watchman, on a staggered round, had hidden and observed as the robbers selected which crated appliances they wanted to take. Powder answered the call himself.

One of the uniformed officers on the scene criticized the second watchman severely for hiding when his friend was down and might be dying.

Powder put the uniformed man in his place.

A coward, Powder told the cop, would have run to the farthest dark corner; a stupid man, being afraid of what people might say, would have charged like the cavalry with his dog against six armed men, to get Custered. Instead this guy keeps close, watches everything that's being done and takes notes on what he sees. Accurate description of the truck they use. Clothes and builds of the men. And a useful bit of observation: that one of them has a clipboard and is reading off numbers. Some of the boxes in the warehouse they take and some they don't.

"They haven't been out of here twenty minutes and there's a call on them all over town."

"The guy should have been carrying a gun," said the cop.

"But he wasn't," Powder said. "What do you want him to do, point his finger and go 'kuh kuh'?"

The injured guard had a skull fracture.

Before he left, Powder asked the uninjured guard why neither of them carried a gun.

"We did until last year," said the man, middle thirties, dark, thin and nervous. "But the boss decided a guard being armed was too much responsibility for one man, so he took away my gun, put an extra man on and gave us dogs. And put up the fences to sixteen feet. That's why I didn't try to climb out, see? There was just nothing I could do."

"We should have them in an hour," Powder told him. "I'll bet on it."

"Sure hope so," said the guard.

But an hour later, a little past twelve, they didn't have them and Powder was on the first floor at Headquarters cursing Uniformed Operations.

"Take this lunatic away!" Captain Mallin said. His men had had the truck's description minutes after it had left the warehouse. "If the truck isn't on the streets, then my men can't spot it on the streets. Go away, Powder. Go back upstairs. You may dish it out to your fairies up there, but we don't get shoved around that way down here."

Walking up the stairs, Powder cursed Mallin some more. But fumbling for the key to let him out of the stairwell onto the fourth floor, he laughed. They'd always said he put too much pressure on people; but pressure got results. Funny. Nobody ever notices that.

Powder walked back into the Night Room, sat at his desk and, head in hands, thought about the way he dished out pressure. From behind his hands he called out, "Smith!"

Pause.

"Sid Smith!"

"You want me, Lieutenant?" asked Sid Smith.

Powder came out from behind his hands, frowning.

Smith got up and came reluctantly up to the wall of Powder's cubicle. "Yessir?"

"Come in, sit down, Sid."

Smith hesitated, uncharacteristically for one so young and confident.

"Come on, then."

Smith complied.

"I've got a question, a hypothetical question that will make a better cop of you."

Smith raised an eyebrow. Powder saw it. Ignored it.

"You've got a warehouse, right? Big joint. Television sets, all kinda junk." He waited.

"Yeah," said Smith, thinking, Sure, I've got a dozen of them scattered all over the Midwest.

"You've got a warehouse and it's protected by high fences

and two unarmed guards, each with a dog, and then one night a gang comes in with a truck, kills one dog and hits one guard on the head so he's bad in the hospital."

"Yeah?"

"Now the other guard hides and watches, takes down good notes on everything that happens. License number on the truck, descriptions of the men. And soon as the guys leave, the guard runs to the nearest phone. Four minutes after he calls, the description of the truck is on the radio, on the radio! Within four minutes our guys are there, have talked to him and have got the description out."

Smith nodded, still uncertain where this unhostile conversation was leading.

"But with all that speed, two hours later every buck on the force, *plus* the Sheriff, *plus* the State, nobody's seen this truck."

Smith frowned, had to frown.

"So there you are," said Powder. "What kind of cop are you? What do you think about it?"

Smith took a breath. "One: it's a job with inside contact if they know exactly what to take."

Powder shrugged; he let Smith warm himself up.

"Two: if we haven't picked up the truck, it's probably under cover somewhere fairly close to the warehouse."

"Aah," said Powder, pointing a finger at him. Thinking, *Kuh kuh*.

"And if that's so," Smith continued, "they must know we're after them. Maybe they're listening to the police radio."

Powder watched as it unfolded.

"But if they know to listen," Smith said slowly, "and if they have a place to hide so close . . . It sounds like they knew we'd be after them fast."

Powder nodded, in grudging but complete agreement.

"If it's an inside job," Sid Smith continued, "they should have known about the second guard. If they thought they'd taken out the only guard, then they wouldn't have expected us to be after them so soon, and they'd be on the road somewhere."

"And we'd have had them by now."

"So you have to doubt the witness," Smith concluded. "The second guard."

"Get your coat."

"What?"

"There are a lot of possibilities, but I want you to cover us. I'll give you four men from Mobile Reserve and I want you to cover the area of the warehouse, discreetly. In a couple more hours I'll take the call off, make it clear on the air that we've given up. We'll see what happens."

"Yessir."

"Well, don't just stand there!"

Powder watched Sid Smith methodically gather his belongings and leave the room. Then he looked at Alexander Smith banging furiously at his typewriter, writing a report. How long would it have taken old Smith to follow the markings on the trail of logic which Sid Smith had picked up so quickly? Powder rubbed his face, made the call which gave Sid Smith his posse. Maybe Alexander Smith should grow a beard. "Hey, Smith."

"Me, Lieutenant?"

"You drink sarsaparilla?"

"What?"

"Forget it."

"What?"

"I said forget it! Finish that damn report."

## 14

There aren't many places to eat in Indianapolis at four in the morning.

Powder didn't know whether he wanted to eat, when 3:00 A.M. and the end of his duty rolled around. He considered hanging around the station till he found out what really

**NIGHT COVER**

had happened at the west-side warehouse. But when he saw Big Jack Monroe waddle into the Night Room to cover till 7:00 A.M., Powder decided to call it a day. Turn it over instead of listening to Jack's version of his family life for three or four or five hours.

Powder couldn't help it if he didn't enjoy the company of most cops these days. Not that I hate *people,* he thought to himself.

Before he left Headquarters he stopped in Communications and had them abandon the active search for the warehouse-robbery truck. They were surprised at the order, but obeyed it. Then Powder phoned back upstairs to explain Sid Smith's operation to Big Jack.

"Suspicious bastard, aren't you?" Jack said. But he hadn't sweated it. Big Jack never complained unless a job required him to physically leave the office. Rumor had it that he was too fat to get into a police car, but that wasn't true. He could get in, and drive it. It didn't even hurt, he had a callus where the steering wheel rubbed his stomach.

Powder left the police parking lot a little after 3:30, desk clear. He chose the Han Restaurant, twenty-four-hour Belgian-Cantonese Food. He would probably have eaten there more often if it weren't on the opposite side of town from his house and pretty far out at that.

"Pork Lo Mein tonight, Charlie."

Place run by Charlie Chuteh.

"How's business, Lieutenant?"

"High turnover but no profit."

"I know the feeling," Charlie said. "If there's anything worse than not having anything to do, it's working like hell but not having anything to show for it."

"Oh, I got something to show for it," said Powder. "Kid gave me this the other day for services not rendered." Powder flipped him the copy of Mao's Thoughts which he still carried in his overcoat pocket. "Ever read it?"

Charlie held the little red book at arm's length, studied the cover. "This an investigation, Lieutenant?"

Powder laughed. "No," he said.

Charlie looked at the book again. "Tell you the truth, I did look at it once. Or try. I couldn't really make heads of it, you know? Doesn't read like a book, you know?"

"Just wondered," said Powder meditatively.

"We're Taiwanese, anyway. My grandfather, I mean."

"Hey, I don't want you to think that just because you're Chinese . . ."

"I know, I know," said Charlie. "You ask all the people you meet whether they ever read this Mao stuff."

Powder realized that without thinking about it he had . . . just because Charlie was Chinese. Ah, screw it.

"I find it kind of interesting," said Powder. "I'm not very far into it, but there's some of this stuff—here, give it to me."

Charlie gave the book back to Powder.

From inside the hatch a voice said, "One double Pork Lo Mein," and someone slapped a plate on the sill. Powder found his page and Charlie brought the plate of food around to him.

"Here," said Powder. " 'Imperialism is a paper tiger.' "

"Oh yeah?"

"Well, I don't know much about the imperialism. But paper tigers I like."

"Oh yeah?"

"I like the idea that problems are tigers because they're problems, give you trouble. But they're paper because you can solve them. I have to deal with that every day."

Charlie pulled his ear lobes. "Oh yeah."

"And," Powder chuckled, "there's a guy down at Headquarters who's having all kind of fits because a case he's on turned out to be more tiger and less paper." Chuckled some more. He was thinking of Brindell, who could learn from Mao about handling mistakes, come to think of it.

"Yeah, well," said Charlie, "like I said, I never finished it."

"I'm going to finish it," Powder said. Picked up a fork and took a bite. "Kinda cool, isn't this? No, I don't read much, but if I start something, I like to see how it comes out."

"Yeah?" said Charlie. "Like I said, we're Taiwanese."

**NIGHT COVER**  |

---

Powder drove back through town to the west side after he'd eaten. He considered driving by Sid Smith's area. Half hoping to find the kid asleep. But instead he went out of town to the south, to an all-night bar. Nearly empty, but the jukebox was blaring.

"Whyn't you turn that thing off?" said Powder to the proprietor, Gabriel Wollenden.

"I think it cheers the place up."

"Bull. Not much business tonight."

"You only just missed the action, by three hours." Wollenden was wiping glasses.

"Scotch," said Powder.

"Single or double?"

"Fifth."

"Sounds cheerful."

"And two glasses. Look, Gabe, I want to ask you a hypothetical question to make you a better cop."

Wollenden opened the new bottle and poured.

"Look, you got a guy, he can hardly walk."

"This isn't going to be about Korea, is it?" Powder and Wollenden had served together in Korea during the Second World War, after the A-bombs were dropped on Japan.

"Naw. Look, he can hardly walk. Now, he robs a place, takes some money and an office typewriter. Now, what's wrong with that?"

"I don't know, what?"

"You're not trying!"

"How true." Wollenden pulled on his drink. "Hey, this is good. Where did you get it?"

"Well, I'll tell you what's wrong," said Powder. "If the guy can't walk, how's he supposed to be able to carry a big heavy fucking typewriter all the way out to the street? Now, that I don't understand."

"Neither do I," said Wollenden.

Powder was surprised to see his wife's car pulling out of the driveway as he approached the house. Hadn't realized she was back. But hadn't thought about it one way or another.

She glared at him as they passed. He thought it was a glare. He glared back. She didn't look so good. At the sight of her, Powder drove past the driveway and accelerated.

Their house was a large ranch-style place with an acre and a quarter, and much grander than you'd expect a fresh detective sergeant to have been able to buy at age twenty-four, no matter how good his prospects in the department. But it was a burned-out shell when they bought it; most of the inside had been destroyed. The man who'd built it, owned it for its three years, had neglected to insure against the misfortune. The Powders, stretching everything they could stretch, made a mortgage of it. Neither of them had had a childhood. It seemed a chance to buy a dream which they shouldn't let get away for lack of trying.

They'd got the house, but hadn't had the petty cash even to celebrate when it became secure.

It was the house that blocked a divorce. Who got Ricky was no problem. Especially now, when the answer would be neither of them. But the house!

Powder didn't turn around after he'd gone past it. He decided to go out to the garden for a few hours instead. Took a couple of pulls on the remains of his bottle.

By the time he got out to Allisonville Road, it was drizzling. Pretty cool, too, but he'd expected that. Eight in the morning? What else?

He worked anyway. Boots through the mud. He spread fertilizer, natural and processed. Checked tree ties in his orchard of the future. Fixed a leak in his shed roof.

At 10:30 he clambered into the car, having had the most terrific time in ages. He drove home leisurely and sang half the way.

**NIGHT COVER**

---

At ten past five the phone rang. Powder thought it was the alarm for a minute, for two minutes. Then he realized what it was and answered it.

"I get you out of the shower or something?"

"I was asleep."

"Oh, sorry. Look, Powder, this is Miller. I just wondered if you could come in a few minutes early. I got something I'd like to talk to you about. Not urgent, but I'd appreciate it. That OK?"

"Yeah, I guess so."

"Good. Thanks."

Powder placed the phone in its cradle. Sat a minute. Problem was he'd gone to bed too happy. Miller hadn't given him time for his bad temper to catch up.

What's he want to talk about? Chaperones for the Police Ball?

Powder had just about gotten comfortable, lids were just about to close for the last time. When the phone rang. Only it turned out to be the alarm.

Oh yeah. Intended to go in early anyway. Damn.

Shower. Big breakfast.

---

**15** At quarter past six Powder was climbing the stairs to the fourth floor. Wondering what the hell Miller could want with him. That's the problem with phone calls. The person who does the calling knows what he wants and is ready to talk about it. The person who gets called is less prepared, misses chances. What's Miller got to do with me anyway?

He unlocked the door and stepped into the corridor. From inside, the stairwell doors at Police Headquarters in Indianapolis opened only by key. So that a prisoner who escaped onto the stairs found only a fool's-gold freedom.

Powder walked straight into Miller's cubicle, stood hands on hips in front of the desk. "What's this shit about wanting to talk to me?"

Miller, reacting slowly—a defense—just raised his head and said, "Ah." He tidied a pile of papers which had nothing to do with anything and said, "Sit down."

"No."

Miller leaned back. "What's the matter?"

"You're the one with something the matter. You're the one that waked me out of a sound sleep."

"Sorry. But I've been talking to Albert Samson. You met him, I understand."

"What was the name?"

"Samson. The private detective whose name I gave you."

"Oh yeah," said Powder.

"We've got a situation on our hands, that's all."

Powder relaxed into a chair. "I hate losing sleep," he said. "I don't get enough as it is." What with digging in the rain.

Miller paused. Couldn't quite make up his mind whether to say "You're a good cop, but you make too much needless aggro"; something like that. Decided it wasn't his place.

Powder said, "Well, you've been talking to your buddy Samson."

"You know anything about him?" Miller asked, figuring this was the best way to the center, the long way.

"I know he's your buddy. I know he works out of a cruddy office over a carpet store. I know his mouth—" pause to remember—"is going to get him in trouble someday."

Miller smiled, too. "Yeah, well, he says he hates his showers being interrupted."

"He doesn't get enough of them. Yeah. Yeah."

"Well," Miller continued, "what maybe you don't know is that over the last couple, three years he's had a pretty good record of coming up with the goods. Now, maybe it's luck, and maybe it doesn't mean we should pay attention to him just because he's got that glint in his eye, but I've given up betting against him."

"So I've heard," Powder said ambiguously. But meaning clear to both of them. It was all around the department that Miller's promotion had been helped along by a non-department case.

"Yeah, well, don't believe everything you hear," said Miller, who knew damn well that he'd been up for the promotion anyway.

"So what has your golden boy got his golden eye on now?"

"You sent some school kid to him, right?"

"More or less." More.

"And the kid was complaining about a girl and her grades."

"Yeah?"

"And the kid has come up complaining that the girl has gone missing."

"Oh?"

"Well, Samson is hot about this missing girl."

"Then he knows something that I don't."

"He thinks he does."

"What?"

Miller twisted uneasily. "Well, I don't know quite what. He wouldn't tell me."

"Terrific," said Powder, rising. "Been nice talking to you, Miller."

"He did tell me—" waiting for Powder to sit down again—"that the girl is definitely missing. She's been leading a routine life and then last Friday she never came home from school."

"How old is she?" Powder asked.

"I don't know exactly. Eighteen maybe."

"Big girl."

"Yeah, but Samson says she has a background which makes her more interesting than just maybe a runaway."

"What is it?"

"Well," said Miller, "my impression is—"

"Impression! For crying out loud, Miller, do you know anything or not?" And before Miller could answer, "And besides, what the hell does it have to do with me?"

"Well, Samson thinks it would be smart to take the pressure off this kid, this . . ." Miller looked for his notes.

"Rex Funkhouser." Thinking: China Charlie.

"Yeah, Rex Funkhouser, about that break-in at the school. Samson implies that the missing girl will be bigger."

"'Implied.' 'Impression.' It sounds to me like your friend is trying to fix the case for his client, that's what it sounds like to me."

Miller's turn for indignation. "I don't fix, Powder."

Powder shrugged.

"But I know this guy, I know how he works. And if I were in your shoes I'd ease off on Funkhouser for a while. It's not as if he murdered anybody."

Powder said, "It's not my case anymore."

"I know," said Miller. "Been assigned to Groce. Know him? Dean Groce?"

Powder shook his head.

"Well, I had a word. He says because you gave special attention to the case he's been leaning pretty hard on Funkhouser. He wouldn't want to back off unless you said so."

"Leaning hard? Christ, I had the kid set up to bring in a signed confession."

"I don't know about that," Miller said.

"So you want me to call Groce off because he's been leaning too hard on one of your friend's clients. Have I got it right?"

"Not call him off, Powder. Just relax a little while and give Samson a chance to do the work for us."

"Funkhouser tell Samson that he did the break-in?"

"Samson wouldn't say."

"I see," said Powder.

"Well?"

"Tell your friend that I won't play."

"What?"

"That's all. I don't do things on the advice of flea-bitten private detectives who come in and act like they know the secrets of the universe but just don't care to pass them on. Your friend wants to put his cards on the table, I'll consider talking to him."

"Well," said Miller, "if that's your attitude."

"That's my attitude," Powder said. "And don't wake me in the middle of my night again. I'll start calling you in the middle of yours."

Powder left Miller's office and went over to check his day desk. Couldn't. Nothing left to be said. Nothing on the desk either.

Powder had walked halfway to the Night Room before he turned on his heel and walked back to the Day Detective receptionist.

"Leave a note for me, will you?"

"Sure, Lieutenant Powder."

"To Sergeant Groce. Ask him to see me tomorrow, five thirty, about the Funkhouser case and bring his notes."

"Sure, Lieutenant Powder."

The business with Miller threw Powder off his track. He knew he had something he wanted to do. But couldn't remember what it was. Fuck it.

Fuck fuck fuck.

Something on the mind.

What was it he wanted to do?

Powder walked into the Night Room. It was completely empty.

"Fuck," he said to the assembled throngs of assembled throngs. "No dedication left in this business."

He walked to his office, casually threw his coat on his desk. It slid to the floor, taking the In-Tray with it. Powder hesitated, sighed audibly and then got down on his hands and knees to clear up.

"You've got to admit he's a damn good cop." Sid Smith was entering the room.

"He here yet?" Schleutter.

"No, nobody here."

"He worked it all out before he talked to you?"

"Yeah, brought me in for one of those 'hypothetical questions.' "

Schleutter laughed.

"He thinks he's a goddamn teacher. That's what he thinks he is," Smith continued. "But, by God, I'm sitting outside the warehouse gates cursing him at five in the morning when a guy walks up to the gate and the night watchman lets him in. Guy goes behind the warehouse and drives out in a big semi. We stop him; the semi's full, only the cargo sheet says it's empty and going to Fort Wayne."

"Damn well would have been empty by the time it got to Fort Wayne."

"But look at it. If Powder'd just sat on his ass, turned in the report and waited for Day to come in . . ."

"Oh, he has a nose for the job," said Schleutter. "No question about that."

"I knew he was smart enough. That's what you hear, anyway. But he's such a prickly bastard. How'd he get stuck on nights, anyway? You know?"

"It's a long story," said Schleutter, who knew.

"Come on, tell me."

"Tell me, too," said Powder, rising.

Schleutter and Smith stood in shocked silence.

"Mouths in the cookie jar, boys? Come on, Schleutter, tell us how I got stuck on nights. That's an order."

"There was a little trouble about a special investigation, and there was a rearrangement inside the department, that's all."

"I see," said Sid Smith, nodding vigorously and trying to help.

"What the hell were you doing on the floor anyway?" said Schleutter. "You sick?"

"Tell your nodding friend to put a stick under the fur on his chin or I'll send him down to the Drug Squad to check for needle marks."

Smith said, "Did you hear how the warehouse thing came out

last night, Lieutenant? We got the whole load about five A.M. An hour later we broke the night watchman. He set up the whole thing—"

"Save your breath, kid," said Schleutter.

"But I just wanted to—"

"He's giving you good advice," said Powder. "When you want to talk behind my back, do it out of my territory. I can't afford electronic equipment, but you can never tell where I'll be hiding. Get the hairy caterpillar out, Schleutter."

"Right."

Schleutter led the confused Sid Smith away. Powder hung up his coat, replaced the In-Tray and sat at his desk. Wondered if Schleutter would tell Smith who should have been Chief by now.

It unfolded as a quiet night, as nights in Indianapolis go. Some street action, but not much that required a detective on the scene.

A report came in for Powder at 8:30, from Tidmarsh.

Now, what the—Oh yeah, I remember.

It was an outline summary of the multiple killings over the last year and a half.

Brindell and his square hole. Too many Brindells these days.

Powder's interest in multiple killings was because he had the impression there'd been quite a few series-type cases like the battered women of the last few weeks. Seemed worth putting Alexander Smith on—till Smith turned reluctant.

But the report was still interesting. Four cases of series murders in eighteen months were quite a few. The previous three groups had been two, two and three killings, respectively. Superficially . . . very different kinds of cases.

Phone call. "What was that?"

"I said," said the uniform duty officer downstairs, "we've got a burglary in which ninety-three wind-up clocks were stolen. Do you want it?"

"More clocks? I don't understand it."

"What's that, Lieutenant?"

"Nothing. Yeah, we want it. Give me the details."

Which he passed on to Schleutter.

"Look," said Schleutter, "I know I was out of line talking to Sid Smith, but there's no reason to put me out to pasture."

"You'll do what I tell you, damn you. We've had, I think, three thefts of wind-up clocks now. It's an epidemic. I want you to check this one out. Get lab men out there if you have to. You wouldn't want all the wind-up clocks in town to be stolen, would you?"

"Wouldn't I?"

"Go do it, Schleutter."

"Yes, sir, Lieutenant Powder, sir. Yes, sir." Schleutter goose-stepped out of the Night Room.

Powder didn't really care. Lot of Smiths in my life. A Robert Smith had pushed the guy he owed money to off a quarry lip. Most people have the decency to knock a guy out before they throw him into a quarry lake, but not Smith. Not for his loan shark. But three nights later he did knock out his local pusher before sending him over the same quarry lip. Convicted for two at the price of one.

Now, that's something, Powder thought. Why did he knock the second guy out?

Of the other two series, Powder had dealt with one of them himself in January before he left for his vacation. Fairly straightforward; three men shot and dumped near Weir Cook airport. Consecutive nights. Straightforward in that the killer had been picked up the day after the third man was found. He'd had the gun on him and said he was hunting for his fourth victim. Protection men, and the guy had been fed up with having to pay the guys off.

What did I think that case was? Powder thought. Oh yeah, had it tagged as a gang war.

He went down the list, the third series killing. And there it was again, two people bashed with pipes or sticks. Unsolved, this one. Victims: a shopkeeper who got robbed, and a robber with a long record of violent robberies. An irony there, but nobody caught.

In day-to-day business they blended into the miscellaneous killings of the city, but separated because he'd asked for them, they felt like a lot for one town like this in eighteen months.

"Hey, Schleutter?" he called without looking up.

"He's out, Lieutenant."

Oh yeah. Was going to ask him if he thought we'd been getting a lot of these series murders.

Hell, he probably wouldn't know anyway. Mentally, he mimicked Schleutter: "One mudder's a lot like anudder mudder."

Settled for sending another project to Tidmarsh.

Powder called Tidmarsh on the phone. "Yeah, well, give me the same kind of records for the last ten years. What? Naw, don't break them up into anything. Oh yeah, year by year. Naw, year by year's fine. No. No charts. No crazy graphs. Jesus, Tidmarsh!"

## 16

"I'm beginning to spend my days here as well as my nights."

"Oh yeah?" Groce was a crew-cut detective born fifteen years too late. "Well, it seems like *I'm* spending my nights here as well as my days, and that ain't good. I got a pretty little wife to look after, you know what I mean?" Nudge nudge; wink wink.

"I want to know about that case I did the groundwork for."

"Oh, the Commie kid and the school break-in. I don't know why everybody's making such a goddamn fuss about it. Doesn't seem to me like it can be worth all the sweat."

"Yeah. What I want—so that you can get home to that pretty

little wife of yours—is what you've done the last couple of days."

"Well," said Groce modestly, "she ain't that pretty. But my daughter, you ought to see my youngest daughter."

"I'll go out and arrest her if you don't snap it up." Powder was chronically impatient when it came to other people's results.

Groce laughed. "Haw haw! That's a good one. Better not do that, buddy. I got pull down at Headquarters." Reined himself. "Well, first day I had a couple of the boys stop the kid on the street. Next I pulled him in."

"Funkhouser?"

"Right, the Commie."

"And what's he say?"

"Well, I thought he was going to be easy, but I worked pretty hard on him and he didn't say anything."

Powder sighed.

"Which ain't to say that he didn't say anything, but he kept on bitching about his girl friend not coming to visit him or something. I think he's off his nut, you ask me. It was like he didn't understand the questions. Just kept asking about this girl."

Powder frowned. "How long did you interrogate him?"

"Well, to be honest and frank with you, not very long. I let him sit for a while in Lock-Up, see how he liked the company, but I didn't actually work very long. I got a lot of cases to work on, you know, Lieutenant. I don't know what caseloads were like in your day, but now, wowee." Groce fanned his hand.

"Did you read my report?" Powder's smoldering coals were fanned by Groce's wind.

"Sure."

"Including the advice about what to do, and not do, about Rex Funkhouser?"

"To be honest with you, Lieutenant, I honestly figure you were playing it wrong. You got to lean on these guys, it's the only way. Now, I don't know what punks were like in your day—"

"In my day sergeants took advice from lieutenants."

"Yeah, well. It's my case, isn't it? And if you want my opinion, I give it to you for nothing. I think you missed the important angle on this kid and that's the Commie angle. If we keep after him we can probably come up with a whole little cell."

"But you haven't got anywhere yet?"

"Give me time. Give me time. I deliver the goods. But I got a lot of cases. I got this guy who's been hustling old people about fixing their roofs so that—"

"You haven't made any progress on physical evidence—the money or the typewriter?"

"No."

"Nor any witnesses?"

"No. But I know you're interested in this one, Lieutenant. I'll keep after it."

Powder thought for a few seconds.

Groce got restless. "Gee, Lieutenant, you think I can go now? I'd like to get back to that little woman."

"You know, Groce," said Powder. "This case feels pretty dead-end, doesn't it?"

"What do you mean?"

"Well, school insured. And if you haven't pinned it on them by now."

"If you don't want to make it a personal thing, Lieutenant, that's OK by me." Puzzled, but quick to catch the drift.

"You go on home, then."

"Yes, sir. Good night."

Powder felt no guilt, he'd expected some.

Over a steak—didn't this $3 steak used to cost $1.25?—he chuckled out loud once. Rex had some strength, whatever his weaknesses. Groce said Rex kept talking about the missing girl. If so, he'd taken the initiative away from Groce. And it's the initiative, the unfamiliarity, the reputation, and the fear of the police and consequences which make police interrogations effective. Talk about something else, determinedly, and there's nothing much the police can do. If they don't try too hard.

It was five past seven when he walked into the Night Room.

## 17

Powder had a caller about ten. A disgruntled private detective who said, "I want to talk to you, Lieutenant."

"Samson, I believe," Powder said as he decided whether to be too busy. "All right, take a pew."

Samson sat.

"And you want . . . ?"

"What I want," said Samson, "is for the people in this police force to squint hard and take a look at the noses on their faces."

"You got nice technique for asking people to do things for you," Powder said. Ho hum, another private detective.

Samson laughed. "Yeah, I suppose I do," he said. "You didn't catch me at my best the other night."

It was an offer to be more friendly, but Powder didn't take it. "Just what the hell *do* you want?"

Which rehardened Samson. "What I want is for you to stop wasting your time rousting my client every day and start to work on the more serious case that's involved here. Now, I've been to Miller and asked him nice, but he says that Groce leans on Funkhouser because Powder wants him to. I don't know what Funkhouser ever did to you, but one of you clowns ought to get to work on this missing girl, Cherry Cable. She may be in bad trouble, and your pigheadedness may cause her to end up dead. For all you know, she may already be dead."

Powder shrugged. "I'm listening, gumshoe, but I don't hear anything."

"All right," Samson said, "I've been working on this case four days now. It started out with Funkhouser worried about the way this girl was going to get flunked. That she threatened to kill herself, that kind of thing. He said he told you."

Powder sat motionless.

"All right. Then he and I spend a little time talking about ways I might be able to help him out. Nothing looks like value for money, but there are things I can try." Samson spread his hands to encompass disparate elements. "He says go ahead. We leave it at that. Until the next day, Monday."

"He gave you money."

"The money you took off me Sunday night."

"That's right. Where did he get it?"

"I can't swear."

"You don't ask a kid where he gets the kind of bread you cost?"

"You want to get fancy?" Samson asked. "I have, in the past, had cause to find out whether I can be legitimately hired by a minor. I can, it's legal."

"Didn't you ask where the money was coming from?"

"Not necessary, but I did. He said he got it from savings bonds his grandmother had given him for college."

"And no doubt he told you nothing about a robbery he committed, or helped to commit, last Saturday night in which four hundred and eight dollars and an electric typewriter were stolen from the University School?"

"He certainly didn't. Though I've heard enough about it since. You guys really are crazy bastards, you really are. Rex can hardly walk. The idea of him staggering out the door with an office electric typewriter in his arms is ludicrous."

"Not so ludicrous if you figure he has a friend with him."

"Who?"

"It's not my case," said Powder.

"Hopeless," said Samson. "And on these grounds you hold

Rex for eight hours on Monday and you have him rousted by passing cops twice in the last three days. You guys are too much."

"I still haven't heard you say anything, Samson."

Not each other's favorite people.

"The girl has been missing since Friday night."

"Run away from home."

"There are reasons to believe that she would not run away from home."

"What?"

"Staying in school this year was important to her. Besides that, she had appointments and plans with various people. And she didn't take anything with her. Her stuffed lion, for instance. Her aunt says she'd never go anyplace without it."

"How old is she?"

"Eighteen."

"Big girl." Powder rubbed his face.

"And she's not stupid. From what I hear, she just wouldn't leave without telling anybody."

Powder shrugged. "This is evidence?" He thought for a moment. "If she's not stupid, how come she's going to flunk these courses? What's she doing in the University School at all?"

"She's had some problems," Samson said quietly, "but she's supposed to be over them."

"Come on, gumshoe. I still can't hear you. You may baffle kids with tones of voice and enigmatic faces, but I want facts. Tell me something, damn it, or go away and leave me to my crossword puzzles."

"You do crosswords?"

"No," Powder said. And sat to wait.

"All right. *If* you dimwits had any interest, you could find out, too. Cherry Cable had some problems when she was fifteen. Like drug problems which led to sex problems. She was packed away for a while. But her aunt got her out of care last summer and part of the deal was going to this University School. The only school in town, I gather, that would take her."

"Aunt?" said Powder.

"Her parents died when she was fourteen. Now, I don't know if you know anything about depression syndromes in teenagers"—Powder yawned—"but this was a sick girl."

"If she was so sick . . ."

"She got better. They let her out in the care of the aunt. Things started out all right, but have been getting worse. And the reason is that so-called school."

Powder waited.

Samson said, "Miller told you, I suppose, that besides this grade manipulation to make sure they come back next year, Jefty, the principal—"

"I met him."

"Jefty occasionally dabbles with some of the older girls, on the premises."

Powder shifted in his chair. "Dabbles with? You mean—"

"Sex is what I mean."

"How the hell do you know something like that?"

"I have it from a good source."

"Jefty?"

"His wife."

Powder thought about it for a minute. The physically fit French teacher. "She never told me that."

"You probably never asked her."

Powder laughed. "True. Women confide their troubles to you, do they?"

"I don't know for certain it applies to Jefty and this Cable girl," said Samson, rejecting Powder's mild thaw. "But Jefty held her future in his hands. Then Rex found out money is what's important to Jefty, not kids' futures. He came to you and drew a blank. Meanwhile, the last time Cherry Cable's been seen is Friday in school."

Powder sighed, but listened.

"The point, Powder, is that there's a sick girl who may have been taken advantage of. It looks like she may have been thrown into a bout of depression. Now, I don't know whether you know it or not, but depressives kill themselves. You're already responsible for the police not looking for her for three days. You may already have killed her, but you should damn well take the brakes off. Unless you like to see kids kill themselves."

Powder paused. "All right. There's a case for looking for her. We'll look for her. But if you'd told us this stuff before now, you'd have saved some time yourself."

"You may not know it, copper, but it takes longer for one man to get information than a police force. You could have put it together in half a day."

"And let me tell you something, gumshoe. This stuff still doesn't absolve your client from his responsibility for breaking into that school and filling his pimply pockets. He got me to help him. And then in return he committed a crime. I don't forget that kind of favor. I want him for robbery. I think you ought to tell him to give us a little help, save us a little time, for that one."

"I don't think he did it," said Samson.

"There are things you know?"

"I know plenty that you don't know, Powder. I'd be afraid you couldn't take it all in at once. When you find Cherry Cable, or dig her body out of the river, then maybe we'll have a little talk about the University School."

"You know what obstructing justice is?"

"I know, Powder. Do you? It's talking tough when you should be on the phone getting your beef out looking for eighteen-year-old girls. Ones to help, I mean."

As Samson walked away, Powder rubbed his face with both hands.

## 18

Powder signed off duty and walked down the long staircase to parking-lot level, frowning. He shuffled along the long corridor to the garage, purposely dragging his heels. When he got into the car, he rubbed his face twice and thought about slapping it. He couldn't quite put his finger on what was troubling him. Or which of his troubles was troubling him most.

He felt embarrassed to sit too long without going anywhere, so he started the car. He drove, though slowly, out of the lot. Sighed to himself. Shook his head. What am I doing? He couldn't answer himself.

He drove to All Knight Ribs.


"Let me ask you something," Powder said halfheartedly, trying to form a hypothetical question. He was working on the second half of a double order of ribs. Not that he was hungry, but he felt a need to maintain appearances.

"Sure," said Knight amiably.

"Hey, is that a new gold tooth?"

"No, man. Same one. That's what you want to ask me?"

"Where would you go to find a girl?"

Knight raised an eyebrow. "A girl?"

"A girl."

"You mean a girl?"

"No, of course not," said Powder. "I mean a girl like who's missing."

The way he approached it was backhand. He told himself that he couldn't think of anything else to do, so he drove home.

Knowing that Margaret should be home, he parked on the street and walked up to the house. Let himself in quietly. With luck she wouldn't know.

He walked through the darkness to Ricky's room. Undressed and slid in between the sheets. Within three minutes he was asleep. Only a quarter past four, almost like a normal person after a late night.

At eleven, when he woke up, the first thing he noticed was his door was ajar.

On the breakfast table he found a note. "I heard you come in last night. You know the rule, you bastard." At twenty to twelve, as he walked to the car he could see something was wrong.

When he walked around the hedge he saw exactly what. The two front tires were flat.

He turned around and walked back to the garage for an old hand pump he had found there when he was working on the shelves on the weekend.

After pumping up the tires he looked under the hood. The leads were intact. She must have been in a hurry. He tossed the pump on the back seat.

Of course she was in a hurry, he thought later. Only two of the tires.

He caught Gartland just before the captain left for lunch with a revolver manufacturer's rep. Powder put his case quickly and Gartland was surprised.

"Aren't you taking this a bit seriously, Roy?"

"I feel responsible, but I figure if I want to work on my own time, you can't really knock it."

"I can," said Gartland.

"But you won't."

"I don't understand. So you made a mistake, maybe, and the kid took advantage of it. If you were bucking for promotion . . ."

"I don't want to be responsible for making work for people. Maybe I gave this kid too much time. If I did, it's my responsibility to clean it up. If Groce doesn't mind, I don't see why *you* should."

"I don't," said Gartland as he shrugged the conversation to a close. "I just don't see why after all this time . . . You'll be asking for day assignment next."

Powder decided to treat it as a suggestion.


"I never heard of nothing like this, Lieutenant, if I may say so."

"What's to hear you've heard."

"Look, if this is a job you want done, just tell me. But the way you were talking yesterday, it sounded like you wanted me to ease off." Groce, like almost every detective sergeant, had the sense to suspect something worth hanging on to when a superior wanted to take a case off him.

"You pick up the con man you were telling me about yesterday?"

"No," said Groce. "This afternoon, if it all breaks right."

Powder just nodded. But it was a sign-off. Powder wanted this case done after all. Powder wanted to do it. Groce would complain loud and long to the little woman when he got home that night.

## 19

To rest content with a smattering of knowledge, says Mao, is to behave like a blind man groping for fish.

Christ, thought Powder. I'll be taking the pledge next. Or whatever they do.

There were more than a dozen kids standing in front of the University School as Powder pulled into the No Parking Zone. Ordinary-looking kids, they parted like the sea as he strode to the door and went inside.

Powder didn't knock at the office door; he walked right in to find Jefty pointing a finger at a young woman and saying, "... financial aspect." He turned to Powder, angry at interruption, then uncertain. "Don't I know you?" He turned the stubby finger in Powder's direction.

"Detective Lieutenant Powder, Homicide and Robbery."

The young woman started.

Powder said, "I want to speak to you alone." Pointedly he held the door for the young woman, who left without hesitation.

Jefty did hesitate. "You ... you're the one who was here last week."

"Sunday, yes. I have some more questions I want to ask you."

"I don't understand what all the fuss is about."

"You didn't help us a great deal," said Powder. Jefty, in his school role as commander-in-chief, started to contradict him, but Powder projected chin and voice, "So I want some more help now."

Jefty paused, thought, and sighed. "What can we do for you?"

"The scope of this investigation is widening," said Powder, trying to inspire fear of the unknown. "I want the names and addresses of your current students and the teachers you've employed in the last five years."

"Oh no!" said Jefty. "That would take hours."

"You don't keep such records in a tabular form?" Powder said as if he knew a law that required it.

"Well, no," Jefty said. "We have record cards for the students and a book we keep track of instructors in."

"Let's see," said Powder. It was partly abrupt and partly conciliatory.

"Which?"

"Both."


Powder left Jefty muttering in his office, trying to decide whom he could take out of class to type the lists Powder still claimed to want.

Powder drove off toward Guilford Avenue north of Kessler Boulevard East. His dual object at the University School had been to stir Jefty and to get Cherry Cable's home address.

6218 North Guilford was a modest brick house which peeked from behind and beneath two woolly evergreen trees.

Powder walked up the path and knocked on the door.

A woman answered the door after tens of seconds. She opened the door less than a foot and showed an eye. "Cha want?"

"Are you Mrs. Maxine Tedesco?"

"To you?"

"Police," said Powder. He showed her his identification, held it up for quite a while. "Are you Mrs. Maxine Tedesco?"

"Yeah?" said the woman.

"May I come in and talk to you, Mrs. Tedesco?"

The woman hesitated and seemed in discomfort.

"It's about your niece, Cherry."

The face nodded, though the eye frowned; the woman stepped back and opened the door for Powder, who wiped his feet before he came in.

Mrs. Tedesco weighed a good 250 pounds; she led him to a dark living room.

"S'down," she said and she went to the window, where she drew back the net curtains. It didn't improve the light; the two spreading trees saw to that.

The choice was between two settees and a couch. Powder took the couch. Mrs. Tedesco sat down across from him. She looked uncomfortable.

She said, " 'S it bad news?"

"I haven't brought news, good or bad," Powder said. "I've come to try to get help from you."

"Oh," said Mrs. Tedesco. She seemed to relax. " 'S a relief."

"When did you report Cherry missing?"

"Didn't," she said. "Got worried last Friday. She didn't come home. Called them up when it was Saturday."

"Who?"

"You," she said, meaning the police. "Said to come downtown."

"Did you?"

" 'S not easy. Sunday morning her friend came here, said he'd take care of it."

"Which friend?"

"Rex," said Mrs. Tedesco.

"It's not usual, then, for Cherry to go missing for a few days?"

"Oh no. No. Part of probation."

"Probation? Have you told her probation officer?"

"No."

"Who is her probation officer?"

The big woman twisted uneasily. "Don't remember."

"I can get it from records. Please don't waste my time," Powder said. "What's the probation officer's name?"

"Think she's in trouble?"

"I'm trying to find her. We'll worry about her trouble then."

"Mrs. Buffington."

"Thank you." Powder wrote it down. Didn't press for address, phone number, other details. "How long has Cherry been here with you, Mrs. Tedesco?"

"November fourth."

"Last year?"

She nodded.

"And since then she's never been missing? Not even one night?"

"No." Said definitively.

"I'm not working for the probation people; I need to know the facts, whatever they are."

"No." Still definitive.

"Does she have transportation?"

"Scooter."

"Do you have the license number somewhere?"

"AR 3952."

"You're sure?"

"Yes."

"Good," said Powder. "I take it the scooter's gone, too?"

"Yes."

"When she left Friday morning, did you notice anything out of the ordinary? Did she leave early or late? Did she take anything with her that she ordinarily didn't take? Was she upset? Anything unusual?"

"Been different for about two months, nervous. Been worried about her."

"Do you know what she was worried about?"

"Things at school, but don't know what."

"Did she have a lot of friends there? Of her own age?"

"A few."

"Do you know their names? Besides Rex."

"Ross Hodge. Arthur Nowlchuk."

"No girls?"

"No. Never liked girls."

"Did she have friends, apart from school?"

"Think maybe."

"Did she like school, Mrs. Tedesco?"

"No."

"Not at all?"

"They were unfair. Didn't allow for her problems. She hadn't been at any school for two years."

"How old is she?"

"Just eighteen."

"Do you have a picture?"

"No," said Mrs. Tedesco. "No pictures here."

Powder had a close look at Cherry Cable's room. He almost thought, in the dim light, that he'd found her in her bed, but when he went to it he saw the figure tucked under the blankets was an enormous stuffed lion.

"Called Frank," Mrs. Tedesco said from the hall. "After m' . . . m' brother."

To see better, Powder turned on the reading light over the bed. It was as bright as all the other lights he'd seen were dim. Mrs. Tedesco drew back from the doorway.

There was no direct information on Cherry or her activities to be found. But things stuck in Powder's mind. Frilly lace curtains and bed trim. Books which filled the bookcases. And when he closed the room door, he found a now familiar poster photograph of Chairman Mao.

Powder spent half an hour in the room, but without much reward. The girl was on the tall side, from the clothes and the fairly large shoes. Variety of tastes: full-skirted square-dance dresses to the gray of the liberated. Reading, less than there appeared to be, because two of the three bookcases were filled with children's books. Powder hadn't realized so many Bobbsey Twins existed. But the third bookcase was interesting, too. *Lord of the Rings, Jonathan Livingston Seagull, Unsafe at Any Speed, Manchild in the Promised Land, I Never Promised You a Rose Garden, Jeeney Ray,* the letters of George Jackson.

Before he left, Powder tried to think about what wasn't in the room. Photographs and letters. That's what he missed most.

NIGHT COVER |

He turned out the light and went back to the living room. Mrs. Tedesco stood before the window looking out.

He surprised himself by standing silent in the doorway watching her, a prisoner of flesh.

Then he said, "I'm finished now."

Mrs. Tedesco turned slowly. "Find her," she said.

"I'll do what I can," Powder said.

" 'M responsible for her. Love her."

## 20

By quarter to five Powder was in the police parking lot. He walked the long corridor to the police basement, but instead of making for the stairs he took the elevator up one floor and got out. The public level.

He walked through the police wing, across the City/County Foyer and studied the index for the other side of the complex. Found the Probation Department and took the elevator. Just another tourist.

At the Probation Department main desk he identified himself and asked for Mrs. Buffington.

"I'll check for you, Lieutenant," said the delicate young man he spoke to. "Would you take a seat?"

Powder stood at the desk until the kid's return.

"I'm sorry, Lieutenant. Mrs. Buffington is out."

"Is she coming back here before she goes home?"

"I'll check for you. Would you take a seat?"

Two minutes later.

"I'm not sure if she is going to return to the office, sorry."

"I'll leave a message."

"OK."

"Well, don't just stand there. Give me a piece of paper."

"Oh, right."

Powder wrote a note. The young man disappeared and when Powder finished the note, he had to pound on the desk.

"All right!" said the kid.

"Do you have an envelope?"

"I'll check for you."

"No, I won't take a seat."

The young man brought a huge envelope. Powder frowned, but put his succinct message inside it.

"Thank you," the young man said pointedly as Powder handed him the envelope.

"You know, kid," said Powder, "you'd do your job a whole lot better if you anticipated the needs of people coming to this desk. If you kept track of where people were and what they were doing. You know that?"

"I'll suggest it to my boss," said the kid. "Care to take a seat?"

Ah well, Powder thought. Mao says we must take care of our troops, give them guidance and help them correct their mistakes. I tried.

"Bastard," the kid hissed behind him.


With a couple of hours to kill before he came on night duty, Powder took a walk. Downtown Indianapolis, he thought, and then went north instead. Up Delaware to the Bash Seed Store. He browsed, letting his mind have the rest of a change. Artichokes? What the fuck are artichokes?

Then he ate dinner at the bus-station cafeteria because he wanted to talk to a guy he knew there. But the guy was off. The cafeteria didn't serve artichokes.


Rubbing his face, Powder walked slowly up to his day desk, where he found an envelope from Tidmarsh. He didn't know whether to read it on the spot or to take it downstairs.

"I found ten dollars."

"What?" In front of him Powder saw a gray-haired, very old

woman holding a purse in one hand and a folded bill in the other. He put down his envelope.

"I found ten dollars."

Powder frowned; tired. "How did you get in here?"

"I found ten dollars," the woman repeated again. "Here." She pushed the bill out to touch his hand.

Powder took the bill and opened it. A $10 bill, all right. "What exactly do you want me to do with it, ma'am?"

"I found ten dollars," she said. "I want to turn it in."

Powder rubbed his face. "You want to turn it in?"

"Whoever lost it might need it," she said.

"Yeah," Powder said and took a breath. "Just a second." He carried the money over to Miller's office. Miller was working through a stack of papers.

"Hey, Miller, where the hell is Lost and Found?"

"Out the East Corridor door, second right," Miller said without looking up.

"Thanks."

Powder returned to the old lady. "Could you come with me, please?"

It wasn't until he stepped through the East Corridor door that he realized Miller had sent him to the toilets.

Powder was late for his shift, and, in the way these things go, his four detectives were in the Night Room ahead of him. Calls started coming in early, which saved him jokey flak.

It was quarter to eight before he realized he had left the envelope from Tidmarsh on his desk upstairs.

On the way he stopped to pick up a cup of coffee. When he got back to the Night Room he found a woman waiting for him.

"Are *you* Lieutenant Powder?" she said, as if she'd asked half the world.

"Yeah," he said. The phone rang. "Hang on a sec." He took a sip from the coffee and answered the phone. "Yeah?"

"Lieutenant Powder, please."

"Speaking."

"Look, Powder, you never heard of Ten Buck Tillie?"

"What the fuck you talking about?" said Powder, then to the lady, "Sorry." To the phone, "Who the hell is this?"

"Lost and Found. Look, Powder, you sent a patrolman to us with a little old lady, had ten bucks to turn in, right?"

"What of it?"

"What floor did you find her on?"

"Fourth."

"Fourth," Powder heard the voice say. "She's up to the fourth. Look, Lieutenant, that's Ten Buck Tillie. Beginning of every month she brings in a ten-dollar bill and says she's found it. When nobody claims it, we give it back to her, then she brings it back in. It's her night out, see? But to us it's just waste paper."

"I understand," said Powder, who didn't like being told there was anything he didn't know. "I hope she comes to me again because I'll bring her down to you personally, and I'll break your arm if you give her a hard time. Got it?" Powder slammed the phone down on its cradle and nearly knocked the set off the desk. He rubbed his face, sipped some coffee.

The woman was smiling; middle thirties maybe. Looked tired, but the smile was friendly.

"Now, ma'am," said Powder, gathering the remains of his face, the public face. "What can I do for you?"

"My name is Adele Buffington," she said. "You left a note saying you wanted some information about Cherry Cable."

"Ahhhh," Powder said. He rubbed and sipped again.

"I don't want to give you any information," she said pertly.

To give me yourself, Powder thought. Then frowned. A thought like that was unlike him, on duty.

"I came over to ask some questions instead. What kind of trouble is Cherry in?"

"Frankly, that's what I want to find out. She's been reported missing. When was the last time you saw her?"

Mrs. Buffington frowned. "She came to her last probation meeting, which was twelve days ago."

"When is her next appointment?"

"Monday. Are you suggesting she isn't going to come to it?"

"Yeah. She hasn't been home since . . . damn . . ." He looked for his log. Then looked through it. "Since the morning of Friday, April 27. Last seen after school the same day."

"But that's a week! What's taken so long?"

What indeed? thought Powder. He felt an impulse to tell her all, but overrode it. "For one thing, nobody reported her missing officially till a couple days ago."

"Not officially? But someone did unofficially?"

"Yes, but we didn't know she was on probation or anything else about her." He spread his hands. She knew; they both had plenty to do with the work which came through on official lines.

"I wish . . ." she began. But stopped.

"We're on it now, ma'am. Can you give me some background on the girl? I've seen her aunt; I've been to the University School; I've talked to one of her friends, Rex Funkhouser. I have some idea of her present. But I have no details of her past, or where she would be going if she went somewhere."

Buffington took a breath.

Powder said, "Look, would you like some coffee, something like that?"

"Yes, I would," she said. "I've come straight here from work."

"Nothing to eat?" Powder said, and felt foolish.

They walked together quietly to the Canteen. At the door she said, "Why did everyone frown when I asked them if they were you?"

Powder chuckled. "Don't ever work for me or you'll find out."

He sat her down, got her some machine food and drink. His public face, full front.

"Cherry was an orphan," Adele Buffington began.

"I know," said Powder. "Parents died when she was about fourteen, wasn't it?"

"No. She was orphaned when she was a few months old. The Cables adopted her. It was they who died when she was fourteen."

"Crash or something?"

"No," she said. "First Mr. Cable died of cancer and then seven months later Mrs. Cable had a cerebral hemorrhage. Cherry came home one day and found her on the floor."

"Rough," said Powder, who felt out of his depth. "What happened to her?"

"There was a brother of Mrs. Cable's who took her into the family, but she didn't fit in. For various reasons."

Powder wasn't up to the psychological machinations. "Were there criminal proceedings?"

"Yes," Mrs. Buffington said briefly.

"What?"

There was a pause while they both realized that Powder could find out, whether Buffington told him or not. "Well, there were a few arrests and fines and suspended sentences. Then when she was sixteen Cherry assaulted an old man with a stick and robbed him."

"Nice."

"Another man coming out of his front door caught her as she was running away and kept her for the police."

"She did it alone?"

"Yes."

"Was the old man hurt?"

"Hurt, yes, but not severely. Cherry was held until he could make a statement. That's when they discovered she was an addict."

"Ahhh."

"... and that she had those three arrests for solicitation, under a false name. And, clearly, having given a false age."

"Considering what you've said," Powder said, "I'm amazed they let her out so soon."

"She was in care more than two calendar years," said Mrs. Buffington. "But you have to understand that what you have here is not a case of a chronically hostile environment which led a weak girl into these acts. She grew up in a perfectly happy home with two parents who loved her. Then they died, both of them, for no good reason. She's a strong, intelligent girl, but adolescence is probably the worst of all possible times of life."

Powder sighed. "I take it she 'responded to treatment.' "

"You don't really understand, do you?" Adele Buffington said sharply.

"No," said Powder. "I don't really understand."

Buffington shook her head.

Which made Powder mad. "But let me tell you something, young lady—"

She interrupted, "Does my being a woman bother you, Lieutenant? Is that it? Probation officers should be men even though a lot of our clients are women?"

Powder waved a finger. "You're letting *your* hostile environment show. You'd do better to keep your problems out of your problems' problems." He cut off her reply. "As I was about to say . . . I may not understand why this girl beat up an old man with a stick or why the people in charge of her let her back on the streets, but at least I *know* I don't understand and I don't pretend that I do. Don't lump me with your prejudices about cops. I don't go around saying she should have been locked up and the key thrown away; I don't say anything. I don't know what the hell we ought to do with felons of any damn kind. What I *do* know is my job. Most of the time that has to do with catching people who break the laws. This time it has to do with finding a kid—eighteen years old, so I guess we have to call her a woman—who's missing. And . . ." He couldn't quite remember how he was going to finish.

Adele Buffington understood his cessation. She said, "Thanks, I needed that."

Powder was still angered. "You sound like a fucking commercial."

"I didn't think they had to advertise it," she said.

Powder paused, blinked. He laughed; they laughed together. When they stopped they were left with an embarrassed silence.

"Ahhh," said Powder.

"Ummmm," said Mrs. Buffington.

"Ahh, where were we?" Powder came nearer to blushing than he had in decades. The mood had changed completely. "What sort of girl is this Cherry Cable, then?"

"She's good-looking. Very blond," answered the could-be-called-blond-if-you-stretched-the-point Mrs. Buffington. "Platinumed."

"Did you have any feeling that she might be going wrong again? I mean, that something was wrong with her. I mean, seeing her, what, every couple of weeks?"

"I didn't think there was a crisis. I know that she was very worried about her grades. While she was in care she made up a lot of work—she is very intelligent, I mean *very*—and the arrangement with the University School was that if she passed her courses this semester they would accept her special work in lieu and give her a high-school diploma. It was very important to her."

"Why?"

"Well . . . it wasn't explicit, but I'm sure she wanted to continue her education. She mentioned the possibility of training to be a nurse and . . . and she had the brains to do well in college if she ever put them to work."

"Not that eager a worker, then?"

"She never worked hard. If she understood something immediately, then she had it. But she wasn't what you could call a worker."

Unite! Powder thought. He frowned. "You didn't have any indication . . . ?"

"Of serious difficulty? No. She did miss one of her appointments, three months ago, but she was sick. Her aunt, Mrs. Tedesco, confirmed that to me."

"When did this Mrs. Tedesco appear on the scene?"

"Oh, she's always been there. She was very fond of Cherry from the time her brother and his wife adopted her. But with a family to place Cherry with—the wife's brother's family—it was thought that would be better than putting her with Maxine alone."

"She was married?"

"Yes. She's had problems of her own, as . . . as you can . . . You've met her?"

"Yeah, this afternoon."

"Well. Her husband left her six months before her brother died."

"Sounds like it was a rough year for the Cables."

"Yes."

They didn't say anything and Adele Buffington sipped at the last of her cold coffee.

"Any idea where she could be?" asked Powder.

"No."

"Any idea where she could go? Anybody she might go to?"

"She has no other relatives. No old friends that I know about."

"Well," Powder said.

"Well."

"Well."

"I would appreciate it if you would keep me informed of your progress, Lieutenant."

"I will, I certainly will. And I appreciate your cooperation."

"Anything I can do in the future."

"I'll certainly let you know if I can think of anything more that I need."

"Good," she said.

"Well," he said, distinctly uncomfortable.

"Oh well," she said, and fished in her bag. Came out with her wallet.

"Please," said Powder, "I'm more than happy to pay for what you ate."

"Here," she said with a smile. She handed him a card. "Oh, let me put my home phone on the back." She did. "You're more likely to catch me there."

"Good," Powder said.

"In the morning until about eight thirty; or late at night. While I'm working there's no telling when I'll be in the office."

"Good," Powder said. "Good."

He was in the Night Room, on the way to his cubbyhole, when he remembered he still didn't have the envelope from Tidmarsh, and simultaneously Schleutter mumbled, "Where you been with the lady, Powder? Down in the garage?"

Without saying anything, he pivoted on his heel and walked straight back out.

## 21

There were several pages in the envelope from Tidmarsh and single-spaced at that.

Powder spread them out. What the hell had he asked the man for?

The report was even titled: "Multiple Homicides Since 1950." Asked him for ten years. Oh well. Powder put the pages together again, set them on top of the envelope and put them aside. Too much too much.

Half an hour later he picked them up again. Mao says we must learn from the past, he thought, and chuckled to himself. Schleutter looked up quickly.

"What you want, Schleutter?"

"Nothing, Roy, no way."

"Don't be shy, son."

Schleutter went back to his paperwork.

Powder dug in for the long read through Tidmarsh's tome.

At four, Powder was in Knight's. "We miss you for a week," Knight said, "then bam, two nights in a row." Powder shrugged.

Halfway through his meal, Powder said, "Look, here's a hypothetical question that will make you a better cop."

Knight laughed. "For when I retire here, huh, man?"

"You got a little old lady, right?"

Knight was respectfully silent.

"And this little old lady gets her kicks by bringing in a ten-dollar bill every month and saying that she found it on the steps of Soldiers' and Sailors' Monument and she wants to turn it in."

Powder paused. Knight said, "Yeah?"

"Now, what she does is turn it in and then wait the month and we send her a letter saying nobody's claimed it and would she bring in her receipt and we'll turn the found property over to her. She comes in, takes the bill away and a few days later she comes in again. Same bill, same serial number, same story. So what do you do?"

"What do *I* do?" said Knight, pointing to himself.

"Make yourself a better cop," said Powder. "What do you do? This lady is wasting manpower, you understand. Keeping us from finding who stole your gold tooth."

Knight touched his tooth. "Me, I ask Ella to talk to her."

"But she won't be talked to. She swears she found the money; and she prowls around the department until she finds some poor slob she hasn't given the story to."

"What do I do?" said Knight. "I don't know."

"Come on," Powder urged. "Be a better cop."

Knight sensed some fraying of his customer's edges and tried to play. "Well," he said, "she turns in this money lost, right?

Suppose I go in and say it's mine, I lost it. I claim it."

"Hah!" said Powder, waving a rib triumphantly. "That's what you'd do if you were a cop! But I tricked you this time, because if you were a *better* cop, I'll tell you what you'd do."

"What?"

"Nothing, that's what. She's a member of the public and she's entitled and if you were a better cop you wouldn't complain about it."

"Phooey," said Knight.

"What do you mean?" No answer. "Give me some more of these, will you?"

Knight put together another order of ribs. Unlike most cops, Powder paid his way, but Knight had special quantities: "A Policeman's Plate," he said, pushing it to Powder.

"What do you mean, phooey?"

Knight took a breath. "I mean you make the question like you make a doll out of straw, man. Then because it's straw you say, Look, I can tear it apart easy. You going to make me a better cop, you gotta give me a chance."

It was the first time Powder had ever seen that he annoyed Knight. It annoyed him that Knight had felt annoyed for a long time and hadn't shown it before. If that was it.

"Yeah, well," said Powder and concentrated on his food.

Knight looked at his watch and went to the back room, like he had something to do there. A woman came in and the bell on the door brought Knight back to the counter.

She bought almost more food than she could carry. "A little party?" Knight said, professionally pleasant.

"Jus' hungry," said the woman. She paid with a new twenty and left quickly.

Powder had followed the transaction. "Poker game?" he asked.

Knight shrugged.

"Craps?"

"All I know, someone somewhere is hungry, man."

**NIGHT COVER**

"Look, I'm sorry if I gave you a hard time," said Powder.

"Oh hell," said Knight magnanimously. "I'm just not much of a cop," and he laughed a lot.

"Why do you work nights?"

"You make me a better rib man now, too, huh?"

Powder shrugged.

"Ah, I just find it easier to get people to work here in the day than at night. Besides, I make the sauce at night, and if I'm alone, that way nobody trying to get the recipe from me." Knight laughed again.

Powder did his best to join him.


Powder tried to wait for the sunrise in Holliday Park, but he felt sleepy and desperately wanted to go home.

He settled for a compromise. He drove and parked around the corner nearest to his house. Walked nearly a quarter of a mile to his driveway. As silently as he could, he entered the house, Ricky's room. He fell asleep on top of the covers in his clothes.


## 22

Margaret was in the kitchen when he walked in at 11:30. "What are *you* doing here?" she said.

"Bugger," he said. "This Saturday? This *your* weekend?"

"Yes. Get the hell out." She frowned. "Where did you leave your car? I didn't see it."

"Around the corner, on Sale," he said, and retreated to Ricky's room. Where he found that he hadn't left anything. He was still wearing it all.

Behind his back, Margaret smiled.

Every fourth weekend Powder stayed in town. It wasn't like him to forget the day; but it was like him when he was working on something to forget everything else. On the way in, it crossed his mind to call Adele Buffington and ask her, straight out, to put him up for the weekend.

Somewhat rested, he expurgated the thought. He didn't even know if the broad was married or otherwise . . . With his knees controlling the wheel, he rubbed his face with both hands and tried not to think about his private life. With considerable success. Practice makes perfect.

Powder opened the door from the stairwell on the fourth floor at a quarter past noon. The first man he saw was Howard Brindell, who averted his face.

"Brindell! Hello!" Powder said. Long-lost friend.

"Hello, Lieutenant."

"Hang on a sec."

"I'm in quite a hurry."

"Sure, sure you are. Hang on a sec, I wanted to ask you about something."

Brindell gave up. "What?"

"How are you doing with that murder case, those three bodies?"

Brindell sighed heavily. "What you got against me, huh?"

"I don't understand what you mean, son."

"I mean you know damn well I got lifted off that case. The whole damn force knows about it."

Powder raised an eyebrow. "You know what paranoia means, son?"

"You mind if I go now, Lieutenant? Sir."

"Hang on a sec. Before you got lifted, how did you do on identifying the third body?"

"Before I got lifted I didn't do any good identifying the third body." Brindell walked away.

"Hey, hey. Who's got the case now?"

Brindell neglected to hear him.

Powder chuckled all the way to the records office, where he asked for a check on Cherry Cable.

Brindell's case had been taken over by Detective Sergeant Malmberg, another of the department's bright young things, but a man with a lot more about him than Brindell or, probably, than Sid Smith.

"I appreciate your interest, Lieutenant Powder," Malmberg said after Powder explained what he wanted. This acknowledgment of the extra-curricular nature of his concern won Powder over. A matter of principle.

"How are you getting along?"

"Not much at all."

"Where the problems?" Powder asked.

"Well, there are at least two killers. Ellyson killed his wife. They've sent that one on through, but someone else picked up the details and tried to make the other two look like the first. A copy-catter. The second body, this Hilda Chaney, was in the drug scene. But I haven't been able to do much with that. I asked Drug Squad to put out some feelers, but—"

"Have you identified the third body yet?"

"No," said Malmberg.

"Why not?"

"Well, no fingerprints, for a start."

"None?"

Malmberg shook his head. "And the other thing is her face was kind of knocked around."

"How long was she in the water?"

"Not that long. Same night, we think, but she was bashed on the face with a heavy stick or a pipe."

"That's what killed her, then?"

"Well . . ." said Malmberg, and shrugged. "There was a lot of action in the vicinity of her neck. Hypothesis is attempted strangulation but she fought and had to be hit. It honestly has all the feel of a cold-blooded and well-planned operation."

The feel. Powder liked the sound of that. Saddened him, though, because it showed that the best cops never get assigned to nights. "How long you been in the force, Malmberg?"

"Well, in detective branch now for about four years."

It was half an evasion, but Powder didn't press him. Clearly a college type who came more or less directly into Detective. By the shortest route anyway. Whatever that was, these days.

"Why?" Malmberg continued. "I making some kid's mistake?"

"Oh no," said Powder. "Just wondered."

They both let it ride.

"She killed on the spot?"

"Probably not. Probably dumped."

"But she was killed the same night?"

"Yes."

"Maybe just in a hurry to get rid of the body."

Malmberg nodded tentatively. He couldn't rule it out. What Powder said made sense. Though a lot of things could.

"What were her physical characteristics?"

Malmberg looked them up. Powder wasn't a type to waste time, and if he came in chatting—in a daytime—it seemed sensible to let him get to whatever was on his mind in his own way.

"She was a female Caucasian, twenty to twenty-five years old, height five feet seven and a half inches, weight a hundred and thirty-two pounds avoirdupois, eyes blue, hair yellow. I take it that's the sort of stuff you mean."

"It is. Was she an addict?"

"Subject addicted to heroin," Malmberg read and folded the notebook cover.

"I kind of thought she might be," Powder said.

"Care to tell me why?" asked Malmberg.

NIGHT COVER

"Sure. Because Hilda Chaney was involved with drugs." Then Powder said, "You got a picture of this corpse?"

"We can get one."

"Where is the corpse? Hasn't been packed off somewhere, has it?"

"It's still on file."

Powder, who was playing it so close to the chest that the hairs left imprint marks, couldn't leave without giving a little something away.

"You ever read old records?" he asked Malmberg.

"Not a lot."

"You ought to," said Powder. "Make you a better cop."

"I don't get a lot of time," said Malmberg. "And they're kind of hard to put your hands on, you know. Instructive ones."

"You got to ask for them," said Powder.

"Well," said Malmberg, who was going purely on instinct since he'd lost the drift of things, "if you come across any that might be interesting, I'd appreciate it if you'd pass them my way. Always interested in learning something."

Powder nodded with approval. Got up and left. Malmberg picked up the phone. When Powder walked into Identification, they were already five minutes on their way to laying their hands on a picture of corpse number three for him.

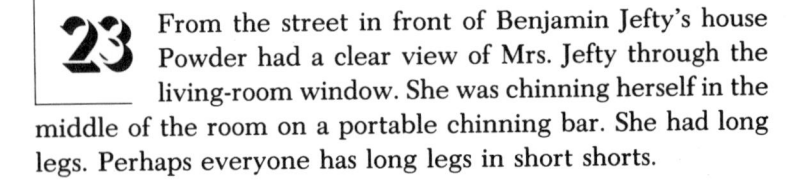

## 23

From the street in front of Benjamin Jefty's house Powder had a clear view of Mrs. Jefty through the living-room window. She was chinning herself in the middle of the room on a portable chinning bar. She had long legs. Perhaps everyone has long legs in short shorts.

She answered the bell promptly and wiped her face with a towel as Powder asked for her husband.

"He's at the school. Are you going to arrest him?"

"Should I?" Powder asked.

"We seem to have been getting a lot of callers of your type recently. I wondered if it was all leading to something. A girl has to be prepared."

Powder expected her to flex a muscle—or do a knee bend—but she didn't. So Powder left and went to the school.

The University School front door was locked. Powder banged on it for a long time before he saw movement within. It was still longer before Jefty appeared to peer out through the replaced panes of glass, and finally to unlock.

"Sorry to wake you," Powder said. Many things in his tone, but no sorrow.

Benjamin Jefty said, "I'm supervising the typing of the list you asked me to prepare. With the sound of the typewriter, I didn't hear you knocking at first."

In the background a typewriter started.

"It will be finished in just a few seconds, Lieutenant."

Jefty made no move to usher Powder into the school. So Powder walked past him.

"Is there anything else I can do for you?"

"You can tell me where Cherry Cable is."

"Wha . . . Cherry . . . I . . ." The question caught Jefty completely by surprise.

But Powder couldn't press the advantage. A dark-haired teenage girl opened the principal's office door and came into the front hall with four sheets of paper in her hand.

"They're finished, Mr. Jefty."

Powder stepped in front of Jefty and took the papers. "Thank you, miss," he said.

Jefty, struggling to recover, said, "This is Rosemary, one of our seniors."

Rosemary beamed.

"Thank you, Rosemary," Jefty continued. "I appreciate your typing these for me very much. We'll see you on Monday."

"Oh," said Rosemary. "OK. I'll just get my things." She went back into the office."

"Excellent typist," Jefty assured Powder. "But a little slow, you know what I mean?" He pointed to his head and crudely changed the gesture to scratching his ear as Rosemary, carrying a sweater and a handbag, pranced from the principal's office to the front door and waved goodbye.

Without saying anything, Powder walked into the principal's office. Jefty, still off balance, followed close behind him. "What else can I do for you . . . ?"

Powder stopped and scanned all the office's inanimate objects.

"Just wondered if your typewriter had turned up," he said. "If maybe it had been misplaced."

"Tha . . . tha . . . that's ridiculous."

"Is it?" Powder said menacingly. "Get your things, Mr. Jefty. And lock your doors."

"Wha . . . wha . . . what do you mean?"

"I'm going to have to ask you to come downtown for a little chat."

"What about?"

"We'll talk about it there. Get your things."

"This is outrageous. I see no good reason why I should—"

Powder cut him off. "I told you yesterday that this case was bigger than a tiddly shit break-in. I'm going to take you in, voluntarily or otherwise."

Jefty stood dumb for a few moments. Unable to believe what was happening to him. "I . . . I . . . Of course I want to cooperate. . . ."

"Then get your things." With force and resolution.

"But my wife . . ."

Powder took Jefty to the reception desk of the Day Room and asked the receptionist in a loud voice, "Can I fit this man onto the lie detector now"—Powder winked—"or shall I interrogate him first?"

The receptionist glanced through a few papers. He didn't have anything to do with the two polygraph rooms on the third floor, but he tried to make it look good, sound good.

"I'm afraid the lie detector is solidly booked this afternoon, Lieutenant Powder."

"Right," Powder said. He pointed Jefty to the door.

Then the receptionist said, "Lieutenant?"

"What?"

"The case records you asked for have come through. And there's someone waiting for you." He gestured to a chair against the wall in front of him.

Rex Funkhouser sat holding a magazine so limply that half the pages were dragging on the floor.

"Good Lord," Powder said. Then, gruffly, "Tell him to wait."

Powder marched Jefty down the hall, took him past the first two interview rooms and sat him down in E454. "Don't go anywhere," Powder said and then left.

Walking through the halls, he gave his face a good rub.

On his Day Room desk he found the police file on Cherry Cable. Five arrests, two quickie convictions and fines for solicitation. And the story of a rather brutal robbery. The one which led to her being held long enough to have her habit and real name discovered.

Powder surveyed the Day Room. And at that moment Howard Brindell stood up and told someone near his desk that he could be found in the Canteen.

Brindell, Powder thought, and smiled inside. "Brindell!" he shouted.

Brindell started, though his hand was in no visible cookie jar. He said something Powder couldn't hear.

"Come here!"

Brindell had no choice but to come to Powder's desk. Powder stood up to greet him.

"I was just going—"

"Howard," said Powder, putting his arm around Brindell's shoulders, "I've got something I'd like you to do for me."

Brindell couldn't believe it.

"I've got a man in 454 who needs softening. I'd appreciate it very much if you'd take a crack at him."

"I . . . I . . ." It was so unexpected a request that Brindell couldn't think, quickly, how to start to get out of it. He said, "I don't know anything about what you want . . . or . . ."

"There's a missing girl and I think he knows what happened to her. Take him through the when-did-you-last-see-her routine and he'll tell you all you need to know. I think there was something between them. If you want to pace yourself, get him to tell you about a robbery and press him about whether he did it. You got it?"

"I . . . I . . ."

"Thanks a lot, Brindell. I appreciate it. I really do." He really did. Powder strode quickly from the Day Room proper to the reception area.

Rex saw him come. When Powder got to him, Rex was on his feet. "Are you really going to give Mr. Jefty a lie-detector test?" he asked.

"Come on, son," Powder said. "Let's have a little chat."

They walked down the hall slowly and were overtaken by Howard Brindell. "You not at it yet?" Powder said.

"No, I was writing down what you said to interrogate him about."

"Good," Powder said. "Good procedure."

"What was the name of the girl? You didn't tell me."

"Cherry Cable," Powder said crisply and didn't look at Rex. Rex reacted enough for Brindell to realize Powder was working on the same case and to suggest to Brindell that it might be hot. "Right, Lieutenant. 454?"

"Yeah."

Powder steered Rex into Interview Room 408.

The room was steely and spare. A heavy metal table and four chairs. Walls bare except for one panel, which was in fact an observation window. All interview rooms have third-party observation facilities. Microphones; tape recorders which never malfunction or run out of tape.

"Sit down."

"You're finally looking for Cherry," Rex said. He intended it to be tough, but he was out of his depth.

"When did you last see Cherry Cable, son?"

"After school, Friday, April 27."

Powder checked his notebook. "That was the afternoon two days after you first came and talked to me?"

"That's right."

"Did you talk to her about coming here?"

"Yes."

"Did she approve?"

"She didn't want to get in trouble. She didn't want me to make it specific about her because she didn't want to get in trouble."

"Do you know why?"

"I think she was on some kind of probation or something."

"That's all?"

"It's pretty important, you know. If you're on probation."

"Do you know what she was on probation for?"

"No," Rex said righteously. "And I never asked. It was her business and if she wanted me to know she would have told me."

"When you came in here you told me you overheard your principal—"

"Owner," Rex interjected. A last bastion.

"You heard your principal talking with a teacher about the grades of some kid or kids. Was the story you told me true?"

"Absolutely."

"Were they talking about Cherry Cable?"

"No. Not specifically."

"Did you overhear anyone talking about Cherry Cable's grades any other time?"

"No."

"Did you know of any reason that Cherry Cable might think that she would be doing badly when report cards came out?"

"Some of her teachers told her she was in trouble."

"What sort of trouble?"

"Behind on assignments."

"Was she likely to fail?"

"We didn't know."

"But she was afraid she was in jeopardy, is that right?"

"If she failed, she'd have to stay at the school another year, and she couldn't bear the idea of that."

Powder took a breath. Rex was worried. Not for himself. So was Powder and not for himself.

"How good friends were you with Cherry Cable?"

"Do you always have to use both her names? It makes her sound like a thing." Powder didn't respond. "Cherry was a friend."

"Girl friend?"

"A friend who was a girl."

Powder sighed. "Did you ever have sexual intercourse with her?"

Rex was startled. "No!"

"Why not?"

"Well . . . I . . . We . . . Well."

"So what did you do with her?"

Offended. "I talked to her. I tried to help her."

"What sort of help did she need?"

"She didn't like the school. I mean, nobody does, but she let it upset her. I tried to help her see it as a means to an end, same as it is for me. Nobody wins victories without hard and bitter struggles, without sweat and blood."

Powder raised an eyebrow. "She was part of your cell, then?"

"Cell?"

"Your whatchacallit. What *do* you call it? Kids reading Mao."

"Don't call it a cell. That's a leftover from the Russian reactionaries."

Oh. "But Cherry Cable shared your interest in Mao, did she?"

"She was interested. I spent some time showing her how Mao's Thought could help her through difficult times in her life. She didn't study it much, but she was interested. She liked to listen to me talk about it."

"So your relationship was what people of my generation might call platonic?"

"Yes. Though if I felt she'd needed help on the level of emotional relationships . . ."

"Did she have a boy friend?"

"She had a number of friends who were boys."

"You know what I mean, son."

"No," he said. "Not that I knew of."

"How much did you know about her comings and goings? You saw her at school and after school. Did you see her nights?"

"Not often, no. I talked to her on the phone at night sometimes, though."

"How often did you see her or talk to her in the evening or on a weekend?"

"Maybe once or twice a week."

"Did she see other people at night?"

"I didn't know who."

"But you think she went out?"

"Sometimes she said, 'I've got to go out now.'"

"How often?"

"Pretty often."

"But you didn't ask her where she was going?"

"No. If she wanted me to know, she told me."

"Did you ever go over to her house?"

"Oh yes."

"Often?"

"Quite often."

"So when you saw her after school, it wasn't always at school."

"Oh no. Usually at somebody's house."

"Whose houses?"

"Not mine. Anybody else's."

"For instance."

"Well, Cherry's, Artie's, Ross's."

Powder took names and addresses; wrote them down. Then asked, "And were you all involved in the break-in at the school?"

"What?"

"Did you plan and execute it together, or did some of you do it without the rest of you knowing?"

Rex burst into a big grin. Nervous, uncontrolled, amused. "I don't know what you're talking about."

"I'm talking about a girl who may be dead."

"Dead?"

"—and whose death may be related to the theft at the University School on Saturday night. If you give a damn about her, it's time to tell me. Did you plan it alone, Rex, or did you plan it with other people?"

"I . . . I . . . I planned it alone."

"Did you commit it alone or did you commit it with help?"

"I did it alone. All alone."

"What happened to the typewriter?"

"I never took any typewriter. I took four hundred and eight dollars and I tried to break the intercom. I never touched the typewriter."

Well, Powder thought, there's that little problem muddied up. "I've got a picture I want to show you, Rex. Can you tell me who it is?" Powder pulled out a face of the third body in the recent series of murders. "Do you recognize it?"

Totally agitated now, Rex held the photograph in two shaking hands. "I . . . I . . . I . . . I don't know."

"It's not a very good likeness. Tell you what, let's take a little walk. You can have a look at the original."

"Oh God!"

"You all right?"

"I . . . I . . . I . . . I never . . ."

"Stay here a minute, Rex, old son. I'll get you some coffee."

"N-n-not coffee," Rex said. "Tea, no cream or sugar."

## 24

The slow walk to the morgue seemed to calm Rex. The sheer effort which walking required helped him forget, somewhat, what he was walking to see.

"I never knew there were all these tunnels," was all he said between leaving the interview room and entering the police morgue.

Not many do, Powder thought.

Powder pounded a bell on a table for ten seconds before a mustachioed man in a white coat came from an inner recess. "Now what can I show you gentlemen?" he asked.

There was a little confusion about finding the right corpse. The labeling system had been changed six years before and it was longer than that since Powder had brought someone in to identify anybody. Any body.

But Powder wrung the changes, and Rex followed him and the mortuarist, who pulled out a tray and waited before he drew back the cover.

"Get hold of yourself, Rex," Powder said.

"I'm all right."

Powder nodded; the mortuarist showed them the corpse. Rex let out a gasp involuntarily. Powder was shocked because the face had obviously been beaten severely. He hadn't looked carefully when he'd supervised at Pogues Run.

"You're sure this is the right one?"

"Yup."

"My God!" Rex said quietly.

"Is this Cherry Cable?" Powder asked.

"I . . . I . . . I guess," said Rex. "It's so hard. I never saw her like this before."

"Is it her?"

"I remember her hair a little lighter, and I didn't think she was quite this thick," Rex said, but the way he said it—meditatively—removed any doubt that he believed this to be his friend who was a girl.

Powder said, "Either it's Cherry Cable or it isn't. Is it?"

"Yes," Rex said.

"Right. Thanks . . . ?"

"Eric," said the mustachioed man.

"Thanks then, Eric. Lock it up."


Rex was quiet as they walked through the tunnels, but by the elevator door he faced Powder and said, "Did Mr. Jefty do that to her?"

Powder didn't answer immediately because he'd been thinking.

Rex said, "The capitalist bastard! My God!"

"No," Powder said, "Jefty didn't have anything to do with it." Who could be sure? But Powder knew he didn't want Rex wading in.

"But why are you giving him a lie-detector test?"

"We're not."

"But when I was waiting up there . . ."

"You will do me a great favor, son," Powder said forcefully, "if you will let me get on with my business. I do it a lot better than you do. No one will get away with anything and that includes you."

"Are . . . are you going to arrest me?"

The elevator came. Powder opened it with his key and held the door as Rex got in.

"Are you?"

They got out on the first floor. Rex prepared to hear his fate.

At the Uniform Branch reception desk Powder turned to Rex. "Is the money you took at your house?"

"Yes. All b-but fifty dollars."

"We have that." Powder turned to the Uniform receptionist. "I want an officer to accompany this man to his house to recover some stolen money. The officer is then to bring him back to Homicide and Robbery. OK?"

"Yes, sir."

To Rex: "When you get back here, I want you to make a complete statement about the robbery. Then we'll let you go home, and see how things work out."

Rex protested, "But it ought to be settled one way or the other. I don't want to just hang around at home waiting." In vain.

Powder went up to the Day Room for a little think. He sat with his face in his hands for fully ten minutes.

"There you are, Powder!"

He looked up and saw Brindell's glowing face.

"Yeah."

"I been looking for you. How long you want me to go with this pigeon? You want me to take a statement? If you just wanted him softened up, he's soft, believe me."

"Did you inform him of his rights?" Powder said.

Brindell took a deep breath. Should know better than to be happy around Powder. "Didn't *you?*" Brindell asked.

"Did you inform him of his rights?"

Brindell smirked and said, without credibility, "Yeah."

"Good," Powder said quietly. "Now what did you get?"

"Well, don't get me wrong. He hasn't confessed to having murdered this girl, if that's what you wanted. But he screwed her. To listen to him, she was a hot little item."

"He what?"

"She was a pupil at his school, I gather. Disgusting," said Brindell. With disgust.

Powder rubbed his face. "How often?"

"Only once, or so he says."

Powder shook his head. "God damn. When was it?"

"End of last week."

"Which day?"

"I don't know. I couldn't get him on the money in that robbery you talked about. But he tried a cheap play with the typewriter. Says he wasn't insured for the money in the lockbox. Figured he ought to get some compensation, so he hid the typewriter. Seems to think we never solve simple theft cases. Thought he wasn't taking a chance."

"Where is it?"

"Upstairs in his house."

Powder nodded.

"Oh, is that all you want from me, Lieutenant?"

"That'll do just fine, Brindell," Powder said. "Good work. And thanks."

Before he went to mold the softened educator, Powder took care of loose ends. He called the Probation Department and left a message for Adele Buffington. He looked for Tidmarsh's file on multiple homicides since 1950. It was downstairs in the Night Room. Powder made the effort, walked downstairs and then back up, and left the file on Malmberg's desk, after scribbling, "Return to Leroy Powder" at the top.

"I ought to charge admission," said Eric, the mortuarist. He rolled the body out for Jefty and Powder to get a good view, then drew the cover back with a flourish.

"Take a good look," said Powder. His tone of voice fitted the chilled surroundings to an icicle.

Jefty took a good look.

"Is that Cherry Cable?"

"I just don't know," Jefty said. "I never knew her that well." Intimately, but not well. "That's all, Eric."

Eric wasted no chipper chat on them as they left the morgue. Powder wasn't hiding his feelings.

"Are you going to arrest me?" Jefty asked.

Brindell had broken him, to a point. The facts were unattractive, but they'd lost something in Brindell's telling. When Jefty repeated his confessions for Powder and a stenographer, he made it sound like God had given him permission to steal the typewriter and Cherry Cable had undone his fly and put it in for him.

Jefty was not Powder's favorite man, but they had agreed on a statement before looking at the body.

Powder led Jefty to the Uniform reception desk. To the cop behind the desk, Powder said, "This man wants us to search his house for a typewriter he says is upstairs in his bedroom. That's right, isn't it, Jefty?"

"What? Oh, yes."

"Here is the house key." Powder put out his hand. Jefty fumbled for the key, found it. "And I'd like one of your guys to pick it up."

"Yessir."

"And as for you . . ." Powder took Jefty to the prisoners' elevator and dropped him off on the fifth floor in the Holding Room.

Didn't book him. "You're not really my case. And I thought you'd like to tell your story to Sergeant Groce."

"Not again!" Jefty whined. Powder left him.

It was a few minutes after six before Powder got a chance to go out to eat. With the typewriter and the money recovered, with Jefty turned over to Groce to do what he liked with because it was Groce's case, with Rex sent home to sleep because Rex's case was his to do with what he liked, Powder was beat. Working all day before he worked all night. No future in it.

Powder was late to work. Schleutter and the two Smiths watched him weave slowly between their desks. To his own night hidey-hole. To work, perchance to dream. Before he sat down he turned to face his men. Frowned. "Where's Harold?"

No volunteers because Salimbean was not particularly well liked. No one suggested he was out making a phone call. Salimbean was just late.

"Whatsa matter?" Powder asked the dumb faces. "Nothing to do?"

On cue, the night phone rang.


When it rains it pours. Before one they had calls for no fewer than four domestic shootings. And Salimbean didn't show up at all. The only grace the evening provided was a slow period after one.

Powder was almost asleep at his desk. The reports slid through without notation.

When Big Jack came in at five past three to relieve him, Powder was daydreaming about his seven toes. About the three he'd lost. Finders keepers. If they'd been fingers: fingers keepers.

Powder drove to the Illinois Hotel on South Senate. He parked in its small lot and shuffled into the lobby. Behind the desk an old man with soot-black hair combed flat back greeted him.

"Lieutenant! We missed you last night!"

"Yeah, I forgot I was due. Look, Christy, I'm pretty tired. Usual room?"

"That's right, Lieutenant."

"Leave me a call for one o'clock."

"It would be my greatest pleasure."

"And, hey, is there any food around? You got any food?"

"Well . . ." Christy hesitated. "I brought two sandwiches and I only ate one."

"Could I buy it off you?"

"I don't know whether you'd like it, Lieutenant."

"I'll like it. Why, what's the matter with it?"

"It's a banana sandwich. My sister had some bananas she said would go bad unless she used them. So she gave me two banana sandwiches. That's why I got one left."

"I'll take it," Powder said.

Christy hunted for, found and gave Powder a rumpled, grease-spotted bag.

## 25

By two on Sunday afternoon Powder felt refreshed. Partly it was eating a decent meal—he'd splurged on his second steak of the week. And partly it was carrying out a prolonged investigation. In his own time, and a physical strain to be sure, but it had an invigorating "feel." He wondered whether he might just be coming out of a long hibernation.

Before 2:30 he was at Headquarters. On his way upstairs he remembered Adele Buffington. She hadn't called last night in response to the message he'd left.

As he stepped into the fourth-floor corridor, Powder pulled at his shirt collar, which was getting sticky. He frowned, then turned in the direction of the Day Room.

He never made it to his desk. As he entered the Day Room he was accosted from two sides: the reception officer and a day sergeant.

"Lieutenant Powder, Inspector Pugh has been looking all over for you."

"Please see Inspector Pugh at your earliest opportunity."

He gave them each an ear and simultaneously saw Malmberg look up halfway across the room, get up, grab some papers and come toward him in a hurry.

Malmberg said, "Where the hell have you been, Powder?"

"What's it to you? It's my day off."

"Come on," Malmberg said. "Inspector Pugh wants to talk to us."

"He's Operations, isn't he?"

"Come on!"

Powder followed, but refused to break into a trot.

At Pugh's office Malmberg just told the secretary, "We've located him."

"Go on in."

Knocking first, a formality, Malmberg led Powder in.

"So," Pugh said.

There were two breeds of inspector, new and old. Pugh was new; the man someone like Malmberg would look to. Powder hardly knew him; hardly knew anything about him. Wasn't he born in a train?

"We've had quite a time locating you, Lieutenant Powder. Your wife says you weren't home last night."

"I was here last night. It's my job."

"All night?"

"Close enough."

"But it's nearly three. . . ."

Powder shrugged. "So when's someone going to tell me what's been going on?" *You found out I'm a Maoist? What took you so long? I've been a Maoist nearly a week.*

Pugh tensed his lips. "This report is veiled dynamite."

"What report?"

"This," said Pugh, who waved a manila envelope. "You were responsible for it, weren't you?"

Powder looked and recognized the file which Tidmarsh had given him. Which he had passed on to Malmberg. "Oh."

Pugh looked to Malmberg. "Didn't you brief him, Sergeant?"

"I just brought him here as soon as he was located," Malmberg said. "You didn't say to brief him."

"I didn't realize it would be necessary." Sarcasm aimed at Powder. "You mean to tell me that you don't realize the implications of what's in the file you passed to Sergeant Malmberg?"

"Who ever knows all the implications of anything?"

Pugh reflected in perplexed amazement. Like a company director hearing that his second-in-command had never seen a $100 bill.

"You going to tell me what's going on?" Powder asked finally. "Or do I wait to see it on television?"

"As far as you're concerned, Lieutenant, what was that report about?"

"Are you asking me how I came to have it compiled?" No demurs. "Well . . . I've had a feeling that I've been seeing a lot of multiple killings lately."

"A feeling?"

"Yeah. And there's a new guy, Tidmarsh, in ID and Records, so I thought I'd help break him in. I had him make me a report over the last year and a half. And when that was in, I had this one. I asked for the last ten years, but he gave me since 1950."

"And your conclusion from reading the contents?"

"We have had more series murders in the last three years or so than we usually do."

"A feeling . . ." Pugh spoke it like the word was bitter. "Do you know how *many* more?"

Powder considered briefly. "I'd say eight or nine series when we should have had two. Roughly that."

"And do you know the statistical chances of that happening randomly?"

"Don't tell me."

"Tell him, Malmberg."

"On superficial figures, at least twenty to one against."

"I said don't tell me!" Powder said sharply. "You want to emphasize the point that it's unlikely. OK, it's unlikely. That's why when I heard Malmberg had responsibility for the current case I thought maybe he'd be interested in reading Tidmarsh's file. So he is. So here we are." Powder didn't quite know what the moral was. So he said, "By the way, I may have a make on your third body."

"What?" the two men said in unison.

"I've had a preliminary identification. Not formal. We can take care of that now, if you like."

They liked, and Pugh arranged personally for Mrs. Maxine Tedesco to be brought in to look at corpse number three.

"Tell them to treat her gently," Powder told them.

"Which leaves us—" said Pugh as he put the phone down. A compact man, nearly bald, with wire-rimmed glasses.

"Which leaves us," Powder intercepted, "with the problem of what you think is causing this outbreak of multiple murders."

Pugh inhaled. "And what do *you* think the cause is?"

"Dunno yet," Powder said.

"Malmberg," said Pugh. "Suggestions?"

"There *are* a lot of possibilities, sir. Without knowing more, it's hard to eliminate many."

There was general agreement on a moment of silence. Then Pugh nodded slightly. "Well, how it shakes out, we shall see. For now, what I want is a special investigation team to work with, what's his name, Tidmarsh? To work on the current case and to verify the background to this preliminary report. We have enough to go that far. Will you need a third man, do you think?"

"Oh no," said Powder.

"Good," said Pugh.

"Oh no!"

"What do you mean, 'Oh no,' Lieutenant?"

"You're not roping me into any special investigation. Thanks, but no thanks. You get yourself some other boy."

Pugh was dumfounded. Malmberg was surprised. Unspoken but understood: special assignment was a plum, high-reward work. Cops slit throats, metaphorically, to get on special.

"Or your boy here can do it alone," Powder said.

"What's the matter? Why don't you want to work with Malmberg on this?"

"Nothing to do with Malmberg. I don't like special teams. I have a job I like. I'm good at it and I'm too old to change." Then he added, "Besides, I come up for retirement in two years."

Didn't need, want the promotion boost such an assignment—if it broke—would give.

The two other men had heard Powder was difficult to work with. Pugh's attitude was firm about men who played personal games with department priorities. Malmberg shrugged. Pugh said, "I can't make you do it." Though he could.

"Keep me informed. Happy to work informally with you guys. Whoever you set up."

"There will be no informal work on this case," said Pugh icily. "It will be a secret operation. Top secret."

Meditatively Powder said, "I thought it might be." He felt uncomfortable. So he stood up.

"You intend to retire then?" Pugh asked.

"Not necessarily," said Powder. "I'm just happy doing what I do."

And Powder left the two men to their top secret.

Walking down the hall, he rubbed his face hard. Too close to home, that. He'd tried a special assignment once; hadn't liked it.

## 26

Powder sat alone in the Canteen for nearly three quarters of an hour. The urgency of whatever he had come in to Headquarters to do on a Sunday—Sunday! —had passed and he sat, uneasy in his mind. Three times he tugged at the uncomfortable collar. It made him wonder, just wonder, if his night duty wasn't a collar. One worn too long. But retire? Christ, what the hell would I do? Become a private detective?

When he finally left the Canteen, he spoke out loud, to no one in particular. "Time for a change."

The only certainty in the words meant the shirt.

At the door of the Day Room he asked loudly, "Anybody got a spare shirt?" No response. "I said, has anybody got a spare shirt I can borrow?"

He walked away muttering, not quite willing to repeat the performance in the doorway of every other room in the building.

Instead he went upstairs to the prison floor and intimidated a young Medical Room officer into issuing him a clean prisoner's shirt. He had to sign for it, for all that. It was too large: an all-purpose size. Powder changed shirts on the spot. He carried his dirty shirt ostentatiously through the Day Room to his desk against the wall.

From the desk he made a call to Adele Buffington's home.

"I got your message, but couldn't come in last night," she said distantly. "I called your house this morning, but your wife didn't seem to know much about you."

"She doesn't," Powder said.

"What she said was 'He doesn't live here this weekend.'"

"That's right," Powder said. Rather than elaborate, he rubbed his face with his free hand. "Look, what I wanted to know was whether you have a washing machine. I have this dirty shirt. . . ." Listening to himself, it didn't sound nearly as romantic as it had in his mind when he first thought of it.

"And . . ." Powder scrambled to continue, "er . . . last night what I wanted was for you to come in and have a look at a body we've got here, but the officer I've, um, passed the case on to has already sent out to have Mrs. Tedesco brought in to look at it."

"Body," said Buffington. "Cherry Cable's body?"

"We think so."

"What happened to her?" The voice was disturbed.

Powder wanted to tell her the whole thing. "It's pretty complicated," he said. "Can I tell you over lunch?"

Ice on the line. "I've already had lunch."

"Then dinner?"

"If you want to ask me out, my married policeman friend, then ask me out. But don't use Cherry Cable's body to do it."

"I . . ." Powder wanted to say that he needed her as much for her social-worker capacity as her private capacity. But he realized before trying to say it that she wouldn't consider that a particularly apt approach either. Besides, she was a probation officer, not a social worker. "Shit," he said, "I must be going out of my mind."

She took this, not incorrectly, as an apology.

Powder said, "We found a woman's body a week ago. Friday night. Floating in Pogues Run. She'd been strangled, with hands and face mutilated. She's finally been tentatively identified as Cherry Cable. The only other thing we know is that she was an addict."

"Oh dear."

"There are aspects . . . Well, I can tell you with absolute honesty that we're working on it here, it's a priority case."

"Are *you* working on it, Lieutenant?"

"Not officially. I was asked to work on it," he had to tell her, "but I declined."

"Why?"

"I'm not sure," he said. Then, "But I'd be particularly pleased to talk about it with you over lunch or dinner or in a launderette."

She laughed, but not easily. "I just wish I could," she said, which he tried to believe.

"You're spoken for," he said and then wished he hadn't, because it was an old-fashioned manner of speech and this was not, from his point of view, an old-fashioned girl. "I mean today," he added hurriedly.

For once she missed the undertone of his original words because she had been thinking. "Look," she said, "I don't know exactly what my plans are. Can you hang loose?"

"I guess so," he said uncomfortably.

"Can you give me a number where I can get hold of you through today?"

When he hung up the phone, Powder had contradictory feelings. The call had cheered him up enormously and somehow compensated for the disturbing interview with Pugh and Malmberg. But he also felt uncertain. He was drifting toward uncharted waters when he'd spent decades in a canal between locks. Anything but ambiguity. Even his home life, so-called. The only thing to be said for it was that it was all written down on paper.

Powder stopped at the Day Room's reception desk on his way out. Any messages which came through were important, not to be lost or delayed. Relay them through Communications.

No more time to sit around the Canteen. Whatever else happened, Powder felt and responded to a strong urge to wrap up loose ends.


In Eagledale, Nicki Funkhouser answered the door.

"Yes?"

She appeared not to remember him; he extracted his ID. "Lieutenant Powder, ma'am. Is Rex here?"

She was silent and tight-lipped long enough that Powder considered saying something more.

Then she opened the door. "I think you better come in," took him by the arm. "Come in, sit down," led him to the living room. "Sit down, sit down," pushed him into a chair.

"I don't know what to do," she said, now tearing. "I really don't know what to do." She whimpered.

Powder brought himself to the front edge of the chair. "Is Rex here?"

"Is Rex here! Yes, he's here. He came in last night and locked his door and he's been in there ever since." The tears stopped, but she looked at Powder wildly.

"Oh yes?"

"Oh, I know he has some cookies in there, some nice chocolate-chip cookies in a box. I don't think he thinks I know, but I do." She paused. "I have to clean his room. Nobody else does it. What I don't understand is what's happened to his body functions. I just don't understand, I listened all night."

Powder stood up.

"His father went round outside and looked through the window, but I knew he was all right. I could hear him typing. All through the night, typing, and his father snoring. Of course *he's* off at Baba's now."

Powder left the living room.

"Hey, where do you think you're going?" She scurried after him.

Powder banged hard on Rex's door. "Open up, Rex. Lieutenant Powder here."

There was silence, then feet hit the floor. Key turned in lock and Rex opened the door. Powder walked in; Nicki tried to follow, but Rex barred the way. "Go strangle a cat," he told her and slammed the door in her face.

Nicki took the words without protest. They watched the door and listened to her walk away.

"I was resting," Rex said. "I was going to come in to see you later on." Rex's eyes were bloodshot and shiny. He looked very tired.

"I saved you the trouble," said Powder and he pulled up Rex's chair and sat down to face the younger man. The idea had been to offer an old-fashioned deal: Rex keeps out of trouble and we forget his indiscretions this time. Jefty's excesses provided certain extenuations. A first offense. The urge to protect the friend who was . . . dead.

"I've been working on a confession," Rex said with some sting in his voice. "All night. I've put it all in here." He picked up a sheaf of papers from the bed. "And I mean it's *all* in here." Now he was aggressive. "Including how you let her die."

"What's that supposed to mean?"

"I came to you, didn't I? I told you, didn't I? You can deny it, but I told you she'd kill herself if you didn't do something about that evil capitalist school. You can't deny that!"

It's what you get trying to be nice in this world, Powder

thought. He rubbed his face and said, "We found the body the same night you first came in and talked to me. She was probably already dead."

"Oh God." Mournfully.

"Besides, she was murdered. She didn't commit suicide."

"What?"

Powder explained, in a limited way, and left. Good cops don't make deals, he thought. He took the "confession," twenty-seven pages of it, and he told Rex not to leave town. Powder's remaining compassion went only as far as telling Rex to get some rest.

As Powder walked out, he found Nicki reading a magazine in the living room, *Cat in Health.* She shot out of her chair. "He hasn't done anything, has he?"

"He's in a pretty bad way," said Powder. "A friend of his has died and he's very distraught."

Nicki's eyes narrowed. "Distraught, is he? And what am I?"

## 27

The reception officer shook before Powder's wrath. "That's the message, Lieutenant. I don't know anything else about it!"

"Jesus Christ! Can't anybody do anything around here?"

Powder stomped through to his Day Room desk. His weekend was slipping away. Again. Another one.

On his desk was a slight typed note. Powder picked it up roughly and glared around the room. Nobody glared back. Lucky for them.

Lieutenant Powder.
  *Re* body of unidentified female admitted Friday, 26th April. Mrs. Maxine Tedesco of 6218 Guilford Avenue was

shown the body at 3 P.M. today, Sunday, May 6th. Mrs. Tedesco rejected the hypothesis that the body was that of her missing niece, Cherry Cable. Rejection was vigorous and did not admit of doubt, though she refused or was unable to specify why it was not her niece. She could not identify the body. Attending officer: Patrolman Charles Plzak.

"Oh, for crying out loud!" Powder said to nobody in particular. "Oh, for God's sake!"
He put the sheet down and put his head down on top of it.

Behind twin towers of empty coffee cups, Powder had settled in to read Rex Funkhouser's "confession" by 4:30. His day for typed documents.

I first saw Cherry Cable on February 7th. I was standing outside the University School where I had been a student —a junior—for one semester. Miss Cable arrived on a scooter, parked directly in front of the school, despite the signs, and walked to the door. We all noticed her. There were five or six of us outside—there usually are because we get there early and the school owner, Benjamin Jefty, keeps the door locked until five minutes before classes begin, even on very cold days. I remember she tried the door handle several times. Then she turned to the bunch of us watching her and she said, "What's the matter with this joint? No school today?" Nobody answered her. I don't know why, thinking about it, and then she took a step down and said to me, "Hey, cutie pie. I asked you a question!"

It was a very full account of the history of Rex and Cherry. Cutie Pie and Cherry.
On page 19 Powder's phone rang. He tore himself away and answered before the end of the first ring.

"Ah, you're there!"

"Sure I'm here," Powder said. "Who is this?"

"Oh. It's Adele." Then as an afterthought she added, "Buffington."

Powder shook his head to clear it. "Oh. Oh." Then, "Good."

She was not certain of her ground, hadn't realized he had other things to think about while she'd been working on the problem she'd called to report solution of. "I've managed to extricate myself," she told him. Her style, hard won, of directness and strength. "If you're still available. And willing to feed with me."

"Yeah. Yeah," Powder said, wrenching at his mind to bring it to a social face. "When are you free from?"

"Look, are you all right?"

"Oh yeah," he said, "I've just been reading a report that's heavy going."

Lightly she said, "I have not the faintest notion of what kind of hours you lead. You always seem to be on duty."

"Not always," he said, struggling to reproduce the will to light chat, struggling to remember the reasons he'd made overtures to this woman. Surprises fatigued him—blanketed his emotions—and Mrs. Tedesco's failure to confirm Rex's identification had surprised him profoundly. "When are you free from?"

So businesslike, Jesus. Regret the extrication, but, "Well," she said, "Pretty well any time now."

"Good, good," he repeated while he looked at his watch. "It's five to five. Can you be down here in about half an hour?"

"Can I . . . Well . . . I suppose so."

"Good," he said. "Good."

"Look," she began, irritated. But held it. "Oh well, where should I meet you?"

Idea. "Do you know where the morgue is?"

Powder was ten minutes late. "Sorry," he said. "Sorry." And he smiled.

He took her arm, but she resisted. "Look, Lieutenant," she said. "I just want to tell you this was not at all what I had in mind."

His mind, which in the intervening forty minutes had caught itself up considerably, said, "I didn't exactly plan it this way either."

"So you say," she said, believing him, but trying to get him to consider, momentarily, that she didn't. "And what would you have done if I hadn't extricated myself?"

"When I got around to it, probably gone out to your place to bring you in."

"Dragged me by the hair out of my lover's arms?"

"Look, you want to see a body before dinner or not?"


"It's definitely not Cherry Cable."

Powder rubbed his face. "You're sure?"

"I'm sure."

"How can you be sure?"

"Well, this girl looks more solid than Cherry, for one thing."

Powder shrugged, but Adele persevered. "How tall is this girl? Was this girl?"

His notes were upstairs. He looked around for the particulars on her. "Hey," he called to the college student who filled in Sunday nights. "Get me the measurements on this body."

Adele raised an eyebrow.

"Cherry was five feet nine inches tall and weighed a hundred and nineteen pounds. She also had artificially colored hair."

"She wasn't blond?" Powder asked, surprised.

"Not the shade she carried. She had light brown hair with a vivid imagination's worth of red in it. She called it cherry blond, meaning strawberry blond. Only it wasn't either. When she started school she had it platinumed so she would start a new personality with a new life."

"Oh yeah?" Powder said.

Adele walked up to the head of the body. "Look, after you're dead, doesn't your hair keep growing? This girl's roots are the same color as the rest of the hair."

Powder took her word for it. "I've been reading . . ." he began, but from behind him footsteps took his attention.

"I've got the measurements," said the night attendant.

"Just read to us. What's the height and weight of this body?"

"The height and weight?"

"That's it."

"Well," the kid said, "the inmate measures sixty-seven and a half pounds—I mean inches in length, and weighs one hundred and thirty-two pounds."

"Thank you," Powder said, dismissing the boy. "That's dead weight, of course. Got to add a little for lost blood and the weight of the soul."

"And sixty-seven and a half inches makes five seven and a half, the way I count it."

"Well, everybody knows the soul is one and a half inches high."

"And makes you lighter by thirteen pounds."

Powder said, "I never thought it was Cherry Cable. Doesn't make sense, does it? I mean, Cherry Cable didn't have the same color hair, did she?"

He took her to Vinnie's, a rambling restaurant in a large house on the way to Beech Grove. Picking it was a gesture to her.

As they walked up the steps, Powder said, "I don't know many decent eateries; most of what I know is greasy spoons."

She stopped on the step. "So let's go to a greasy spoon."

"Naw," he said, "we're here. I got to show off the only decent place I know."

When they went in, Vinnie's mother greeted Powder like a lost son. Powder was only slightly embarrassed. Adele was immediately conscious that none of the attention rubbed off on her. That meant disapproval, but she also noted from the conversation that Powder had not been to the restaurant for a long time. To listen to Vinnie's mother tell it.

"So, come and eat in the kitchen, eh?" said Mother. Even here she didn't look at Adele.

"No. We want to talk."

"OK, you go where you want."

They went. Adele felt strongly she was supposed to gush at this dousing in his world. The world he was important in. Especially when wine and antipasto arrived without being ordered. She was not particularly good at being led.

As he poured wine into her glass, Powder said, "If Cherry Cable isn't dead on that slab, where the hell is she?"

"This is where she came in, the lady answered," Adele answered. "When do you go off duty? Or are you one of these compulsive types?"

"My duty sheet puts me on from seven P.M. to three A.M. Tuesday night through Saturday night."

She frowned. "Lovely," she said. "I didn't realize detectives did so much detecting in the middle of the night."

He explained the night cover system to her. She understood immediately the contradictions between what he said and the situation as she knew it. "If you're the man who sets the cases up for the day people, how come *you* are running around trying to find Cherry Cable?"

"A hypothetical question," he began. "To make you a better cop."

"But I don't want to be a better cop. You may, but I don't."

Powder conceded gracefully. He explained at some length his original mistake in handling Rex Funkhouser and how he'd tried to make up for it.

"But you must have made mistakes before."

"Not many," he said.

"But some, damn it. Do you go out and be a sleuth in your spare time for all of them, too?"

"Not really," he said. And he left it at that.

She exhaled sharply.

"I was offered . . ." He started to say it before he realized why he was saying it. Must be the wine. ". . . a job on a special investigation today. Would have meant working days."

"But you turned it down."

"Yeah." He no longer knew exactly why.

"Why?"

He rubbed his face with both hands. By way of an answer.

"I'm no expert," she said, "but I would have thought you'd be a pretty good investigator."

"I was," he said. "I am." Brave face, because he felt she was leading the conversation. It was uncomfortable, yet not without its pleasures. Marked the difference for him between social occasions and business occasions. He was rarely out of the lead in conversations, and rarely had social occasions. He was uneasy, and yet . . .

"So how'd you get stuck for nineteen years in a job like night cover, Lieutenant?"

"Swing shift," he said, and thought of the real dead-ender, Big Jack Monroe.

She shrugged.

"Time was," he began, and then two plates of food came, followed by several supplementary bowls.

"Did we order?" Adele asked.

"Not exactly, no," Powder said.

Adele frowned.

"Time was," he persisted, "when I was the department's golden-haired boy."

Instinctively she looked at his head, regretted it. What there was was gray. Powder missed her mistake, though, because he enjoyed the prospect of telling his story. It was the one where he was the handsome prince punished for his virtue. It was the story about the departmental investigation of internal corruption he was on and of his vigorous dissent at what would be called a cover-up now and then was called protection of the police public image.

"If it happened today," Powder said, as Adele Buffington listened quietly, "I probably would have resigned. But in those days . . . you thought more about security, and I had a big mortgage and . . ." He paused. ". . . you just didn't rock the boat like they do now."

"And they shunted you into night shift? Sorry, 'swing shift.' "

"It suited me."

She laughed aloud. "The golden-haired boy and you were happy to get put on nights and prepare cases for other people?"

"And we took the idea of teamwork a lot more seriously then, too. I do a good job. Better than anybody has ever done it before."

It didn't faze her. "Look, Lieutenant . . ." She caught herself. "What is your first name anyway?"

"Leroy." Before she could repeat it, he said, "Call me Roy."

"A hypothetical question, Roy, to make you a better cop."

"What?"

"Suppose you have a guy with talent and you give him a job and make him keep it so long he can do it in his sleep and he becomes an institution. Now, how do you get the best for the team out of him? Leave him in the job to become completely fossilized, or change him to something else which will make him grope a little bit and then use those talents?"

"It's not as simple as that," Powder said. But he sensed it was a weak defense. But damn it, it wasn't as simple as that.

"What's the matter," she said, "don't you want to become a better cop?"

"Of course I want to be a better cop." He said it so earnestly that it stopped the conversational flow and they made up some lost time on the food until she said, "You got a terrific line in small talk, Lieutenant, you know that?"

"Yeah," he said, a little embarrassed. He liked stories with him as the hero, but this one didn't sound as heroic as it used to. "Say, did you know I only have seven toes?"

**NIGHT COVER**

Later, in his car, Powder came out of a short period of silence to ask if he could talk about business for one last time.

"Can I stop you?" she asked.

"I just wondered if your impression of Cherry Cable was that this last year she was still pretty promiscuous."

Adele inhaled sharply. "Whatever brought that kind of idea up in your tiny mind?" Defensive.

"Huh? Oh, I just wondered. This friend of hers, Rex, the one who spent all last night trying to write out his non-relation to her. He spent a long time talking about his good intentions and about 'saving' her."

"Saving her for himself?" She identified immediately with the savee.

"He says he spent a lot of time with her, trying to help her with her schoolwork. And he taught her about Maoism."

"Like Chinese Mao Tse-tung Maoism?"

"That's it." Powder smiled. "He even gave me a copy of Mao's Thoughts."

"Oh yes?"

"I read them. Surprising how much applies to police work, if you read them that way."

"And just what did your goodhearted friend think he was saving you from?"

Powder, now very relaxed, more relaxed than in months, laughed. Once, shortly; but aloud. After a moment he said, "Not your impression of Cherry Cable, then?"

She sighed. "Well. If you're asking whether the real Cherry Cable, down in the core, was a slut and a whore and a dropout, then I'd say no. But how far she'd go again to keep the world from throwing more stones at her . . . well, she went pretty far before."

Powder thought about it. "So something like having her grades tampered with might . . ."

"Might undo a lot of hard work by a lot of good people," Adele said coldly.

"That goddamned Rex was right. It's a crime."

They drove in silence for quite a while, until Powder turned a corner and said, "Which one is it?"

"Third house on the right."

## 28

Powder got to the Police Department at 8:30 A.M. First time in years.

He walked up the stairs to the third floor and didn't rub his face once.

While he stood waiting for Inspector Pugh's assistant to get off the phone, Inspector Pugh himself walked in.

"Morning," said Pugh. Then recognized him. "Oh, Powder. What can I do for you?"

Deep breath. "I'd like a word with you, you don't mind."

"All right. Hang on a minute out here, will you? While I settle in."

Powder waited a good deal more than a minute.

"Yes?" said the assistant, just off the phone.

Powder was about to explain when Pugh opened his inner door and said, "Please come in, Lieutenant Powder." Pugh closed the door behind him.

Blunt. "I've reconsidered the special project we talked about yesterday," Powder said, "and I've decided I'd like to be assigned to it."

Pugh frowned. "I thought your reasons for wanting to be dealt out were pretty cogent," he said.

"Oh, for crying out loud," Powder said, annoyed now, "I didn't think there was going to be any trouble about it. What's the matter? You assign someone else?"

"In fact, I decided that Sergeant Malmberg would work

alone, for the time being. To restrict the number of people with knowledge."

"Good," Powder said, as if it were settled. "Then he'll be happy to have me around. Extra head and hands and legs without extending the number of people privy."

"What I still find hard to understand," Pugh said, "is why exactly you want to sign up for what would mean a change in your whole way of life here. Depending, of course, on how long this investigation takes. Frankly, are you a straw in the wind? Am I to expect you to come to me tomorrow and ask to be taken off again?"

"I've thought it over," Powder said seriously—it had been a very long time since he'd asked for something important to him—"and I think I've been on nights too long. At least, long enough. If I don't get this, then I'll ask for day assignment again anyway. I think the change will help make me a better cop."

"So you aren't thinking about retiring anymore."

"I never was," Powder said, "sir."

"I see," said Pugh, and sat looking at Powder for a few moments.

"I would have thought," Powder said, "that a case like this was a pretty heavy responsibility to leave entirely to a youngster like Malmberg." The comment didn't help his case; Powder could see it in Pugh's eyes. These modern sons of bitches!

"Frankly, my worry is a little more down to earth, Lieutenant. After you left yesterday I assured Malmberg that he would be in charge of this investigation and I feel his plans for work on it are pretty impressive. Can you take orders from a man who is inferior in rank to you, as well as younger?"

Why was life so complicated? Visions of Sid Smith. "Surely the operational structure would be essentially cooperative."

"But in the end you would take orders from Malmberg. Can you abide that? Because what I can't have, won't have, is you trying to jump on and off an important investigation like a cowboy trick rider. Believe me, the only reason I consider you at all is because the original damn idea for this was yours. If that wasn't so, you wouldn't get the time of day from me. I like men who know their mind and stick to it."

The thought of going on nights again, after deciding in the night not to. "I want on," Powder growled. "That's a fact. Do I get it or not?"

Powder found his heart thumping as he left the office. Like a kid, he thought. But not entirely deprecatingly of himself. He was rather proud of his actions.

He didn't quite know what to do next, so he went down to the vending machines and nursed a cup of coffee.

Fifteen minutes later he was joined by Malmberg, who was annoyed. "This is how you start a new assignment?"

"You don't tell me how to conduct myself in this business, son."

"Coffee was more important than coming up to see me about . . ." Malmberg looked around and saw that people were looking at him.

Powder looked into his face smugly. They both knew Malmberg had remembered the assignment was "top secret."

"I'll see you in E258," said Malmberg.

"But that's a Juvenile room."

"Where else?" Malmberg said crustily. For public consumption. "Consider it a break. You'll be able to oscillate between there and here without climbing any stairs."

"I'll be along in about half an hour."

"Half an hour!"

Powder swirled his coffee and fished in his pocket for change. Malmberg left. Kid has to be upset, Powder thought. Like Dewey. Went to bed last night thinking he was king of the castle.

"Always under somebody's fingernails, ain't you, Roy?" The speaker was also named Roy, a uniformed patrolman and one of Powder's oldest acquaintances on the force.

"Call me Truman," Powder said as he downed his coffee.

NIGHT COVER

Roy chuckled without understanding. "Always under somebody."

Powder got up. "How things been treating you, Roy?"

"Pretty good, Roy, and you?"

"Could be worse. What you on now?"

"Oh, traffic control, special events. Working out my time."

"Look," Powder said, "make yourself a better cop. Everybody on this team is important. Critically important. Without you everything in this whole force would grind to a halt." Powder nodded goodbye and walked toward the door as Roy said, "Hell, I retire in two months."


## 29

"Hey!" Powder shouted. "I'm forty-eight years old and I only got seven toes. I don't have the time or the durability to wait forever for someone to come to this counter!"

Behind the counter a door to an interior room opened and the vaguely familiar face of the young roster officer Powder had dealt with before presented itself. "You're Lieutenant Powder, aren't you?" the kid said.

"That's right."

"Well, could you hold it down, please? I'll be back in a minute, but we got a crying woman in here."

What could he do? Powder stood and waited. Then felt uneasy, because the roster kid was so much more confident now. Damn. They learn so quickly. For the first time it crossed his mind that on his new assignment he might well not be the Sid Smith—the hot shot—but the Alexander Smith. Too old to be making the change; too stuck in old routine for a new job.

The thought sobered Powder's mood. Especially when it

crossed his mind how much better Malmberg fitted the Sid Smith role.

The roster officer came back and Powder explained, more quietly than he had envisioned doing, that he had been transferred, as of a few minutes ago, to a special assignment and that tomorrow, Tuesday night, a new man would have to be found to direct Swing Shift Detective.

"You can confirm it with Inspector Pugh."

"I appreciate you letting us know promptly," said the roster kid.

"If you want something for nothing, I'd put Sergeant Schleutter in charge. Suggest it to whoever's in charge of you. Schleutter's spent a lot of time with me, and he knows how things should be done."

"I'll make a note," the roster kid said. "Schleutter. If he knows how you run things, then it'll be easier for you to work back in when this assignment's finished."

"Yeah," Powder said. He'd come intending to make it clear that he would never be going back on nights. To mark that in their little books with no mistake. But when it came to the point, Powder said, "Well, we'll see how things work out."

He'd also intended to suggest that they put Brindell on Swing to fill Schleutter's place. But some of the comfortable cantankerousness, the certainty, had been sapped, briefly or no. It looked like being a whole new life.


"This is carrying secrecy a bit too far, isn't it?" Powder said when he walked into E258 and found Malmberg sitting at a table in the middle of a room ringed with shelves and cardboard boxes.

"It's a storage room," said Malmberg, "Inspector Pugh picked it. He's having a phone put in this afternoon." Malmberg was clearly dispirited. Powder felt sorry he'd given him a hard time in the Canteen.

**NIGHT COVER**

"This your first special assignment, son?"

Malmberg smiled.

"There a chair for me?"


It was a two-pronged problem: past and present. Present were the murders of Hilda Chaney and the woman who was not Cherry Cable.

"What have you done with it?"

"Well, I went through all the evidence. They had two guys on it all week before it got to me."

"I didn't know that," Powder said. It meant that the trail must be pretty cold.

"I had to see if I could come up with some way Ellyson could have killed the other two."

"Only you couldn't."

"That's it. Then you walked in. With your identification of the third body . . ."

"Yeah, sorry."

". . . and with that stuff from Tidmarsh."

That was the second prong of the problem. Whether the chance discovery that there were at least two murderers for the current three bodies had bigger implications: that there had been copy-cat killings before. If so, how many? It was urgent to find out. And frightening. If confirmed, it meant that some killer had been at work for months, possibly years, without anyone even knowing it. Much less trying to catch him.

"That's the key," Powder said. "To be sure they exist."

"The idea," Malmberg said. "To think there is some smug bastard killing people and we didn't even know he was doing it. It chills the blood."

Powder nodded. It chilled his blood, too, and Powder's blood had been subjected, over the years, to a lot of temperature extremes.

"You would have had a rough time working on this alone," Powder said.

"I asked Pugh for some help," Malmberg said. "But he said he didn't have the men to spare."

Powder frowned. Surely Pugh had understood the implications of the situation. And already Malmberg seemed much less certain of his direction than Pugh had implied. Powder took a breath; the mysteries of the brass.

"Before we decide which way to go," Powder said, "did you get any ideas on the current two?"

"The only idea I got was that there might be more to learn from the man who found Hilda Chaney. John Daeger."

"Johnny Uncle? No, I know him. He couldn't be involved."

"Well then . . ." Malmberg said.

They gave the first day to pulling the individual case files of all the multiple killings in the last ten years and studying them individually.

I go from night duty to day duty in a room with no windows, Powder thought as they left E258 for Records. Not much change.

And yet . . .

"Wait a minute," Malmberg said. "I'll just drop in and see Inspector Pugh."

"Why?" Powder said.

"He said to keep him up to date with every detail."

Malmberg went into Pugh's assistant's office while Powder stood in the corridor.

They needed a trolley to carry all the files back to their investigation office. The amount of paper, on average, that collects in a murder file—whether the case is solved or not—impressed them both.

In the short time they took for lunch Powder called the Probation Department, but refused to leave a message.

By five o'clock his eyes hurt. They each had to read every file and analyze each case. They were dealing with something important and they had to make sure they were right.

"Only five to take home?" said Malmberg when they decided to call it a day. "I've got ten."

"I'm not as young as I used to be," said Powder, who was thinking: Home, now there's another problem to solve.

But Powder felt younger than he had in years. The forthright Mrs. Buffington had helped see to that.

As Powder went to the stairs, a man brushed past him. Then he stopped. And turned around.

"You son of a bitch," Brindell said. "You goddamned son of a bitch!"

"So I understand," said Powder mildly.

"If you think because you've finally got me on night duty that means you're going to have me cleaning out all your shit piles, you've got another think coming. Believe me, lieutenant or not, nobody is going to make me jump through hoops just because I made one mistake. Everybody makes mistakes, even great God you. And I'll quit this goddamned job before I take shit from a dead-ender."

Brindell dashed away before Powder could say anything. Or so Brindell thought. Powder didn't have anything to say.

He just rubbed his face with both hands.

## 30

On the parking-lot phone Powder called first the Probation Department and then Adele Buffington's home number. Neither with luck, the luck he wanted. It left him ambivalent. Lots of untied strings hanging around and serious things to do. He felt the lethargy associated with having too many things to do. Which is first? Doing none of them.

What he wanted to do was go out to eat. He was hungry. But he wanted to eat with Adele. Treat her two nights running. He felt tired, but there was a coltish side to his fatigue, one which made pushing on attractive.

But she wasn't there.

Strings. Whatever happened to his garden? The vegetable plans? Emotionally he frowned as he looked back. On the Vegetable Powder. Amazing he'd gone so long without thinking.

Dead-ender was right. Was.

He tried Adele's number again. Still empty.

Then he went to sit in his car.

What I ought to do, he thought, is go get a hamburger to tide me over, then take her out to eat later.

But I don't want a hamburger. I've had too many hamburgers in the past. I feel like sauces. New places, new palaces. New solaces.

He rubbed his face again. Shook his head to clear his head. It's what routines are for. To help you avoid having to decide what to do each instant of the day.

Screw this, he thought. I'm a big boy now. I have responsibilities and I make decisions for myself.

To avoid the big decisions, he thought for a minute about his responsibilities. To read some files before morning.

Shift starts at eight. Jesus, what am I doing going to work at eight in the morning?

Then he thought about what he would do for a place to sleep that night. Not allowed to sleep in his own house.

A decision to avoid.

And Cherry Cable? There was another responsibility. Shove her back on Groce? For nothing to happen. And Rex thinks she's dead. And Jefty?

Just for something to do, Powder started the car's engine and drove out of the lot.

**NIGHT COVER**

## 31

There was still some daylight downtown as he turned from Pennsylvania onto West Maryland.

Rush hour out means parking turnover in. Powder locked his car and crossed the street. MAGNIFICENT MAY SALE. Powder looked in the window for a full minute. Thought about laws about advertising.

The street door to Samson's office was still unlocked. Powder didn't mind; he opened it with one hand and reached for his penlight with the other. But things were different; a small bulb lit the landing at the top of the stairs.

The lettering on the door was the same, though. "Albert Samson. Private Investigator. Walk Right In."

Powder knocked.

The door was quickly answered and to his surprise Powder found himself face to face with two people. Samson and a slight middle-aged woman in a head scarf. They were both standing, both near the door.

Samson said, "Good heavens, my six-o'clock patient already." He took the lady by the elbow and said, "You think about what I've told you, and if you think it's really worth the trouble, you let me know."

"Thank you very much," said the little lady. "Very much."

Powder made way; when the woman passed him and started down the stairs, Samson's eyes met Powder's.

"Hi," said Powder. He walked right in.

Samson stepped back awkwardly. "I'm not really in the mood to play punching bag today."

Powder shrugged and sat himself down in what must have

been the chair set out for clients. "What's all that about?" Powder asked chattily.

Samson squinted as he sat down on his side of the desk. "Yes," he said, "well, she was accused of shoplifting in 1948 and wants to clear her name. Delicate case."

Powder restrained his instinctive dislike and said only, "Sorry I asked."

"It's true, it's true," Samson said, "that I lie a lot." He sat up. "I hate to use the same excuse for not offering you coffee, but I have an important engagement soon which will require my turning into a swan. Was there anything in particular that you wanted, if it wasn't to beat me up again? To return my money, by any chance?"

"Not exactly, no," Powder said. "I don't know how you stand with Rex Funkhouser, but—"

"Since you came up with his girl friend, I don't stand at all," Samson said.

Powder corrected, "His friend who is a girl."

It caught Samson, because he knew the truth of it. "Yeah," he said, and softened.

"Well," Powder said, "I thought you ought to know that the body Funkhouser identified as Cherry Cable is not Cherry Cable."

"What?"

"I thought you ought to know."

"Rex doesn't know?"

Powder shook his head. "I didn't think I should call him on the phone and I don't have time to drive out there again. Unless you don't want to tell him."

Samson scratched his head, then nodded it. "I wouldn't have guessed," he said. "But it makes some sense. You're sure this time?"

"Yeah. Rex identified the body as Cherry Cable, but he was upset because he'd never really thought she was really dead and because he'd just confessed to breaking into his school to steal money to pay you with."

"Well, I don't know about all that."

"I do." Despite himself, Powder was running out of patience. He said, "I had a few minutes and I came over here to tell you Cherry Cable is not in the police morgue. I thought you would want to know, in case you and Rex still want to look for her. From now on at Headquarters she'll be a routine missing person and parole violator. We get a lot of each and a lot of both; we're not likely to find her. I hope you do."

"Do you?"

"I'm curious why she ran away. I like to know how things come out." Powder got up. "I've got an important engagement of my own." He went to the door.

But it wouldn't open for him. Samson stepped in front of him, took the handle and with a practiced movement opened the door. But he blocked Powder's path.

"I've been sitting up here all day alone," Samson said. "Then in half an hour I get a woman who wants to make her daughter get a divorce and then I get you. I'm sorry if I don't take life seriously enough for you. I appreciate your coming over to tell me what you did." He stuck out his hand.

Powder took it, shook it and left.

Before he went to his car, Powder walked around looking for a phone. He walked all the way to the bus station before he found one that worked.

"Hello?"

"Is that Adele?" He wasn't certain.

"No, Mummy's not back yet. May I take a message?"

"I . . . I . . . Do you know what time she will be back?"

"She should be back now. But you know Mummy." The voice hesitated. "Or do you?"

"I didn't know she had a daughter."

"Are you the man who was here last night?" the daughter asked baldly.

"Well," Powder said, "I guess I am."

"Aren't you sure?"

"I'm not sure whether your mother would want me to say it like that."

"Oh, she wouldn't mind. We're very confidential."

He almost asked whether she was confidential enough to know whether her mother would like to come out to dinner that night. But he caught his breath as he realized the kid would probably misinterpret the proposition as a more extensive one. Probably it was. Not the kind of thing to arrange through a kid.

"How old are you, honey?"

"Now, that's something I don't know whether Mummy would want me to tell you if you didn't already know she had me."

"Well, maybe you can tell her for me that the die is cast and that I'll call her later this evening. Can you do that?"

"The die is cast?"

"That's right."

"I'll tell her," said the daughter. "But I don't know when to tell you to call her back because as soon as she comes in she's going out, I know that."

"Oh," Powder said. Caught by surprise, he conveyed a lot.

"Uh, yes," said the daughter. "With a colleague." It was a happy word, she thought, to have come into her mind like that. It meant her vocabulary was growing.

"Well, you tell her I called."

"I will."


Powder slouched in the phone booth after he hung up. He hadn't had so many emotional ups and downs in years. Following nose to tail.

He took a deep breath, left the booth and stood in the bus-terminal concourse. This new life was going to force him to change his whole style. The anticipation of the change was good. New broom. Whatever happened. Good. Good for him. Good.

**NIGHT COVER**

Powder went to the magazine counter, pulled out a copy of *Hard Justice,* paid for it and slammed it under his arm. He walked straight up Illinois to Vermont and bounced into a seat at Joe's Fine Food. He had a big meal, and read all about crime-busting heroes.

At eight o'clock he was walking toward his own front door. Car parked smack in the driveway, as if he owned the place. He didn't even knock. He used his key.

"Who's that?" Margaret's voice came with urgency from the kitchen. She hadn't, apparently, been expecting anybody to enter the house with a key. Powder found slight sympathy from an unknown, undrained source. To listen to her talk, when they did talk, she was never alone. To listen to her now, she always was.

"It's me," Powder said. "Just me."

She appeared in the kitchen doorway like a shadow in a cloudless sky. "What the hell are you doing here?"

"There are a few things I need," he said. Walked down the hall. She didn't follow.

When he'd finished packing his clothes, he carried the suitcase through the kitchen to the garage.

It was harder in here. All his lovely tools. By God, why not? He threw open the garage portal and opened his car's trunk. He marched back and forth till the hardware overflowed.

Margaret watched this process at first. Then stopped watching. She knew what was going on.

As she heard cupboards being closed, she reappeared. "Ricky's coming home next weekend," she said.

"I'll leave a number at the department," he said, and it was over.

---

On the drive back to town Powder decided to check in at the Illinois rather than go directly to Adele's. Dashing and romantic to go direct, but presumptuous.

He parked in the tiny off-street lot behind the hotel and made arrangements. Booked his usual room for a month. When he arrived upstairs with his suitcase, he found a spotty paper bag containing a banana sandwich. Where he had left it on the bureau, a day and a half before. He unfolded the top to have a look. Half thinking to eat. But refolded the bag quickly.

And there he was.

After some hesitation he dialed Adele Buffington's number again. When the phone was answered he felt disappointment, but asked for Adele anyway.

"She's out," said the daughter. "Who may I say was calling?"

"This is Roy Powder," said Powder. "I just wondered if she left a message for me."

"No, she didn't," said the daughter. Was she cooler than before? Hell.

"Sorry to bother you, then. When do you think I should call back?"

"Well," the daughter said, "maybe she could call you back tomorrow. Does she have your number?"


Powder went out for a walk. Downtown Indianapolis on a Monday night. Walking away from the hotel, he scolded Adele. But on the way back he scolded himself with more rectitude. Just because she pops up and is important at a critical time in your life doesn't mean you are going to be important in hers.

At 10:12 he opened the first of the five case files he'd brought home.

NIGHT COVER

## 32

"You're late," Malmberg said when Powder walked in at ten past nine. "We start at eight."

"I overslept. I forgot to leave a call."

"Leave a call?"

"Yeah." No particular inclination to broadcast his circumstances in detail.

"How did you do on the five cases?"

"I read through them," Powder said. Old habits coming back. Bit stiff inside this building.

"And?"

"And I would say one is definitely a candidate for our list, and a second may be."

"Here, you give me your five. There's a stack on the table waiting for you."

"All those?" asked Powder.

By two in the afternoon they agreed about what they had found. The suspicious cases and the possible cases went back as far as June 1967, but no further. "That just about fits with a graph I made last night from Tidmarsh's figures. Look, if you extrapolate his multiple-murders figures, it shows the increase starting the summer of 1967."

"Graphs, is it now?" Powder said negatively. "You're sure it doesn't show it's past time for lunch?" The atmosphere of the little room was oppressive and he very much wanted to get out.

"Lunch?" said Malmberg.

At twenty past four they reported to Pugh. By quarter to five they had convinced Pugh of the existence of systematic duplication of murders since 1967. Apart from the sheer increase in multiple-killing cases, it was a matter of paying more attention to small differences between subsequent killings and the first. In the most recent case, for example. Leonora Ellyson had been strangled and her fingers had been smashed with a large hammer which was not left at the scene of the crime. There were a few blows to the face, but not many.

But Hilda Chaney had nine fingers mutilated and her face smashed pulpy, these with a brick left on the scene although the killing had taken place elsewhere.

The third body was closer in treatment to the first, granted. But by then the certain killer of Leonora Ellyson had killed himself. The sledgehammer found in his car. That case wrapped up.

"Bad luck for our subject," Malmberg said. "If he'd realized that the first killing was a family affair instead of something less personal, he probably wouldn't have copied it."

Pugh said, "If this is the first we've suspected of it, he's chosen his opportunities pretty skillfully."

Both of them looked at Powder, who was the man who had picked up scent first.

"It's the bureaucracy of this place," Powder said. "Everybody stuck in one part of one job. Nobody sees the whole." As part of his new self he'd have to write a series of suggestions to build an overview into the system. Maybe work it out with Tidmarsh.

"Right," Pugh said. "We're back where we started. We have a subject. How do you two propose to identify the subject?"

"The key," said Malmberg, "is where our subject gets his information. He has to know the details of a killing before he can copy it. Either he gets his information from a public news source, say newspapers. Or he gets it before it becomes public."

"And you think you can track him down by studying his information?" asked Pugh.

NIGHT COVER |

"Well," said Malmberg, "I suggest what we do next is assemble newspaper reports in each of the cases."

"How many cases do you suspect?"

"Eleven, since June 1967. If we get the newspapers and study our files, then we can make a graph with time zero set at the first of each group of murders. We can enter on the time axis when each stage of information was reached, and when each of the duplicate murders took place. If none of the duplications took place, say, until we released details to the press here, but did occur before the stories got into the papers, well, that would indicate a police reporter. I suggest that kind of treatment."

"You think it might be a reporter?" Pugh said.

"We don't have any way of knowing yet. But I'm hopeful we'll find a pattern."

Pugh nodded slowly. Then turned to Powder, who'd sat stiffly listening to Malmberg's graphs. "And are you agreed, Lieutenant?"

Powder shrugged. "Malmberg's in charge."

"You're a great help," Pugh said with all the disdain an efficient ambition could command. "All right, Malmberg. Get all the information you'll need. But don't, whatever you do, give anyone an idea of what's going on. This is top secret."

Malmberg nodded.

Powder frowned.

---

## 33

At quarter past six Powder walked into the Night Room. He wanted to clear out his stuff. By 6:30 he'd emptied the drawers and filing cabinet and corners and the hiding place in the light shade. Everything piled on the surface of his desk. Though he could still see over the top, he didn't think he had a prayer of removing the stuff without one of his suitcases or at least a large bag. He rubbed his face and then realized that one of the turfed-out items, an old trench coat, could be used to advantage. He unbuttoned it and spread it out on the floor. Selectively he started to shift the pile from the desk to the coat.

"Caught in the act."

"What?"

Schleutter stood in the entranceway grinning ironically.

"I figured to get my stuff out before you came," Powder said. "But there was more than I remembered." He felt unaccustomedly sheepish before Schleutter.

"So what's all this about?"

Powder stood up and realized he was sweating. "I wanted to get my stuff cleared out before you guys came in."

"Cleared out? I thought you were just cleaning house."

"Nope," Powder said, and looked down at his trench coat. All he could see were the arms at each side ready to embrace the artifacts of his nineteen-year stay.

Schleutter pressed. "You leaving permanently? That what you saying?"

"Yup."

"My God!" said Schleutter. He saw uncomforting visions of change. A period of adjustment, transition. "So that's what they were on about."

"Who?"

"Oh. Gaulden, in Personnel, asked me if I wanted to take over for you."

"And?"

"And I said no. I didn't realize he meant permanently."

"I don't know whether he knows. You're not taking it, then?"

Schleutter shook his head. Regretfully.

"A good cop would have filled the gap," Powder said without pity.

"Well . . . " Schleutter drawled, "I kinda figured he was a-gonna put me in the hot seat n'matter what I said."

"So you said no. And so you get to work under some other son of a bitch."

Schleutter wrinkled his nose. "I'm happy where I am," he said. It was true enough, enough to allow him to adjust to the reality as it lay before him. "Hell," he said, "I know what I can do and what I can't. I'd be pushing it to take on more responsibility."

Powder didn't answer as he pulled the arms of the coat up around the pile of papers and trinkets. They wouldn't tie. "Who's replacing me, then?"

"Oh, for crying out loud!"

Schleutter and Powder looked toward the night doorway, where Howard Brindell stood fuming, hands on hips.

"Those fucking liars downstairs," Brindell said savagely. He turned on his heel and left.

"What's that about?" Schleutter asked.

"I guess he doesn't like your looks," Powder said.


Schleutter helped Powder carry the corpse to the elevator. While they waited, Sid Smith walked by and asked pleasantly, "Who's your drunk friend?"

"Aren't you late for duty, Sergeant?" Powder snapped.

Smith just sighed. The story he'd heard was that Powder had been relieved of his night command. No tears from Sid Smith.

The elevator came and Schleutter helped Powder load the coat and contents. "Oh hell," Schleutter said, "I'll help you get it to your car. Doesn't matter if I'm late."

"Not a good way to break in your new boss," Powder said.

"Begin the way you're going to go on."

The two men carried the coat to Powder's car, where they found the trunk already full of tools.

They opted for the back seat instead of trying to fit and juggle.

"You coming back in?" asked Schleutter.

"Yeah," Powder said. "A few more odds and ends."

## 34

On the way upstairs a uniformed officer stopped Powder and said, "Did you get your message, Lieutenant?"

"What message?"

"A lady called twice. Since you're not on nights anymore, I didn't know where you were. I left it on your desk in the Day Room."

Powder guillotined the man with a scowl. Then turned upstairs, leaving the officer to smart under the injustice of being unheaded for doing a good turn.

The Day Room was depopulated, but lit. Powder went to his desk and found, as advertised, two telephone-message forms. Their gist was that Adele wanted him to call her.

Despite a lifetime's carefully developed control, Powder's heart raced.

He sat down and dialed.

"Hello?"

"Adele?"

"No, this is Lucy; who is that?"

The daughter, ah. "This is Roy Powder, honey. Is your mother there?"

"Just a minute, I'll see if she's here." Childlike belief in the caller's acceptance of words at face value. *I'll see if she wants to talk to you.*

Powder waited, confident.

"She's in the bath," came the news. "But if you can come over, she'll be ready to go out with you when you get here."

Oh. "Oh," he said. Then, "Won't you mind her going out with me and leaving you alone?"

"Good heavens, no," said Lucy, sounding like a ninety-year-old spinster aunt for the moment. "It's important that Mummy have an active social life. She is a healthy woman, you know."

The same world, producing Lucys and Brindells. Powder smiled.

He walked down the stairs to the ground floor, and along the subterranean tunnel to the Police Garage.

As he turned toward his car, he saw a movement in the edge of his vision. He looked in the direction of the movement. And saw nothing.

Which was enough to stop him walking toward his car.

Policemen are sensitive to movement; it becomes habit to look in all directions one after another. Called eyeballing.

Powder saw nobody in the whole garage.

He frowned and doubted, uncharacteristically, that he had seen anything. But worried again that Marlon, the man who oversaw the garage, was not there. That, by itself, wasn't enough to worry about.

But with a movement . . .

He took a breath. Drew his gun and moved slowly. Between cars, behind cars. Waited. Moved along the wall. Waited. Moved.

He took ninety clock seconds to get to the end of the garage —close to the exit—where he had seen the movement. Ninety seconds—an hour in real time, emotional time.

In the end it was simple enough.

Another step and there was the motion, crouched between the two end cars.

Powder raised the gun and stepped into the gap. "OK, son, hold it right there." The gun pointed at the head, but Powder's finger was on the trigger guard, not the trigger.

A boy, thickset, twelve years old at most, jumped up from behind the car door he had crouched next to for so long. He screamed with fright at being so startled. His clipboard and pen flew out of his hand, bounced off a police fender and clattered to the concrete floor. The clipboard went face down in a puddle of oil. The boy instinctively bent to retrieve it.

And then grew angry enough to speak. "Aw, there's oil all over it."

Powder took a position which prevented easy flight and holstered his weapon.

"What the hell are you doing here, son?" Powder bent to pick up the pen, a fountain pen.

"It's all dirty! Why'd you have to do that?"

To show who was asking the questions, Powder grasped the boy's jacket firmly. "I asked you what you were doing here, son. Now you tell me and make it snappy."


"And it was a kid!" Powder said genially. "Here. Allow me, ma'am." He held the door open for her.

"A kid?" she said.

Powder walked around the car to let himself in. "A goddamned raggedy-assed kid."

"But what was he doing in the police parking lot?"

"With a pen and taking notes. Yeah." He paused.

"Well?"

"Completing his collection of police license-plate numbers."

"No!"

Powder started the car and pulled away before saying, "Well, I didn't believe it at first, so we took a little walk back into the department. But this kid has been collecting information on us for a couple of years. It's his hobby. You wouldn't believe the things this kid knows. The call numbers. All sorts of stuff he can rattle off. He listens to police calls at home. And he already knows most of the department license numbers. He comes into town sometimes, he says, and has a look around to find numbers he doesn't have. We don't broadcast the numbers on the radio;

he has to come in and get them. It's a matter of which cars are in at what time." Powder chuckled. "Goddamn kid!" he said approvingly.

"What happened to him?"

"Oh. Well, I took him back out to the parking lot and introduced him to Marlon, that's the lot attendant. Let him run around whenever he wants to."

"You don't think . . ."

"No. He's all right. I'm sure he's just what he says he is. I'm going to have him shown around the inside of the department on a weekend. Lay on some police coffee—or hot chocolate—in the Canteen. That sort of thing. I'll leave a note with the PR fellas."

Adele Buffington sat still in the car, looking forward for a moment. Then turned to him again. "You love your work, don't you?"

"Well . . ." Love it? Not a word he had used about work, in his mind or in his mouth. But, "Well . . . I'm kind of married to it. I used to love it, I guess. But now more I need it. It provides me with about all the real pleasure I get out of life." He hesitated, then plunged, "Until I met you." He stole a moment's attention from the road to glance at her. She watched the road in front of them and did not apparently react to his words. "You know, you're good for me, you really are. I won't say that I wasn't gradually coming to realize what I wanted out of life. I was. I have a little piece of land that I grow vegetables on. That I want to live on one day. I bought it a few years back. But you really kind of, well, shook me up. I . . . I think you're great."

She remained quiet and still for a moment. Then, in a bouncing move, turned to face him. Foursquare. "I don't want to mislead you, Leroy. I'm not really free."

Innocent to the end, he said, "I know you have a daughter. I met her just now, remember?"

"I'm not talking about Lucy," she said.

After driving quietly for a while, he said, "I don't understand."

"I have a friend I'm emotionally committed to."

"But the other night . . . ?"

"The other night was the other night. I am my own boss and I do what I want to do. If I'm good for you, it's because I'm a missionary and think everyone should be like me. I do what I want to do; maybe it wasn't fair to you. Maybe I shouldn't have."

"But what are you telling me?"

"Just not to plan for me, Leroy."

"You're not married or something, are you?"

"If I were, in the way you mean, I wouldn't have come out with you in the first place. Please don't be upset. I was afraid you might have misunderstood me. I guess I was right."

He drove quietly for a few minutes. Then pulled off Madison into the parking lot of the Oasis Tavern. When he had parked he sat back and rubbed his face with both hands. "So I'm the other man, huh? They have good catfish here. You ever have catfish, good catfish? Unless you don't want to eat with me anymore."

Firmly she said, "It was important to me, to us both, that you knew exactly how I was fixed. Now you know. The question is whether you still want to eat with me."

Powder actually thought about it for a few moments. Then he got out of the car. Before he could walk around to open her door, she got out, too.

"There's something else I have to tell you about, too."

"Oh God. You have VD."

"That's not very nice to say."

They were inside the tavern before he apologized. And explained, "I'm just a little out of practice at the courting and escorting game."

When they had ordered food and received drink, Powder said, "You had another bombshell you wanted to drop."

Adele sighed. "Just some news. It's why I phoned. I thought you'd want to know. We've located Cherry Cable."

"We?" he said. It took him a moment to realize who Cherry Cable was. Then he did and it hit him. He said, "Dead or alive?"

"Oh, alive. She's in Evansville."

"Evansville! What the hell is she doing in Evansville?"

"I don't know exactly."

Powder frowned. "How did you find out? Police pick her up or something?"

"No. The private detective that friend of hers—Rex Funkhouser—hired. He found her."

"The hell he did!"

"Today. Another friend of hers from school, Artie something, gave him a lead to some people she spent time with in the evenings. She seems to have run off with one of them, to get married."

'To Evansville?"

"Look, Roy . . . I want to ask you something."

"What?"

"I have a feeling Cherry may want to come back."

"But you said . . . get married."

"Cherry doesn't really want to get married. She can't!" As if marriage could hardly solve problems for someone. "Maybe I'm wrong, I don't know. But what I want to ask you is *if* she were to come back, would she face any trouble with the police?"

Powder thought for a minute, then said, "There's no warrant out for her on parole violation, as far as I know."

"If I could fix it with my people . . . ?"

He frowned and then shrugged. "I'm not the expert on what's best for the girl. We're not going to push it without the parole people wanting us to."

"Good," Adele said, and relaxed in her chair.

There was a pause. Powder said, "This detective guy told *you?*"

"He left a message."

"Has he told Cherry's aunt?"

"Mrs. Tedesco? No, not as far as I know."

Powder mused. "Samson," he said, with some distaste.

"You know him?" asked Adele, interested.

"Vaguely. I put Rex on to him in the first place."

"I didn't know that," she said, as if she should have. "Your tone of voice suggests you don't like him much."

"I don't really like him or not like him. It's just hard for me to understand anyone who really cares about justice working outside the police force. And if he doesn't care about it, then I don't care about him."

Adele raised her eyebrows. Smiled.

"I know, pretty speech," Powder said. "Did Samson say anything else about the girl?"

"He'd only just found her and is seeing her again this evening. He'll bring her back, if it's possible."

"Do you think he has the tact for the job?"

"Yes."

"I suppose he's worth something," Powder said. "At least he could look for the girl when I couldn't. And go to see her. Who's paying for him?"

"I don't think it's quite clear."

"These guys," Powder said. "He'll probably take that kid Rex for everything he's got. The kid already stole money to pay for this Samson, did you know that?"

"No," said Adele, who was surprised.

"Yeah. Rex b-and-e'd his school and picked up the loose change."

"What'll happen to him?"

"I don't really know. Not too much, probably. First offense. This business about the girl. And the guy in charge of the school isn't exactly . . ." Powder hesitated. Thought he'd better go out and see Rex again before long. Have a little chat about his future. If he'd learned his lesson: that you either go whole hog and become a guerrilla or you stay inside the law except over some specific principle. . . . Probably there were ways he could help Rex.

Revolution is not a dinner party, Powder found himself thinking. Even the little revolutions in a man's life. He shook his head.

"What's wrong, Leroy?"

"What? Oh. Nothing. I was just thinking."

"I managed to figure that much out. I was just going to say," Adele said, "that my impression of Samson is that he isn't particularly mercenary."

Powder didn't quite pay attention. "Good," he said. "I'd like to know how things come out."

They sat quiet for a moment. A waiter brought two bowls of salad to the table. "That's a happy little party we got here," he said. But didn't wait to reap a riposte.

"Are you happy, Leroy?" Adele asked as they poked at limp salad with forks.

"I haven't caught up. I mean. Well, nineteen years I been dealing with a slew of cases every night. But recently things seem to be happening too fast for me. All of a sudden everything is different." He rubbed his face with both hands, a fork still in one. And he felt better for it. "Yeah," he said, "I'm fantastically happy." He'd been saving up for a long time.

When the waiter brought the catfish, Powder looked closely at them and said, "These look pretty small."

"Yeah," the waiter said. "Prices have gone up so much we can hardly afford the micefish to feed them anymore." He retreated quickly.

Powder said, "I'm tempted to go into the kitchen and give them a ticket for not having the lids tight on their garbage cans."

"But what if their lids were on tight?"

"I'd knock them off. What do you think?"

"Do you really do things like that?"

He smiled. "No." Then speaking for the force as a whole, "Well, not very often." Then he said, "Did you know that I have a kid? A kid in college?"

"No, I didn't."

"Hasn't got a ball in his body."

"What?"

"I think she cut them off when I wasn't looking, when the kid was a baby."

Adele forked a mouthful of cat.

"Do you know the only thing I regret about my new circumstances?"

"No. What?" She was less warm to him than she had been, but it was less important that she be so.

"I don't know how I'm going to get my vegetable patch dug and tended."

"What do you mean?"

"Now that I work days. I'll have to go out there nights and weekends."

"Like everybody else."

"Yeah," he said. "Like everybody else."

Powder took her straight home after the meal. He didn't quite understand, but when they shook hands and he left her, he felt no sorrow.

## 35

It was not yet eleven P.M. by his watch. For most people it was late. But Powder had driven to Guilford Avenue on the off-chance, and there was a light in the house. He could see it through the trees.

He parked and didn't give his impulse time to dissipate.

"Who's there?" The disembodied voice came lightly, if uneasily, from behind the slightly opened door.

"It's Detective Lieutenant Powder, Mrs. Tedesco. I was here a few days ago. I have news about Cherry."

Maxine Tedesco unchained the front door, unlocked the screen door. But then retreated, leaving Powder to make his own way into the house. In the living room the overhead light went out, leaving only a weak side light. The massive Mrs.

Tedesco sat on the couch. She let Powder arrange his own comforts.

"Cherry has been located." Then, lest there be confusion, "She's alive and, as far as we know, she's well."

It set off a short explosion. *"Told* you it wasn't Cherry. *Told* you. *Told* you." And then it was over.

Powder sat for a moment. "You mean you weren't really sure?"

"Was sure. Oh, was sure," she said. "At the time."

With no news about her niece, she'd had nothing to do but sit thinking about whether she could conceivably have made a mistake. Whether Cherry was, after all, lying still on the slab in the refrigerated vault.

"This must have been very difficult for you, Mrs. Tedesco." He considered trying to say something about the emotional violence which lack of knowledge does. He looked around the dark room he shared with Mrs. Tedesco.

"Will she be coming home?"

Powder rubbed his face. "I'm sorry," he said to apologize for being quiet.

She took it differently. "She won't come home."

"I don't really know. I'm afraid it's not us, the police, who have found your niece. I wish it were," he said. "I wish it were. But I just found out tonight that a private detective who was hired by one of her friends has located Cherry in Evansville."

"By . . . one of her friends?"

"Rex Funkhouser."

"Rex," she said with doubt in her voice. Powder couldn't see the expression on her face.

"Honestly, I only happen to know because the detective told Cherry's probation officer, who happens to be . . . a friend of mine. I found out earlier tonight and I thought you ought to know that she's, well, alive."

"See," came the voice from the darkness.

After a moment. "I'll leave now. Let you get some sleep."

"Wish . . ." she began to say.

"What, Mrs. Tedesco?"

"Thank you for coming." She hoisted herself to her feet. At the door she said again, "Thank you."

## 36

"You're early tonight."

Powder smiled. "I'm late," he said.

"Late, man! You never come here before the respectable people are off the streets!" Knight chuckled richly.

"Just single tonight, with a salad," Powder said. "I already ate once. I'm going to end up looking like you."

"Could do worse," said Knight. "Could do worse. The women flock around me. Your problem is you such a skinny little fella."

"And I only got seven toes, too," Powder contributed.

Knight frowned. "How you do that?"

"When I was a kid I blew them off with my grandfather's rabbit gun."

"Aw," said Knight, trying to perceive whether Powder was making an obscure joke.

"It's the truth," Powder said. "But don't tell anybody—" He was interrupted as six young men filed into the restaurant.

"Hey, man," the first of the line of customers said, "when you finish rapping with this dude we want a little service because we hungry, man, hungry." These sentiments were echoed.

Powder turned to the young men and eyed the speaker coolly.

"Hey, man," said the spokesman. "You must be a cop. You a cop? You must be a cop because ain't nobody but a cop look at me like that."

Powder turned back to the counter, where Knight had just put his plate.

"Nobody except your father," said one of the supporting cast.

"And your auntie."

"And your granma."

"And a little baby."

"And that girl you was out with last night."

Powder's interrogator turned on the last speaker good-naturedly. "That was no girl, man."

"That was a man?" Laughter. "Didn't look like no man."

"That *girl* gonna be my wife," said the interrogator with mock solemnity. "Or so she think." Laughter.

Powder sat at the table he habitually used. He had brought more files Malmberg wanted him to look at into the restaurant. Optimistic to think he could work on them. He remembered the general quiet of his early-morning meals at Knight's, but hadn't asked himself whether it was likely to be equally calm in his new hours of patronage. But . . .

Top of the pile, the current case. Funny, in nineteen years he'd hardly ever had occasion to look again at the reports he'd started a case rolling with. He opened the file and read it. Leonora Ellyson, munch.

He was in the middle of a nibble on a little middle rib when he frowned at a detail of an interview he had conducted two weeks before. With John Daeger, Johnny Uncle. He read the interview report again.

Then thumbed through the pages in the case folder slowly.

Powder looked up and saw Knight serving a teenaged girl. The six young men had gone, he hadn't noticed.

"Knight, can I use your phone?"

Knight hesitated.

"Just a short call."

Decision, then conviviality to back it up. Knight was deeper than he liked people to know. "Sure. Sure, man. Over there."

Powder walked to the end of the counter and pulled the

phone toward him. Looked through his notebook for the number he wanted.

The phone rang. And rang. Powder waited it out. Asleep and not yet one A.M. The kid was going to have to learn.

"Yeah?"

"Malmberg?"

"Yeah, who's that? What time is it?"

"It's ten past three. I didn't think you'd be in bed."

"Who the hell is this?"

"Leroy Powder. You busy? Because I just noticed something and I'd like to come over and ask you a question. OK? It'll make you a better cop."

## 37

Even Malmberg was late the next morning. When he found Powder in the Canteen at quarter past nine he couldn't complain. Powder bought him a cup of coffee and a machine Danish. "So. How's a boy feeling this morning?"

Malmberg sat silently for a moment swirling the coffee in its cup. "I'll be all right."

"I've never made a chart before," Powder mused. Then, "Let's get the show rolling. Bring the coffee along."

Malmberg gulped his coffee down and left the Danish. They went to see Pugh.

"Sit down," said Inspector Pugh when his Special Assignment Team walked in. "You were working on where our copy-cat killer obtains the details he copies. How are you gettin' on? Does he get his information from the newspapers?"

Powder didn't answer the question. He said, "We want an authorization from you giving us access to roster and assignment files in the Drug Squad."

Pugh was startled. "I don't quite—"

"It's one-sided to chase information sources only," said Powder instructively, in his element. "I've spent nineteen years preparing cases for other people to look for killers. First thing I look at was who got killed. From eleven originals, we have seventeen copy killings. I look at those seventeen people—they've all been done by one guy, far as we know—and I ask myself, Why them? What made them so lucky?"

"Well?" Pugh asked, frowning.

"We don't know why them," Powder said.

"What's he talking about, Malmberg?" Pugh demanded. "Is this serious or have the two of you just decided to waste my time?"

Before Malmberg could answer, Powder said sharply, "It's serious, Pugh."

The two men glared at each other while Malmberg stifled a yawn. His wisdom had always come from going early to bed.

"We don't know for sure what the seventeen extra victims had in common, but last night we went through the information we have and found that eight of the seventeen had some connection with drugs. Some connection we know about. That includes both of the duplicates on the current case."

"Yeah?" said Pugh.

"Do you know the odds against eight out of seventeen people just happening to have drug connections? Tell him, Malmberg."

"What?"

"All right!" Pugh interrupted. "It's not likely to be accidental. So you think the extra victims are chosen—were chosen—because they were associated with the drug trade."

"It seems a reasonable hypothesis," Powder said. Malmberg nodded in support.

Pugh mused. "Possible," he said.

"Right," said Powder. "If that's why they got lucky, we're looking for a subject who knows the local drug business . . ."

"Yes . . ."

"And who has reliable information about each fresh murder case, so he can sort out the ones it's safe to copy. Looking at it that way . . . who has access to police information and knowledge of the drug trade?"

Pugh took a breath. He didn't want to say it, but he did. "You think it's a cop."

Powder looked him in the eyes and said quietly, "That's what all this top-secret shit has been about, isn't it?"

Pugh didn't deny it. "It's possible," he said. "And you worked this out from—"

Powder interrupted, *"I* didn't work it out. Malmberg and I worked it out together after I woke him out of sweet dreams and told him about our witness."

## 38

It was an intensive day of work in the Juvenile storeroom. Digesting roster information from years of assignments even in a relatively small squad like Drugs required concentration and skill in accounting. When the piece of paper they'd set aside for charting the assignment of personnel turned out to be too small, Malmberg and Powder both got depressed.

"This chart-and-graph brigade is a blunt instrument," Powder said at three in the afternoon, with a final certainty worthy of Mao.

At six Powder rubbed his face with both hands. "We can't go on like this straight through the night."

"I guess not," said Malmberg, who had been humanizing steadily. "It'll keep till tomorrow. God, I'm tired."

"You know what I used to do to people who woke me up in the middle of the day—while I was sleeping?"

"What?"

"I used to call them in the middle of *their* night. About three A.M. when I went off shift." Powder paused. He had intended to do that to Brindell. But he hadn't. He sighed. "Look, Malmberg, *will* this keep until tomorrow?"

"It won't go anywhere."

"But what happens if there's a murder tonight and our friend decides to copy it?"

Malmberg scratched his nose. They'd concentrated on past cases and on the current case. But it was certainly conceivable that they would walk into a future case, any time now.

"And another thing," Powder said. "Why can't we work on this stuff all night?"

"What do you mean?" Malmberg asked, and couldn't help himself. He yawned.

"We forgot about Tidmarsh. He's on nights."

Malmberg took what they had done and what they were looking for down to Tidmarsh while Powder went up to the third floor, to the Night Room, which he had left, forever, the night before.

It took him a moment, standing in the doorway, to realize what had happened. Behind the desk, his old desk, sat Harold Salimbean.

My God.

"I'd like a word with you, Harold."

The Acting Night Leader didn't know whether to leave his post. But he decided to be easy about it. Start of his second night on the job. He was an old hand now. "Where, Lieutenant?"

"In private, Harold." Powder turned to the door, then turned back. "It's business."

As they walked down the hall, Salimbean found himself nervous. "I read your Notes, Lieutenant."

"Notes?"

"Didn't you write up Notes about night procedure? They gave me a set to read and I read them last night."

"Oh yeah," Powder said.

They went upstairs to E462, an observation room. Observation rooms—because they're used to monitor interview rooms—are the most soundproof rooms which a cop can use casually.

"Harold," Powder began slowly, "what I'm going to ask you to do will seem strange." He hesitated. "You are in charge throughout this whole week's shift, aren't you?"

"Lieutenant Gaulden said if it works out, I'll be on permanent appointment."

"Ahhhh," Powder said. Then, "Good." Then he began, "You are the last night man to see the case reports before they go to the day boys."

"Yeah."

"What I want is this. If you get a suspicious homicide in the next few days, any killing which might conceivably be a murder, I want you to add a bit of information to your report."

"Add . . . !"

"I want you to say that around the body's neck was a nylon scarf."

"A nylon scarf! But why, Lieutenant?"

Unity between officers and men. Explain your plans, for an enlightened soldier is ten times as fierce as one left in darkness.

"We're trying to catch a killer, Harold. His trademark is a nylon scarf around the neck of his victim. Until we can push our major operation, we want to pressure him by having the press pick up stories that look like his work, only he didn't do it."

Truth only goes so far: quotation from Lieutenant Powder.

Salimbean blinked. Then, because he felt he was supposed to, he nodded. Though it sounded crazy. But everything sounded crazy to him the last couple of days. Gaulden calling him in on Monday, for instance, and then offering him this permanent night assignment, with responsibility bonus. When it rains it pours. "Whatever you say, Lieutenant."

"It's just in case you get a murder, Harold. It probably won't happen. But it's important that you do this if the circumstance comes up."

"I will."

They walked silently most of the way back to the Night Room.

"How's your wife taking your step up in the night world, Harold?" Powder said when the Night Room door came into sight down the corridor.

Salimbean stopped. "She's not."

"What?"

"She left me," Salimbean said.

"What?"

"Saturday night she never came home. She ran away with the guy who sold us our freezer." Salimbean was trying to act like he didn't care.

"My wife left me several years ago." For all practical purposes.

"Gee, I didn't know that."

"Good luck, Harold."

"Thanks, Lieutenant. I appreciate it." Salimbean turned to the Night Room, took a breath and went in. As the door closed behind him, Powder rubbed his face.

Then followed to the doorway. Opened it: Salimbean was just sitting down. "Sergeant Smith!" Powder called. "I want to see you. Not you with the beard! The other Smith . . . Methuselah."


"Just wanted to wish you luck, Alexander. Didn't see you when I left last night."

"Gee, thanks, Lieutenant," Smith said heartily. "Did you hear about what happened last night?"

"No. What?"

"Well, I went out last night on a gunshot. Turned out to be a suicide. Neighbors heard the shot and called us."

"Yeah?"

"Well, while I was waiting with the patrolman, for the lab team and that, I had a look around and I happened to go down into the basement. And guess what I found."

Powder didn't guess.

"I found stacks of clocks."

"Clocks?"

"You know, those wind-up clocks we'd been getting reports on the last few weeks."

Smith's luck. "Guy committed suicide?"

Smith nodded. "Yeah. No question."

"Did you find anything that gave you an idea what he took the clocks for?"

"Gee, Lieutenant, I didn't think about that. I just thought you'd be interested to know that we found them."

"I appreciate it, Smith. Thanks."

"You're welcome, Lieutenant. And, hey, good luck to you, too."


Powder walked downstairs and to his car. Feeling tired. Maybe luck would be enough. Got to be a place on the force for luck.

In the parking lot he saw Marlon, the attendant. Which reminded him of the kid he'd found there the night before, which reminded him of Adele. Adele. Who reminded him of Cherry Cable. Which reminded him of some business he wanted to know the come-out of.

He went to the phone and looked up Albert Samson's number. But all he got was an answering service. "No message," he told the pert voice on duty.

Then he went to the Illinois Hotel and slept twelve hours.


## 39

"Why was it we didn't go to Tidmarsh in the first place?" Powder asked Malmberg.

"Because he works nights and you don't approve of calling people in the day who work nights."

"If he's on this special assignment, he ought to be here on

special assignment," Powder said cantankerously. The sleep had helped, he was feeling better.

"Well, he's saved us a lot of time."

"Yeah," Powder said.

They shared an appreciation of the gravity of the moment.

"I suppose," Malmberg said, "that we better show Inspector Pugh what we've got."

"You do it," said Powder, who didn't like having to *ask* the likes of Pugh for permission to set up a series of line-ups which might well solve seventeen murders. "I'll go see if I can find Johnny."

"I thought you were going to do that last night."

"I was, but I fell asleep."

Malmberg shook his head slowly. That was the Pugh in him. But then he said, "I doubt he's gone anyplace."


Johnny Uncle was easier looked for than found.

Powder had been sure, for instance, that Johnny's wife would know where to find him. But when he got to the house, he found she had died in 1971. That disturbed him. He ought to have been able to keep on top of information like that.

What if Johnny had died in the last couple of weeks? What a turn-up that would be. He wished that they'd had Alexander Smith on the case with them. For luck.

Powder checked a couple of cafés. City Market. Some old hangouts.

It was after two o'clock when he finally found Johnny Uncle asleep in the sun in Military Park.

Powder hated to wake him up.

But he did.

## 40

"Aw, Roy, you told me I was gonna look at some people. What's all this stuff? I don't understand."

"I told you what I thought was so. But I'm not in charge around here. When Inspector Pugh says let him go through the personnel photographs first, I got to make you look at pictures."

Lieutenant Gaulden, a wrinkled cherub, looked on benevolently. It wasn't often his personnel files were used to solve a crime.

"If you just do your best, Johnny, try to help me, I'll see you clear. You know me. Believe me."

John Daeger looked at the stack of photographs and wiped his dripping nose. He looked up at Powder again. "I wouldn't trust nobody but you, Roy."

"I'll see you clear."

"OK then."

Powder turned to Gaulden and nodded to the door in the interview room. "I'll be back in a minute, Johnny. Gotta talk to this guy."

"OK, Roy." Johnny Uncle was looking through the pictures slowly. The instructions were to eliminate those he could with certainty. Positive ID if he could, but eliminations would save time, Pugh said. Powder supposed they would, but didn't like having his plans changed from on high.

Malmberg was waiting in the observation room overlooking Johnny Uncle's languid hunt.

"So," Gaulden said, "what's all this about, then?"

"It's about you not worrying about it," said Malmberg.

"Just because goddamn Pugh says it's confidential," Powder said, "doesn't mean it's a big deal. We're just having our guest expert pick out the handsomest cop in town. It's a national contest."

Gaulden looked guilelessly through the one-way glass at Johnny Uncle as he sorted through the stack of pictures. "That the truth?" he asked Malmberg.

"Whose pictures you got in there anyway?"

"Everybody currently employed," said Gaulden.

"And Drug Squad from the last ten years," Malmberg added.

"Yeah and Drug Squad from the list you gave me. Hey, why the Drug Squad?"

" 'Cause everybody knows they're the prettiest," Powder said.


Powder took the first turn nursing Johnny through the pictures. Then made way for Malmberg and went to look for a hamburger and boiled potatoes for Johnny. On the park bench he'd promised Johnny food and a warm place to sleep and pocket money if he helped out. "Johnny," Powder had said on the park bench after the older man had been roused into wakefulness. "You remember the body you found a couple weeks ago?"

"Not likely to forget that, Roy. Am I? Am I?"

"Do you remember the car that turned around and followed you before you found it? And the two guys in it?"

"Ooooo, I sure do." Johnny spent his life avoiding threatening contact with people, except for the month he'd been married. "At first I thought they was going to ask me a question, or directions or something. But then when we went under a streetlight I saw how they was looking at me and I thought they was cops. I got the hell out of there."

Powder nodded and rubbed his face. "Do you think you would recognize them if you ever saw them again, Johnny?"

## 41

In his least-guarded moments Powder had hoped that it would turn out to be either Brindell or hairy young Sid Smith, or both, but his luck was never that good.

By eight o'clock and two hamburgers, Johnny had picked out two faces from the collection of photographs. Powder, who knew better than Johnny's appearance and present life, knew that these were the two men Johnny had seen. Pugh treated it as the first step toward tentative identification, and immediately hesitated over plans for putting the two men into a line-up. Pugh talked to Malmberg about his doubts that Johnny would be able to pick out the actual men, about his doubts because the men picked were older than expected. One retired now, the other fifty-seven with a game leg, but working as a reception officer. Granted, Pugh said, working as a reception officer in the Drug Squad.

For Powder the fact that the faces in the car were in the police personnel records at all iced it. What were a cop and an ex-cop doing in a private car together in the Haughville renewal district at night? Why did they follow a bum walking along the street? Were they afraid he'd seen something?

Their luck had just run out. They happened to pick a bum who'd been a friend to a classmate in school a hundred years ago. A classmate who'd become a better cop than they were.

Yet these guys had had their run of luck. Seventeen murders. Some would call it luck.

NIGHT COVER |

---

Powder booked Johnny Uncle into protective custody on the fifth floor and left Pugh and Malmberg arguing the pros and cons of a line-up in the morning—when they were usually held —or in the afternoon.

He intended to drive straight to the Illinois Hotel, but detoured to West Maryland Street. Where he parked and crossed to the unlocked street door of Albert Samson, Private Investigator. At the top of the stairs he stood outside Samson's door and heard voices inside. He knocked.

The voices stopped.

"Who the hell can that be?"

Powder knocked again.

There was a pause. Then the door flew open, as if in anger, and Powder was bathed in light. He rubbed his face.

"My God," Samson said, "the cavalry to the rescue."

Powder walked in. There were two other people sitting in the room. A tall girl with platinum-blond hair and luggage under her brown eyes. And Rex Funkhouser.

When Powder came in, Rex stood up. His hand extended, Powder walked over to the girl. "Miss Cable, I believe."

"Yes," she said hesitantly. Must have an identity problem.

"Well, don't let me interrupt what you were talking about." Powder looked for a seat and found a bench along the wall by the door.

When no one moved or spoke, Powder said, "Sit down. Sit down. Make yourselves at home." Everybody sat. "Well, Miss Cable, how long have you been back in Indianapolis?"

"A . . . About an hour," she said.

"Good. And what have you decided to do with your life?"


Powder got to bed a little past twelve, but he didn't go to sleep right away. He had a drink to celebrate. Murderers identified.

And Cherry Cable was alive, and at least temporarily back in the fold. He was glad that he had stopped by because he was able to answer questions for the little group that would have been left dangling otherwise. Yes, Jefty would be prosecuted, but no, he was not likely actually to go to jail. But yes, Powder would impress on Jefty the wisdom of turning the school over to a manager forthwith. Certain incontrovertible facts would not make good reading in the newspapers, from a business point of view. And the press just might get a hold of the story somehow. Good at coming up with stories to make people uncomfortable, the press. With Jefty off the scene, Miss Cable could be persuaded to return to the school. To learn what she could—or would—but at any rate to conform to the terms of her probation.

Powder found Cherry Cable a puzzling person. Lightweight, yet desperately serious. Thrown into a depression by Rex's report of Jefty's arbitrary grading system. Then taking precipitate action when, from a former student, she'd heard of one way to encourage Jefty's beneficence. But unable to stay to repeat the intended benefit. Cherry laughed at her obligation to let her Aunt Maxine know she was back in town when Powder brought the subject up. Then cried when Powder explained how desolate and involved Maxine Tedesco had been while Cherry was away.

Cherry called her aunt on the spot, oblivious to the three men, who would have preferred not to listen. But each in his own mind felt that the effort to bring this mixed-up girl back to the world of the living had been worth their various efforts.

"Tell Frank I'll be home soon," Cherry said to her aunt. "Tell him I'll never leave him alone again. I missed him so. I'm sorry." The stuffed lion.

"And what about Rex!" Cherry said apropos of nothing when she hung up the phone.

"What about Rex?" Powder had asked.

"Will he go to jail or what?"

"In the circumstances," Powder began.

# NIGHT COVER

"He's got to get off with a warning to be a good boy," Samson interrupted.

Powder didn't like being interrupted and showed it.

"But I'll need him. To help me," Cherry said plaintively.

The matter was settled.

"When the revolution comes," Rex said, "we'll remember this."

Powder didn't like the sound of that, but realized after studying Rex's nervous grinning face that it was the kid's idea of a joke.

Powder actually fell asleep a little before one. About the time Harold Salimbean, Acting Night Cover Leader, was arriving to take charge of a gutted corpse found behind some shrubs flanking a north-side gravel pit. The head had been caught in the parking lights of a courting couple edging toward a favorite haunt.

At three A.M. Salimbean was breathing hard as he tried to decide whether this was the kind of corpse Powder had meant. Probably it was, but a nylon scarf! No one would believe that! And what color?

## 42

Rank held sway.

"Why isn't anything going on?" Powder asked Malmberg in the detective room. At eight Powder had gone straight to Line-Up on the fourth floor at the foot of the stairs from the prison floor. But nothing was happening.

"You left before it was settled, I guess," Malmberg said.

"What was settled?"

"Inspector Pugh decided that we couldn't get a decent lineup together by this morning."

"So it'll be held this afternoon. OK."

"So it'll be held tomorrow morning at the earliest. Maybe the day after."

Powder shook his head. "I don't understand."

Malmberg stood up. "We can't talk here."

"What do you mean, we can't talk here?"

"People will hear us."

Powder let Malmberg lead. The kid was colorless and humorless, but Powder respected his dedication.

"I thought we'd come out from hiding after yesterday," Powder said as they sat down in the windowless storeroom.

"Not according to Inspector Pugh. He says we still have to handle this very delicately."

"Has he had warrants issued?"

"Not yet, no."

"Seventeen murders!"

"Pugh says two things about that. First, nothing's been proved. Second, it's precisely the fact that it was seventeen murders and has been going on so long. People will ask why we didn't know about it before."

"I should hope so."

"Honestly, Powder, it won't help the department. You know the kind of press we've been getting. It'll make us seem like damned idiots."

"I think I've been here before," Powder said.

"He wants us to go to Converson and Wray today and ask them to take part in the line-up."

"*Ask* them?"

"Well, yeah."

Powder got up. "OK, kid, I understand your position. You got a life ahead of you. But do me a favor, will you? You ask those two murderers if they'll volunteer for a line-up. I don't think I'll have time to help you out with it today."

"Come on, Powder, a day isn't that big a deal."

"Got a little business to see to." Powder walked out of the room and went straight to the stairwell without even stopping for coffee.

**NIGHT COVER**

But walking down the stairs he wasn't quite so certain. Maybe he shouldn't be hasty. Instead of getting out on the first floor, he continued down and went to his car.

By 9:30 he was on his plot of land and changing clothes. Growing weather. Weeds were growing like mad things and he hadn't even got his early seeds in. That's the problem with weeds—when they've begun to show, it's almost too late. Hoe when there are no weeds and there'll be no weeds.

Powder worked up a draining sweat in the humid heat before he took a breather. Just too many bits and pieces for one man to keep under control. You've got to husband personal resources in a garden. The idea is just to keep the good plants ahead of the bad plants. Not to try to excise all the bad plants completely and forever. One man working alone can't do the impossible.

When he had rested for a few minutes, Powder rubbed his face and said to his plants, "Hang on, will you, fellas? I got a little business to see to."

He went to his shed, changed clothes and drove back to town.

On the first floor he found the Press Room almost empty. But not quite.

Later he returned to cultivate his garden.

## 43

"You've finished yourself here, you know that."

That's just one inspector's opinion, Powder thought the next morning as he sipped coffee in the Canteen. What Pugh didn't understand was that there is here and here. So he would never make it back into the mainstream of detective life. It didn't mean he had to quit the force. That might be what Pugh would have done, would expect him to do. But Powder had been there before, and it wasn't his way. For a man with principles, Powder was very well able to compromise. Pragmatic, Mao calls it. At ten o'clock he went to keep his appointment with Lieutenant Gaulden in Personnel.

And at noon Powder found Malmberg.

"How'd it go?" he asked.

"Positive ID, but we expected that."

"When did you pick them up?"

"You made me feel like a fool, Powder, you really did."

"Why?"

"I spend two hours talking Converson and Wray into filling out a line-up and next thing Pugh calls me in and tells me that somehow the papers have got a hold of the story and we've got to go arrest them."

Powder smiled. Then shook his head. "You find out why they did it?"

"I couldn't keep them from telling me. They were proud of it, the sons of bitches."

"What was it? Kid die from an overdose or something?"

"Nothing like that. They said they both got tired of having the cops in the squad constantly in danger. These guys are old buddies and hatched it together a few years ago when Converson hurt a leg and got taken off front-line service. He trained for reception duty. Got juggled around till he landed in Drug Squad, where he had access to records and gossip. By that time Wray had taken early retirement and they decided to do something about the state of the world. They took anybody—addicts, pushers, didn't matter."

Malmberg and Powder contemplated the state of the world.

"You got them all right, did you?"

"Yeah," Malmberg said and looked sour.

Powder said, "Can't be bad. Want some coffee?"

"I'm supposed to see Pugh," Malmberg said. Then, like a burst of sunshine, "Hell, why not?"

"Coffee. You're a prickly bastard, you know that?"

"I ought to, kid. But keep trying, you can be like me when you grow up, too," Powder said. "This case should do you some good."

"Guess so," said Malmberg, for whom it had been a tiring, deglamorizing time.

"As soon as you learn to keep your mind on what the hell is really going on when something happens."

"What do you mean?"

"Here, let me ask you a hypothetical question."

"Oh yeah?"

"Suppose you get an inspector who doesn't want the world to know a cop and an ex-cop killed seventeen people. How's the world going to know whether they killed seventeen instead of a hundred or just one?"

Malmberg hesitated. "If somebody tells the world, I suppose."

"But suppose you only prosecute them for two that you have a witness for, two that only happened a couple of weeks ago. How does your department look that way, good or bad?"

"Good," Malmberg said. "Good enough."

They sat quiet for a while.

"Don't take what a guy tells you for gospel just because he's higher up than you. You're supposed to be good at this. But you won't be until you can think for yourself, Malmberg. Sometimes I think all you kids came out of the same package."

"Give me a chance, old-timer."

Powder laughed.

"What are *you* going to do? Not going back on nights, are you?"

"Hell, no. Nineteen years is enough of that. I'm going to take over Missing Persons."

"What?"

"And I'm going to take night classes. Yeah—go to college.

Take shit like Adolescent Psychology and Seven-Year Itch. I got years yet. I ought to be able to get Missing Persons into shape."

Malmberg listened quietly.

"You give me a few years there and then just try and lose somebody." And only fitting, Powder figured, to have Missing Persons taken over by somebody who'd only just found himself.